Fleur Blüm is a Melbourne-based writer, performer and musician.

Her blog can be found at https://fleurblum.com/blog

Also by Fleur Blüm

Sophie's Path
Discovering the Franklins
My Mother's Secret
The Sins of the Father: a Barrett Women novel
The Mother's Fault: a Barrett Women novel
Singular Focus
Singular Purpose
Morgana, My Queen and other stories
Pillion for a Police Officer

Poetry Collections:
My Body. No Apology
Consider the Watchmaker
Smells Like Teen Angst

First edition 2025

Copyright © 2025 Fleur Blüm
ISBN: 978-0-6483654-9-5

Editor: Annie Seaton
Cover Design: Megan Carter

Published by Fleur Blüm, Melbourne, Australia

Carter & Carter Detective Agency

By Fleur Blüm

For all my friends and family,
who are always patient and encouraging.

Foreword

In his introduction to *The Cambridge Companion to Crime Fiction*, Martin Priestman credits the crime story with driving some of the "main structural transformations of narrative" in modern and postmodern literature. One particularly significant development was the female private-eye, who emerged in the 1970s "from the unlikely soil of the white-male-centred private-eye". Thanks to cultural shifts brought about by second-wave feminism, this was a time when an increasing number of women started to gain access to professional fields traditionally dominated by men. The crime fiction genre gave writers the opportunity to portray women as self-employed professionals who could navigate their way through danger and diligently get the job done. After decades of pulp fiction stereotypes – helpless damsels, wily femme fatales, and deranged villainesses – this development opened the door to female protagonists who were empowered, autonomous, and multifaceted. It's a trend that would eventually give rise to characters like Clarice Starling (*The Silence of the Lambs*) and Dana Scully (*The X-Files*) – two of the most iconic fictional detectives of the late 20th century.

Carter & Carter Detective Agency by Fleur Blüm tells the story of Megan and Louise Carter – two sisters who have made a career for themselves as private investigators in Melbourne, Australia. Although they specialise in the "tawdry" business of "trailing cheaters", they decide to accept a job from Sue Ingles – a wealthy local whose niece Penny has gone missing while trying to establish herself as a "van life" influencer with her boyfriend Stan. Thus begins this mystery in which multiple outcomes are explored via the branching narrative format.

With *Carter & Carter Detective Agency*, Blüm continues the work of Australian writers who have pushed the boundaries of narrative convention. Parallels can be drawn between Blüm's novel and *The Monkey's Mask* (1994) by Dorothy Porter: a verse novel featuring a private-eye who is not only female, but queer. Similar to *Carter & Carter Detective Agency*, *The Monkey's Mask* features an investigation into the disappearance of a young woman, led by private detective Jill Fitzpatrick. Just as the Carter sisters find themselves thwarted by inept policemen and obstructive male suspects, Fitzpatrick's investigation is repeatedly stymied by dead ends and distractions. Although Blüm's novel is set thirty years after Porter's, her female protagonists still struggle to be taken seriously in the male-dominated world of law enforcement. In addition to this, intimate partner violence continues to cast a shadow over a society that considers itself to be civilised, yet often fails to protect those who are most vulnerable.

Blüm's novel also contains aesthetic traces of 'The Chosen Vessel' by Barbara Baynton: a groundbreaking short story that was published in the December 1896 edition of *The Bulletin*. For a woman to be published in *The Bulletin* at this time is remarkable; even more impressive is that this story effectively critiques the ways in which Australia's patriarchal power structures routinely dehumanised women. Although Baynton is now recognised as a pioneering early feminist, her contribution to Australian literature was overshadowed by the towering legacy of her male contemporaries such as Henry Lawson and Banjo Paterson. Baynton was a realist – a writer whose unflinching depictions of colonial Australia as violent and brutal stand in contrast to the rose-tinged romanticism found in the prose and verse of Lawson and Paterson.

'The Chosen Vessel' tells the story of young wife forced to fend for herself in a bush home while her husband is away shearing. The house is in an isolated location, "a day's journey" from the "dismal, drunken little township", and the young wife (who remains nameless) is particularly vulnerable because she has an infant to look after, as well as the livestock. Although her husband's behaviour is callous and cruel, she's even more fearful of the itinerant travellers known as "swagmen" who occasionally knock on her door and ask for food and tobacco. While Paterson's famous bush ballad 'Waltzing Matilda' characterises the swagman as a "jolly" – a good-natured rapscallion prone to a bit of harmless sheep theft – the swagman in Baynton's story is a figure of terror. In 'The Chosen Vessel', a swagman visits the house of the young wife, deduces her husband is not home (despite her attempts to make it seem otherwise), and waits until nightfall to break in. Her murdered body is found the next day by a boundary rider, who has to cut the baby's gown free from the still clutching hand of its dead mother.

Like Baynton, Blüm depicts Australia as a place where the bodies of murdered women turn up in the bush. Despite being set in contemporary Australia, the world of *Carter & Carter Detective Agency* is one where men are still very much in charge. The police in this novel – all male – have decided that the disappearance of a young woman is not worthy of investigation, and they openly undermine the Carter sisters, passing them off as "enthusiastic amateurs". Stan, the chief suspect in this case, is obstinate and volatile, and even the countercultural "van life" movement harbours shady characters who prey upon young women exploring alternative ways of living. Although 21st century Australia has progressed to the point where a pair of sisters can make a comfortable living as private detectives, enjoying snacks of toasted sandwiches while using GPS technology, there remains a background note of menace. One misstep – for a woman on an adventure, or a detective on a job – could be all it takes for their life to be extinguished.

The Australian landscape provides an apt backdrop for a story that delves into the darker aspects of human nature. Following in the footsteps of Baynton, and of literary luminaries like Patrick White and Tim Winton, Blüm incorporates the vastness and wildness of this ancient continent into the plot of her novel in ways that heighten the sense of unease surrounding Penny's disappearance. The Carter sisters spend much of their time on the road traversing large distances, often finding themselves in nature reserves with air that's "crisp and clean", yet with muddy undertones of decay. The mythos generated by Joan Lindsay's 1967 novel *Picnic at Hanging Rock* looms large, with the bush existing as a space of eerie liminality in which innocent girls can go missing – offering little in the way of clues, and hindering anyone who goes looking. Just as *Picnic at Hanging Rock* taps into anxieties around primal forces lurking in the wilderness, *Carter & Carter Detective Agency* explores the risk of leaving an urban environment in favour of a nomadic life. If Penny had decided to stay home in Melbourne rather than go and chase waterfalls, so to speak, a missing persons investigation would probably not be necessary. Blüm presents a vision of Australia in which the bush is sun-dappled and beguiling by day, but foreboding and even perilous by night.

Ultimately, the work of a private-eye is to uncover the truth. Often, that truth is difficult to face – revealing the worst aspects of the society in which they operate. In this sense, a private-eye performs the same function as a novelist – courageously journeying into difficult terrain to confront uncomfortable realities. It's a difficult job, one that takes its toll. But at least there are simple pleasures that detectives and writers can enjoy along the way, such as muffins, coffee, and croissants. And the occasional parma with chips. But not oysters – they're filter feeders – and you should probably avoid over-indulging on the house red, especially if you're above the age of thirty. It's not easy to continue in your quest as a truth teller when you have food poisoning or a hangover. Basically impossible with both. So yeah, avoid the oysters – your sister is right.

Louise Carter
April 2025

Louise is a Sydney-based writer whose poetry collection *Golden Repair* was published by Giramondo in 2023. She holds a PhD from Western Sydney University, and she's spent several years tutoring subjects in Australian literature. When she's not solving crime, she enjoys spending time with her cat Maz and learning how to pole dance.

Chapter 1

'Where have you put my phone?' Megan asked, lifting and shifting pieces of paper across the enormous mahogany desk.

'What?' Louise answered, without looking up from her book.

'My phone. I'm expecting a call from a client, and I need to know the phone is charged and on.'

'What client? Where did you meet a client?'

'Will you stop answering everything with more questions and help me find my phone?' Megan looked at her sister, off in her own world as usual, and not helping to find the phone she had a habit of misplacing.

'This phone?' Louise picked up the mobile from the small table next to her armchair and waved it. 'It's on, charged, and hasn't rung all day.'

Megan took a breath before saying anything. 'Yes. That phone.' She crossed the space between them in two strides, took it back, and checked the screen. There were no missed calls or incoming messages; it seemed the client hadn't contacted her.

Quince, who was more a writhing conglomeration of fur than a cat, meandered past the sisters without looking at them, and settled himself into the sunbeam falling across the burgundy-patterned rug. Maz, her sister's cat, was significantly smaller than Quince, though it was mainly because she had less fur, was also around somewhere, though Megan couldn't see her just at that moment.

'Are you going to give me the client's details?' Louise asked, closing her book and using her forefinger as a bookmark.

'Sue, legal name Susan, Ingles. Sixty something, divorced. I know her from spin class. She reckons there's something dodgy going on with her niece—'

The phone rang as she held it, Louise narrowed her eyes briefly at the sound since she preferred to have phones turned to silent at all times.

'Carter and Carter Detective Agency, Megan speaking.'

'It's Sue.' Her voice was breathy as though she'd been running.

She put the call on speaker. 'Louise is with me; I was just explaining your case—'

'After I spoke to you earlier, I felt really very silly, as though I was being paranoid and should just put it out of my mind but then I got a phone called from my sister— Kate, Penny's mum—and she said the police have been in touch to say they've exhausted all their avenues and don't expect to get any further.'

'What?' Louise asked.

Megan held her hand up to shush her sister. 'You didn't mention the police were already on the case.'

'When Penny stopped doing her vlog posts, Kate was worried and tried to contact her, but nothing. Then she tried her boyfriend, Stan. She finally got onto him, but he said Penny was off on her own finding herself, and then wouldn't take Kate's calls. So, after three days, Kate reported Penny missing.'

Lousie frowned and opened her mouth, but Megan continued. 'How can we help?'

'I thought they were just having a lovers' tiff, she and Stan could be volatile to say the least, and that she would turn up. But it's been over a month, and we still haven't heard from her. Kate thinks I'm overreacting and that Penny will turn up eventually. She knows Penny well, and has a less active imagination than I do, but I can't just do nothing…' She trailed off and there was a long silence.

'Sue? Are you still there?' Megan asked.

'What if she's dead?'

'I hope that isn't the case, but if it is, we'll be here to help you,' Megan said.

'Would you? The police have given up, not that they'd put it like that, and I'm worried about Penny, and Kate of course.'

'I understand. A month is a long time—'

'I have to go,' Sue interrupted, 'I'm getting another call.' The phone call ended, and the sisters looked at one another.

'This isn't the sort of case we should be pursuing,' Louise said, her jaw tight.

'I know you don't want to get involved in anything violent, but Sue didn't know who else to ask.'

'We should leave it to the police. This is way outside our training.'

'Sue just called to say they're stuck! Plus, I want a break from following people around trying to get photos of them in a compromising position. There must be something more to our careers than cheaters.'

'There is, sometimes we follow people around trying to catch them in insurance fraud.' Louise sighed. 'I know the monotony lately has been frustrating, but we need to keep money coming in. People don't have money to throw at private detectives to do the work the police should do.'

*   *   *

Megan pouted; it made her look like a petulant child.

Why do I have to be the sensible older sister all the time?

Quince wandered over and slid into Megan's lap. He bumped his head under her chin, and she cooed at him, stroking his ears the way he liked.

'All that stuff has been driving me crazy, but if we're able to find a missing person, and a murderer? Isn't that so much more… exciting?'

'If, by exciting, you mean dangerous and questionably illegal, then yes.'

Megan grunted. 'You're so annoying'

'So are you.' There was a beat of silence, as though they were both hoping the other would concede. 'Fine. We can take it on, but I want a meeting with Sue, and I want to be crystal clear that the moment it looks like we have actual evidence a crime has been committed, we turn everything over to the cops. Agreed?'

Megan chewed her bottom lip for a moment.

If you don't agree with Louise's condition, keep reading.

If you agree with Louise's condition, go to Chapter 13 on page 178.

Chapter 2

Megan frowned. 'What do you mean, actual evidence?'

'We're not cops, Megan. We can't just go around chasing people down if there is evidence of a real crime that the police don't have.'

Megan considered for a moment. 'You know they're ignoring the case because they don't think Penny's really missing, right? It's bullshit.'

'That might be true, but I'm not going to get charged with interfering with a crime, or perverting the course of justice, or whatever, just because you've watched too many defund the police and ACAB videos online.'

Megan pressed her lips together. 'As far as I'm concerned, the cops have washed their hands of the whole situation. It's up to us to find Penny, and maybe, once we've found her, we can hand stuff back to them.'

'If that's your attitude, I want no part in this. You do what you think is best, but don't involve me.' Louise had folded her arms, her mouth pinched shut, almost a pout. There would be no arguing with her now she'd dug her heels in, there was nothing for it but to agree and maybe come back around to the idea when she wasn't feeling so stubborn.

Such a Taurus thing to do.

'Alright. I'll work the case on my own, I told Sue I'd look into it and I'm not going to break my promise, but I see your point. If you don't want to take the risk, I can't make you.'

Louise sighed and sat back in the armchair. Megan's palms itched with suppressed anger—after all the crap they'd seen in their job, the stalking and abuse that the police refused to pursue because it was "he said/she said", the idea that Louise would turn down an opportunity to help someone who might be in real trouble was both infuriating and disappointing. Megan picked up her mobile, her car keys, and her work bag and turned to the door.

'I'm going to do some research. I'll be back later.'

Louise didn't look up. Megan was tempted to slam the office door on her way out but restrained herself. No need to make the situation worse.

Her work bag was a large black duffle that had a long strap on one side, and two thick straps on the back, to convert easily from shoulder bag to backpack. Both Carter sisters had one, Megan's was filled with her tools of the trade; camera, zoom lenses, a tablet device for research, miscellaneous chargers, and some less than strictly legal items: a lock pick set and slim Jim. Megan had never had to use either of those last two on a job but didn't want to be caught without them should the need arise.

She really had no idea what research she was supposed to be doing, rather, it was a reason to leave the office. Sue had had to take another call, but maybe if she dropped in at her place there would be more information to gather.

Megan drove the short distance from the office, in Northcote, to Sue's house in the wealthy suburb of Kew and parked a couple of doors down. On the walk up, it occurred to her she probably should have phoned ahead, but it was too late now. She pushed the old-fashioned bell and enjoyed the tinkling chimes from inside the house. For a long time, she heard nothing, and considered ringing the bell again, but then she heard the clip-clop of high heels on tiles.

'Coming,' Sue's muffled voice came through the door. 'Megan, you didn't say you were on the way.' She opened the door with a frown.

'Sorry, I—' Megan hesitated, 'maybe if I come in?'

'Of course.' Sue stepped back and Megan followed her into the house. The narrow central hallway had green and cream harlequin tiles, deep mahogany wainscotting and embossed cream wallpaper on the upper half of the walls. It was incredibly tasteful and looked very expensive. They passed a formal lounge on the left, complete with two enormous dark leather Chesterfields, and a couple of bedrooms on the right, before coming out into the open-plan kitchen area at the back of the house. This area had a completely different feel, still impeccably tasteful of course, but more modern, the walls were duck egg blue, and the furnishings looked more worn. Megan wondered if the formal lounge was just for show.

'Can I offer you a drink? Perhaps a cup of tea?'

'I'd love a cup of tea.' Megan pulled out one of the stools and sat down while Sue bustled around the kitchen.

'Now, I don't mean to be rude, but why are you here?'

'I pitched the case to Louise, and it… didn't go well.'

'Oh?'

'She thinks we need to leave it to the police, whereas I think they're a load of incompetent misogynists and racists. I don't see why we can't do our own investigation.'

'She won't take the case?'

'Not unless we hand everything over.'

Sue leaned her hands on the counter, one eyebrow cocked. 'And you don't agree?'

'No. I think we need to find Penny. I'm concerned for her, since you mentioned the situation to me the other day. The more I think about it, the more I think we need to get started straight away. We've agreed to disagree, and I'll be working on it alone.'

'Will that be awkward?'

Megan chuckled, trying to release the tension she was holding in her shoulders. 'Probably. We've disagreed on stuff before; you know how siblings are. If the case works out well, it will be fine, but if anything goes sideways, I might need to do some grovelling.'

'I see.' Sue turned to make a pot of green tea.

'Have you had any news?'

'No. Nothing.'

'Who called you earlier?'

Sue sighed. 'My mechanic to tell me it was time to book in for a service. I told him it wasn't a good time, but of course I need to answer any calls; it could be Penny using a different number, you know.'

'That sounds exhausting.' Megan blew across the top of her steaming tea.

'It's been terrible. I keep thinking we should have acted sooner. Kate was so insistent that we leave it to the professionals, that everything will work out, but the police have done next to nothing. Penny's been gone for too long.'

'Do you know where she was last seen?'

'Yes, I've marked it on a map on my laptop.'

'Let's start there.'

Sue went to the couch to grab her computer while Megan waited at the distressed pine kitchen table. When Sue returned, they sat side by side.

'Now tell me everything you know,' Megan said, placing her phone on the table between them with a voice recorder app open, and opening her notebook. 'Is it okay for me to record us, for my notes?'

'Of course.' Sue sighed and drew her shoulders back as though preparing to take the stage. 'Penny is my sister Kate's child. Her only child. She turned twenty a couple of months ago, but we didn't see her for her birthday; she was already on her trip. Stan Warding is her boyfriend, he's twenty-seven, and a bit of a wastrel if you ask me. He told my sister that he was an emerging entrepreneur but we thought it sounded like a fancy way of saying he was unemployed. He does a bit of landscaping and construction work when he needs money but otherwise seems to live in his van and sponge off whoever is fool enough to let him park in their vicinity.'

Megan nodded; she knew the type.

'They met about a year ago, he was at a university party—though I think that's a bit off a man that age hanging out with uni students—anyway, he charmed her, told her she was an old soul, that they were destined to be together. The usual dross.'

'After a couple of months, he had parked his van outside Kate's place in Ashburton. She didn't want him in the house, fair enough, but he said he didn't have anywhere to stay. So, Kate agreed to let him use the shower and kitchen but Penny wasn't to sleep in the van with him, nor was he to sleep in the house. She might be over eighteen but that didn't mean Kate wanted hanky panky happening under her roof.'

'I see.' Megan was writing down the pertinent details as Sue was speaking.

'Three weeks of this and Penny announces that she's taking a leave of absence from uni that semester to go travelling with Stan. He wants to become a professional vlogger, and she's going to help him. They'll go around Australia, and if they get enough followers, and sponsors and what not, they'll take the van to New Zealand and possibly southeast Asia.

'Kate laughed at first—what a ridiculous career, making stupid travel videos and thinking you could make a living off it, but Penny wouldn't be dissuaded. In the middle of her second year of uni—doing Engineering at Melbourne mind you, she's a smart girl—she takes an open-ended leave of absence, packs up a couple of bags and leaves in a van with a pervert.'

Megan scribbled a note; she would need to look into this alleged pervert. Just because the mother and aunt didn't like him didn't mean there was anything actually wrong; sometimes smoke meant fire, sometimes it meant a hippy with a joint.

'When did you start thinking something was going wrong?'

'Kate was convinced he was bad news from the start, all that sugary sweetness around her and her husband didn't make up for being a bum.'

'There are plenty of creative types who don't have a lot of material belongings.'

'I know, believe me, my sister and I both had our arty phases, but there is a distinct difference between a creep and a man-child. Stan was definitely capable of having a job, and dating women his own age, he just didn't.' She paused, looking over Megan's shoulder and through the large picture windows into the backyard.

'Actually, now that I think about it, perhaps he couldn't date women his own age because they wouldn't put up with his bullshit.'

'Maybe.' Megan waited; pen poised for further information.

'So off they went, in his van, with no particular plan or itinerary and a couple of Go Pros and a nice digital SLR camera Penny had from her eighteenth birthday. They'd set up a YouTube channel and a blog site for their stories—'

'What's the channel called?' Megan asked, interrupting Sue's flow.

'Let me think… it was inane, honestly, VanLyfDiaries I think, all one word, but life is spelled L Y F.' She rolled her eyes.

Megan nodded.

'The first few video diaries were made before they left. They did a tour of the van, talked about how excited they were to be doing the trip, all of that. Mostly it was Penny talking with Stan smiling behind her. I wasn't impressed with it, I thought it was setting up a poor dynamic where they were not equals, but I didn't say so.'

'Did Kate watch the videos too?'

'We both did, sometimes together. While Penny was away Kate wasn't too worried. Her only child was away for an indeterminate period of time but she was sure she'd come to her senses. After they left, Penny would call Kate every so often. At first it was every couple of days, sometimes she would chat for hours while they were on the road, especially if Stan was napping and she was driving, but that died off a bit.'

'Why do you think that was?'

'Penny said he needed quiet to sleep, but I think it was more than that. He didn't want her to have such close contact with her family. So, the long phone calls became check-ins of ten or fifteen minutes. When they got to Adelaide, they took the scenic route and spent two weeks getting there from Melbourne,' Sue shook her head, 'they released a vlog every day, talking about whatever they were doing and where they had been. Some of them were very short, five minutes, others were longer, if they were in an interesting town, or went for a hike or something.'

'It sounds like they were having a nice time.'

'It was fine, mostly. I kept an eye on how much Penny was in the videos too, at first, she was a bit stilted, you know, but as they went on, she was more confident. She talked more, even about their food and cooking in the van—she always like cooking you see.'

'After Adelaide, where did they go?'

'I think they went north, up through the wine country, and a lot of dry yellow countryside, they stayed in Alice for a while, doing bits and pieces, a couple of nights at Uluru, then they went east to Sydney.'

'How long had they been gone by this stage?'

'About three months or so.'

'And was Penny still calling her mother?'

'No, by Uluru we were mostly keeping in touch by watching the vlogs. Kate would call her sometimes, but most of the time Penny wouldn't answer. If she did, it was only a few minutes of cursory conversation.'

Megan nodded.

'By the time they got to Sydney, Kate was calling less often, probably only once a week, but she still didn't answer most of the time. Penny would text back that they were out of phone coverage, or they were in the middle of filming or some such other nonsense excuse.'

'Where did she go missing?'

'The vlogs said the plan after Sydney was to go north up the coast, first towards Newcastle. The vlog showed them stopping at a spot near Gosford for a meal, and then Penny stopped appearing in the videos.'

'Do you know where exactly she went missing?'

'This is where things start to get a bit iffy.'

'How so?'

'Kate has access to Penny's *Find my Phone* data, so when the daily vlog went up and Stan said Penny had decided not to travel with him anymore, she started to panic. She called and called, but it went straight to voicemail.'

'The phone was off?'

'Yes. So, she pulled up the app, and it stated the phone was turned off or out of range. The last known location was a rest area just near Gosford where they'd stopped for the day. It features in the vlog, but I have the exact place from the app. The phone travelled a ways up the road, then turned around and went back to the rest stop, then it was turned off.'

'Why would it have done that?'

'Kate tried to call Stan, and after about two weeks of calling everyday he must have given up and answered, because he told Kate that he had Penny's phone, and he was going to post it back to her place in Ashburton in case Penny wanted it.'

'Kate has Penny's phone?' Megan leaned forward in her chair; this would change everything if she had access to the data.

'No.' Sue sighed. 'Stan said he would post it, but it's still not turned up.'

Megan chewed on her pen. 'And you reported Penny missing when?'

'Three days after the vlog came out without Penny in it. When she saw that the phone was turned off, she gave it a day or so to come back on, but yeah, she was immediately worried.'

'Did the cops search the rest area?'

'Kate said they did. Didn't find anything of note apparently. She said she gave them the number plate of the van, and Stan's name and phone number. After she spoke to Stan, you know a couple of weeks after the disappearance when he said he had her phone, she called the police to ask if they'd spoken to him, they said they had but they weren't worried either.'

'What did Stan tell the cops?'

'They wouldn't say.'

Megan made a grumbling sound in her throat that was almost a growl. 'Bloody useless.'

'Privacy apparently. Ongoing investigation and all of that.'

Megan rolled her eyes. 'Does Kate know you've come to the agency?'

'Yes, she thinks I'm being silly, but she said it was my money and I could waste it on a detective agency if I wanted to. What are you going to do now?'

Megan sat back in the chair and tapped the pen against her lips, thinking. 'I have to go to Gosford. I want to see the rest stop, granted it was a month ago so there's not much chance there will be anything obvious there, and then speak to the police, and maybe try to track down Stan. Is he still doing the vlog?'

'Yes, it's not every day, maybe every few days now. I suppose it's harder when you have to do all the driving and all the filming and editing and whatnot.'

Megan started to formulate a plan; she needed to watch all the videos and get up to Gosford as soon as possible. She would try one more time to convince Louise to take on the case, but was prepared to do it without her.

'The last thing we need to do is negotiate my fees.'

'Of course, I should have asked about that earlier.'

Megan waved her hand. 'It's fine. Most people we deal with are so caught up in the crisis at hand, they don't think to talk about money, but it's best to do it before we get too far into the weeds.'

Sue nodded.

'Usually we arrange a daily rate, which is a flat fee for each day we're working on your case, and expenses.'

'That sounds fair.'

'Given there are some travel arrangements and whatever, it might get pricey, so you might like to think about a cut off, you know if we get to a certain figure, I pull the plug or check in with you about the costs.'

'Money is no issue. I want my niece found and I will pay whatever needs to be paid to have that happen.'

'Okay. I'll call you after the first week, and we'll talk about how things are progressing. After that I'll have a think about a weekly rate, since I'll be working exclusively on this case.'

'Alright, that sounds fine. Do you need an initial payment? Say a week to get started?'

'That would be great.' Megan pulled out her mobile and typed in seven times her usual daily rate. It felt obscene to ask that much money from a friend who was trying to find her missing niece, but a cursory glance around the house reminded her that money wasn't exactly a problem for Sue or her sister. 'Great, I'll send you a proper receipt when I get back to the office.'

Sue nodded, her hands wrapped around the now-empty mug, her eyes glazed over.

'Is there anything else you want to tell me? You can always text or email me if something comes to mind later. Even if it seems silly, or inconsequential.'

Sue shivered and looked back at Megan. 'No, I don't think so, I'm sorry it's all feeling too real right now.'

'I know, it can be hard when you have to wait for me to find something. I promise I'll give this my full attention.' Megan stood up and started to gather her things together to leave. She stopped the voice recording and slipped everything back into her work bag. When she was finished, Sue was still staring off into the middle distance, and Megan decided it was better to leave her to it.

'I'll let myself out,' she said, her voice low so as not to startle her. Sue just nodded and continued to stare.

What a weird day.

Megan got into the car and turned on the engine so the heater would come on. She was suddenly cold as though hearing about Penny's situation had chilled her, though it was probably just the weather. The sky was leaden, dull heavy clouds loomed, and it would probably start raining at any moment, though with Melbourne's fickle weather, it might stay like that for the rest of the day without any rain.

She looked over her notes, trying to figure out the next steps. She had to get to Gosford, but Sydney was at least a twelve-hour drive, including a couple of stops, and Gosford was on the other side, adding a couple of hours. If Megan went back to the office now, and tried to talk to Louise, she might be able to convince her to come along for the trip, leave first thing in the morning and be in Sydney tomorrow night. If she didn't bother speaking to Louise and just ducked in to get a bag packed for a few nights away, she would probably make it to the border by the time she needed to stop for the night. It wouldn't be the first time she'd slept in the car for a job, and at least this time she would have a sleeping bag with her to keep off the chill.

If you decide to speak to Louise again and try to convince her to come with you to Gosford tomorrow, read on.

If you want to get started on the drive to Gosford immediately, go to Chapter 19 *on page 306.*

Chapter 3

You speak to Louise again and try to convince her to come with you to Gosford tomorrow.

Megan walked back into the office, apprehensive. She now had a lot more information and hoped it would help convince Louise to take the job. On the other hand, she had no intention of involving the police since they had stated they were no longer interested in the case.

'You're back.' Louise's voice was flat.

'Yep.'

'Did you research anything useful?'

'I did.' Megan walked over to the desk and started unpacking her work bag.

'Are you going to tell me what you found out?'

Megan paused her unpacking. 'I went to see Sue.' She hesitated, one hand in mid-air. 'She gave me a rundown of the timeline. I want to go to Gosford, where Penny was last seen.'

'You're committed to following the case through, even if I don't work on it with you?'

'I would rather work together; I think we make an excellent team, but I'm prepared to do this one solo.'

Louise put down the book she had been reading and shifted in her seat.

'I don't think the police will be able to help. They've given up,' Megan said.

'You know we can't arrest anyone or take them to court.'

'I know.'

'What happens if we find, worst-case scenario, Penny's body up there? Do you expect me to just sit on that?'

'What? No!' Megan frowned. 'I hadn't thought of it that way. If we find a body, or something, then obviously we bring the cops in. And if we run into a dead end, we can hand everything over and hope they do something. I still think we'll do a better job.'

Louise exhaled. 'I can live with that. Tell me what Sue said.'

Megan went over the information Sue had provided, referring to her notes and the recording she had made on her phone.

'How far is Gosford?'

'It's an hour north of Sydney, a day's drive if we go hard, maybe twelve hours.'

'And you have her commitment to expenses?'

'Yeah, but she's paying a flat day rate. I didn't think you were helping so…'

'It's a friend, we're not doing it for the money. That being said, paying rent is important. If the trail peters out or we get stuck, I'll come back down here, and you can keep working on it.'

'That sounds fair.' Megan flipped her phone over and over in her hand. 'Are you coming with me tomorrow then?'

'Uh…' Louise rubbed her eyebrow. 'I have to tie up one or two things down here. Do you want to start without me?'

'Yeah, I can do that.' Megan's relaxed her shoulders. It was good they had worked out their differences; they had their disagreements as all siblings did, but it was always stressful when they were fighting.

She went upstairs feeling lighter and filled with energy for the case. She pulled out the large duffle bag she used for travelling. She wasn't much interested in fashion, and her wardrobe was filled with nondescript staples: jeans, T-shirts, hoodies, several pairs of the same style of sneakers. She figured, why spend her mental energy on frivolous stuff like clothes when she could be thinking about other, more important matters? She dumped the duffle on the floor, ready to fill. She'd brought her laptop up from the office, and she perched on the edge of the bed, opening it. She navigated to YouTube and typed in VanLyfDiaries, Penny and Stan's channel.

There were recent videos featuring Stan, as well as older content with both of them. She scrolled back and started with the first one, letting it play while she packed.

The first few videos were short, five to ten minutes long, with a lot of Penny talking about how excited they were to be heading off, filmed before they started the trip.

'We're on the highway about twenty minutes out of Geelong,' Penny said, talking to camera while Stan was driving. 'We're making our way to Adelaide via the Great Ocean Road. We'll be going through Anglesea, Lorne, Cape Otway, and stopping in Port Campbell for the night. That is, unless we get lost or distracted on the way.' She laughed nervously, and Megan saw a look of doubt cross her face before she plastered a smile back onto her face.

'It's about four and a half hours of driving, not including stopping for food and pictures. If we time it right, we'll be able to see the Twelve Apostles at sunset, which will be really spectacular, won't it, babe?'

Megan makes a note of that discomforted look in her notebook.

I'll have to keep an eye out for that look, could be nervousness being on camera, or it could be something more.

Stan muttered something inaudible in response, and again Penny's smile faltered briefly before the scene cut to them standing on a beach, the sky grey and overcast, wind whipping Penny's hair into her eyes. Stan held the camera in front of himself, selfie-style, smiling and trying to look like he wasn't being buffeted by the strong winds.

'We're here at Bell's Beach, famous for surfing. Unfortunately, good surf usually means wind, and you can see it's a bit of a tough day to vlog.' He laughed, but his eyes remained cold and emotionless. A shiver ran down Megan's spine.

No wonder the mother wasn't keen on him; he's like a shark.

The rest of the content for that day consisted of footage of the beaches, as well as the massive stone monuments of the Twelve Apostles at sunset, with copyright-free music piped over it. Despite Penny and

Stan's novice vlogging skills, it looked spectacular, the heavy clouds lit up in shades of mauve and orange.

At the end of the day, they both recorded a piece to camera in their motel room.

'I love the motels and hotels in this big brown land. They might be spread all over, but there are a couple of common themes that are comforting; muted floral bedspreads, microwaves from the nineties with knobs instead of buttons, more signs than anyone can possibly read—' he panned the camera around the room to demonstrate each item. 'We're about to go get some food at the local pub—hopefully they have something edible, and then tomorrow we continue on the journey. It'll be your turn to drive for a bit tomorrow, babe.' Stan looked to Penny, who smiled tentatively.

The dynamic between them is seriously weird, but bad content isn't a crime.

Maybe Penny got sick of putting her name to the mediocrity, but something told Megan that wasn't the reason she'd dropped out of contact over a month ago.

Megan listened and kept an eye on more of the vlogs while she packed, and planned her driving route to Gosford. If she left first thing and pushed hard, she would be there by tomorrow night, saving the need to stop over in Canberra or some other small town part way there. She also loaded her phone with podcasts and downloaded Penny and Stan's videos to listen to again as she drove. Getting to know her subjects was at least as important as reviewing the evidence.

She briefly scrolled through Stan's social media and found that he had an older YouTube channel too.

'Hey, Louise,' Megan yelled through the open door.

'What?' Louise yelled back.

'You gotta come see this.'

'Bring it down.'

Megan glanced at the time as she descended the stairs, a little before ten, nearly time to get to bed.

'Stan has a second channel,' Megan said, holding the open laptop in front of Louise in the armchair, her own laptop open on her lap.

'Huh?'

'Stan, the boyfriend who probably killed Penny, he has another vlog channel. Can you add it to your research list?'

Louise looked up. 'What's he vlogging about?'

'I dunno, I've been watching their travel diaries. I'm about to turn in, gonna start early tomorrow, so can you have a look?'

'Yeah, alright. I'm still trying to sort out this other thing.'

'What other thing? We're not working on anything.'

Louise sighed, straightened in her chair, and closed her laptop. 'While you were out chatting with Sue earlier, I had a call from Steph, from the law firm. She wants a day or two watching someone claiming total and permanent disability from a work accident. I said yes because I expected to be free.'

'Right. Why not just say so?'

'I thought you'd be annoyed, it's good money and I wasn't sure if Sue would pay.'

Megan frowned. 'Okay then.' She didn't get the vagueness, but it wasn't worth arguing about, especially since they seemed to be getting on again. 'I'm leaving really early; you might not be up, so if I don't see you, I'll keep you posted on anything I find once I get there.'

'Okay, I'll let you know if Stan's vlogs have anything of note or if Sue gets in touch. Drive safe. I know you can get there in a day, but don't push yourself, especially at dusk, the 'roos can come out of nowhere.'

'I promise.' Megan wasn't sure why Louise thought she was the authority on driving in the country, given they were both city slickers, but it was good advice—getting written off by wildlife wasn't on her to-do list.

Megan's alarm went off at six o'clock, though she snoozed it a few times before pulling herself out of bed. The day had dawned foggy and crisp; late autumn in Melbourne could be chilly overnight, but the days were relatively mild.

She tried to move around the kitchen quietly, so as not to wake Louise, although her sister was a sound sleeper. With her bags packed last night, Megan was able to get in her car and set out just after seven.

Even at that time, the roads were surprisingly busy, mostly tradies and trucks heading north. At least the majority of the traffic was going the other way, towards the city. Megan stopped briefly for a service station coffee, a toilet break, and to stretch her legs in Euroa, then had lunch in Holbrook, another brief stop in Yass, but was disappointed to find the famous, or perhaps infamous, McDonald's sign had been taken down since the last time she drove through the town.

It was getting dark as she left Yass, and while she had hoped to make it to Gosford, her bladder was about ready to explode by the time she reached Bankstown, a suburb in western Sydney. She stopped for dinner and checked her messages and emails.

Louise had sent her a couple of things to look at, but after all day in the car, her brain was mush. She dialled her sister's number.

'Are you there already?' Louise asked.

'Nah, stopped in Bankstown. I might need to find a motel here. I'm cooked.'

'I wasn't going to say anything, but it did seem like a big drive all on your own.'

'I'm not going to try to drive the whole way back in one go, that's for sure.'

'I'll fly up to Sydney in a day or two, then I'll be able to share on the way back.'

Megan was silent for a beat, having forgotten why she rang.

'Since you're on the line, I have watched some of Stan's solo content.'

'Right. And?'

'Nothing I can put my finger on, but I don't like him.'

'Is it the dead eyes?'

'Huh?' Louise sounded confused. 'No, it's… his language. It's as though he's spent too long on those incel forums. He's not completely there, but there are sprinklings of words, like "simping" and a couple of others, that make me really uncomfortable.'

'Red flags.'

'Yes. Lots. I had to take a break, I felt soiled. After a day of following around a guy in a wheelchair hoping to catch him out, that's saying something.'

'You're not kidding. Did you catch him out?'

'No, he seems genuinely injured. I followed him to the local supermarket and his wife tried to help but he seemed to insist on doing things himself. If I were to bet, I'd say he was truthful.'

'That's good,' Megan said absently.

'You sound like you're already asleep. Find somewhere to crash out, and you can finish the drive tomorrow. Maybe try to talk to the cops or something.'

'Okay. Let me know if you find anything concrete in those vlogs, I know he's probably just a regulation creep, but if there's video of him being, I dunno, threatening or something, that will help.'

'Will do. Have a good sleep. Don't let the bedbugs bite.'

'Don't mention bedbugs,' Megan said, with a half-smile. She didn't need to be reminded of the time they'd stayed in a weird bed-and-breakfast place which was infested with bed bugs , not long after Megan had joined the agency. They'd both been covered in bites the next day, and it had taken them several attempts to ensure their clothes were properly de-infested.

Megan opened the search app on her phone and found the nearest, cheapest accommodation she could find—above a pub not far from where she was. She grunted loudly as she pushed herself up from the table and hobbled back towards the car.

I need a shower and some stretches before bed, otherwise, I'll wind up crooked and bent in the morning.

Megan fell asleep almost as soon as her head hit the pillow and woke early the next morning feeling better, though not what she would call well-rested. She packed, checked out of her room, and was on the road again not long after seven in the morning, hoping to avoid the worst of the peak hour traffic, though she only partially succeeded.

The drive was pleasant enough; she stopped in to get a coffee and a sausage and egg breakfast muffin on her way through Hornsby just before she got onto the highway north out of Sydney.

Gosford was a waterfront town on the Brisbane Water—not in Brisbane, the city about a thousand kilometres north, but presumably named after the same guy. It was a city, though small, quiet during the winter season, and busier in summer. She pulled up at a motel just back from the main drag and set herself up—they agreed to let her check in early as they didn't have many people staying—dumping all her bags into the dark, pine-panelled room.

There's something about motel rooms, they're all exactly the same but somehow a little bit different. The bedside table had a Bible in it that looked unused, a small TV, a kettle, and those tiny ceramic cups that never held enough of a beverage to be satisfying. Even the daisy-patterned bedspreads were faded and muted, but the room didn't smell of anything weird, and the surfaces weren't sticky.

The last time Penny had been seen was at a rest stop up near the Strickland Falls, a local landmark a little bit to the north of the town, but Megan wondered if she should start with the police.

If you decide to go to the Strickland Falls rest stop and look around, read on.

If you decide to go to the Police Station to try to get some more information, go to <u>Chapter 5</u> *on page 48.*

Chapter 4

You decide to go to the Strickland Falls rest stop and look around.

Megan opened her phone and searched for a route to Strickland Falls and the car park where Penny was last seen. It was a twenty-minute drive, so she figured she may as well go up there and check it out. Even after a month, there might be something worth finding.

The Banksia Picnic area was a large flat clearing in the middle of the eucalyptus forest. A couple of trails headed off from points around the car park, and the small, covered area with a couple of picnic tables and wood-fired barbeques had seen better days.

I didn't know National Parks let you have wood fires like that, Megan thought as she took a lap of the surrounds. She came to a large, coloured sign covered with information about the forest. It covered the local flora and fauna, some of the local landmarks, and maps of the trails.

The waterfall was the most appealing of the three tracks; they were all marked as low or medium grade, and less than two kilometres.

I might even do a second track if the waterfall track doesn't yield anything; there's plenty of time before lunch.

Megan started for the waterfalls; the track led off from beside one of the barbeques. She'd packed small plastic snap-lock bags to collect any evidence that she might come across on the trail, as well as her camera. She walked slowly, scanning the bush on either side of the track for anything of interest, though mostly she saw the green fronds of bracken, dried brown gum leaves, bark, and the occasional chip packet. Any litter that was within reach of the path she collected in a bag and labelled with the time, date, and approximate location.

As she walked, she travelled gradually downhill from the level of the car park, the terrain to one side of the track slowly changed into a rock wall. At the end of the track, the rock walls towered above her, and there were several streams of water cascading over them into a shallow, crystal-clear pool below.

It wasn't the sort of waterfall she had expected, much more subtly beautiful than the great crashing falls she'd seen before. Megan wasn't an outdoors type and had done very little bush walking before, so her experience with waterfalls was restricted to ones she'd seen on television or in people's garden water features. She sat for a moment on one of the drier rocks and listened to the gentle thunder of the water.

I wish I'd brought a snack.

Though the track was short, she'd spent a lot of time looking at the surroundings, snapping pictures and collecting possible evidence, and it had crept closer to lunchtime than she had expected. The other trails would have to wait for another time, maybe after Louise arrived to help with the search and collection.

She hadn't been sitting long before her bum started to get cold and uncomfortable on the rock. Megan pushed herself up and looked back the way she had come. She hadn't realised that the trail was a loop and decided to keep going rather than retrace her steps. She skirted around the pool and over the small stream before starting on the trail up towards the car. Her tummy growled at the thought of the toasted sandwich she would buy from the place around the corner from the motel.

The trail up wasn't too steep, but she found it hard going, even with her relaxed pace and pauses for photos and collections. She'd have to come back and go around the loop the other way for completeness, as there were sometimes things that could only be seen coming from one direction, but it was already far more hiking than she'd done before—perhaps in her whole life—and she wasn't coming back in the afternoon.

The rock wall shrank as she progressed up the hill, pausing on some stairs to pick up a discarded camera lens cap. She turned, and as she stooped to pick it up, she rested her hand on the rock face. As soon as she did, she realised her mistake the rock crumbled under her weight, causing her to lose her balance and fall forward hard, slamming her right kneecap into the stone step below.

She cried out in pain and tried to stop her fall, which only caused her to tumble further down four steps and bang her shoulder into a bit of rock jutting out from the surface of the wall. She saw stars, and pain shot through her from her knee and her shoulder. It was so much pain Megan couldn't call out or cry; she was too shocked to make any noise, and it took her several long moments to get her breath back, having winded herself.

Once she'd recovered a little, the pain in her shoulder had dulled, but her kneecap was still incredibly painful. She had worn skinny leg jeans and would have struggled to roll them up to inspect her leg, but there was no blood coming through. Very gingerly, she ran her fingertips over her knee, checking for any obvious breaks, but didn't feel anything out of place. Everywhere she touched seared with pain, and even through her pants, she could see the knee had started to swell up.

'Fuck,' she said aloud. She pulled out her phone; no coverage. She shuffled around to a more comfortable position and took a few deep breaths. Her work bag didn't have any painkillers, though she thought there were some in the car. The only thing for it was to try to hobble back and call for help from the car park, or worst case, drive back to town to get medical attention. Megan put her plastic bags and camera back into her backpack and tried to stand, avoiding putting weight on her right leg. Her knee was stiffening, and it hurt to bend or straighten it, and to put weight on it, though at least she could bear it.

She hobbled back to the car park, it seemed to take hours, though it could have been more like thirty minutes in actual time. Megan unlocked the car, sat in the driver's seat, with her feet outside, and checked her phone again.

The relief of seeing the bars of reception almost made her cry. She dialled triple zero for an ambulance and hoped they wouldn't take too long to get to her.

The ambulance took over an hour to get to her, by which time her leg had swollen up to an absurd size. They took her to hospital, where they did an X-ray and found that she had broken her kneecap. Though it didn't require surgery, she would have to wear a knee brace for several weeks and wouldn't be able to continue the case.

Louise flew up to join her the next day; she drove the car back to Melbourne, since Megan's driving leg was out of commission. Megan told Sue they had to discontinue the case and return her money. They never found out what happened to Penny.

You failed, go back and try again.

Chapter 5

*You decide to go to the police station to try to get some
more information.*

The Gosford Police Station was a blocky, brutalist
building; all yellow brick veneer and pale concrete
stained grey with rain, about ten minutes' walk from
where Megan was staying.

Not very promising, Megan thought to herself as she
entered through the brown-tinted automatic sliding glass
doors. It wasn't the worst police station she'd seen,
though three stories, and the few people waiting in the
reception area didn't seem to be drunk or drug affected,
perhaps that was more a sign of the time of day than the
effectiveness of the local constabulary.

The dated seventies exterior continued inside, the
foyer's floor covered with shiny, dark brown tiles, and
the rows of middle-brown plastic bucket seats seemed to
be original, though some were bleached and stained,
possibly where they had removed graffiti.

A young male officer stood behind a glass screen,
clicking around and occasionally typing something into
the computer. He didn't quite look bored, nor did he look
enthused. His light brown hair was trimmed short and
styled neatly away from his face, and though he had
pleasing symmetrical features and pale blue eyes, he
wasn't handsome.

'Can I help you?' He briefly looked away from the
screen to notice Megan's approach.

'I'm here to ask about Penny Bean, sorry, Penelope Bean.'

'What's your relationship to Ms Bean?' The young man typed a few things into the computer but hadn't looked back at Megan yet.

'I'm looking into her disappearance on behalf of the family.'

The cop frowned, his eyes tracking slowly over to meet Megan's gaze. 'Private investigator or enthusiastic amateur?'

'I have a Victorian Investigative Services licence—'

'Have you got a New South Wales licence?'

'Uh, no. I was under the impression my Victorian one would be valid up here.'

'I'll have to speak to a supervisor. Take a seat.' The young man waved towards the rows of seats and looked back to his screen. Megan sat down, facing the window behind which the young man was working, expecting him to call over another officer or pick up the phone, but he did neither; he just went back to clicking and staring at whatever was on his screen.

It was a little after nine thirty in the morning. Megan had had a cheese and tomato toasted sandwich and a scalding café latte at a local café on her way over, and the meal sat greasy in her stomach.

Megan texted her sister:

> **Cops in Gosford gave the impression
> my licence isn't valid. I don't get a
> vibe that they're keen to talk to me.**

How's your loose-end-tying-up going?

The few others in the reception area weren't paying her any attention. Opposite her, a man in his early seventies sat with his walking stick resting on the chair next to him. His eyes were drooping, and Megan thought he might fall asleep before he jerked himself up, mumbled something and opened the newspaper he'd been holding.

To her right, young man and woman, probably a couple, were scrolling through their phones. They were slightly dishevelled looking and smelled vaguely of patchouli.

Might be here for weed possession, possibly other van lifers.

The only other person in the waiting area was a woman, possibly in her forties, well-dressed and sitting bolt upright, tapping her manicured fingernails against the very expensive-looking handbag tightly grasped in her lap. Her eyes darted to the young couple repeatedly as though she expected them to rob her right there in the station, and though it seemed laughable to Megan, the woman was quite distracted by them.

'Jane Connor?' the young police officer called out after a couple of minutes. The uptight woman leapt up from her seat and dashed to the window, her towering stilettos clacking on the tiles.

They spoke in low tones for a few moments before the officer stepped out from behind his desk, opened a door to his right and ushered her into the office behind. The old man's eyes were drooping closed again, his newspaper sagging.

'Have you been here long?' Megan asked the young couple, getting up as she did so to move a few seats closer to them.

The woman, a sallow, thin, brunette, looked up in surprise. 'Me?'

'Yeah.'

'We had an appointment at nine,' said the man, also of slim build, though his skin looked healthier than hers, 'I don't really know why I thought they'd run on time.'

'It's a big building, but the only cop I've seen is that young guy.'

'Yeah, we've seen him a couple of times.'

'How many times have you been here?' Megan asked.

The two looked at each other briefly before the man answered. 'We've been woofing up on a farm and we got pulled over for having a tail-light out on our van.' He rolled his eyes.

'We fixed it right away, but they gave us a fine and said we had to show up to the station to pay it,' the woman said.

'What a pain in the arse. You can't just pay it online?'

'We tried, but it kept declining. I dunno, maybe they want us to come and wait in the cop shop so they can terrorise us.' The man's leg had started jiggling up and down as he spoke.

'Was it that desk guy who pulled you over?'

'Nah, a couple of older guys, but this guy was here last week when we tried to pay last time.'

Megan considered for a moment. 'Are there many people, you know, travellers, working on the farms up this way?'

'Not really. Usually they're further north, but we're just testing it out. We want to go all the way around Australia.'

'Sounds nice. How long have you been in Gosford?'

The woman stared at the ceiling for a moment. 'Is it six weeks now, babe?'

'That sounds right.'

Megan sat forward a little in her chair, *take it easy, don't want to scare them off.* 'You wouldn't have happened to cross paths with another young couple a bit over a month ago, they were going around Australia in a van, doing vlogs.' She reached into her bag and pulled out her phone, looking for a photo to show the couple.

'We've met a few people travelling through. The locals aren't much chop for conversation, you know?'

'I bet. Here we are.' Megan showed the photo of Stan and Penny in front of the van that Sue had sent her. 'Penny Bean and her boyfriend, Stan Warding.'

The man reached forward and Megan handed him the phone. 'Looks familiar, right, babe?'

'Yeah, it rings a bell. Lemme see.' She took the phone and peered at the photo, touching the screen to enlarge it. 'Yeah, we ran into them on a hike, in Strickland State Forest, remember? I thought they were camping there in their van, even though it's illegal. We park our van at the farm. After a couple of fines for camping without a permit, we decided it's not worth it, and we stay on the farms when we can.'

'You saw them? Do you remember what day? Or where exactly?'

'Umm…' The woman frowned, pulled out her phone and started scrolling. 'Would have had to be a day we had off, you said about a month ago?'

'Yeah.'

'This was the fourth of April, it was a Thursday, we had it off, and we took this photo at the picnic area before we went on the walk up to the waterfalls,' the woman handed her phone to Megan, showing a photo of the two of them in a car park, smiling broadly. In the background of the photo was the white van that Penny and Stan were driving, and behind the van, she could just see the outline of the back half of a person with a long, brown pony-tail.

'That's Penny,' Megan said, excited.

'Yeah, we could hear them arguing, the girl was trying to be quiet but the guy was carrying on; the whole picnic area was pretending they couldn't hear,' the young man said.

'How many people were there? What time of day was it?'

'Early—well, kind of, about ten. There were just us two and a family of four sitting at one of the tables.'

Megan pulled out her notepad and hurriedly scribbled down what she'd learned. 'Can you send me that photo? I'd really appreciate it.'

'Sure.'

Megan gave her number to the young woman. 'And what are your names?'

'I'm River, and this is Harry.'

'Such a pleasure to meet you. You've been really helpful.'

They all three sat back in their chairs, River and Harry immediately returned to looking at their phones, while Megan tapped her pen against her notebook, considering.

'Harry Reuben? Will you come through, please?' The officer had returned to his post and was now calling Harry to the window. River went with him, and they both shortly disappeared behind the door marked "Authorised Entry Only".

It's just me and the old fella trying not to have a nap then. Megan's phone vibrated in her pocket; a photo message from an unknown number had come through. She opened the picture of River and Harry at Strickland State Forest, then a second text came through from Louise:

> **Loose ends should be tied up by today. I'll get the first flight up tomorrow; can you get me from Sydney airport? I'll confirm the time.**

Megan replied:

> **Yep, let me know the flight and I'll come get you. Just got a lead from a couple in the cop shop. I'll follow that up, I don't think I'll get anything out of the boys in blue today.**

She stood up, glanced at the old man who still appeared to be asleep, and went up to the counter again.

'Did you get anywhere with your supervisor?' she asked the young officer.

'I've left word with the investigating officer. You're welcome to wait, but I don't know how long it might be.'

Megan nodded. 'This is my business card,' she slid the small white card through the gap below the Perspex, 'I'm staying in town. If the investigator wants to get in touch, they can just give me a call on that number.'

'Okay.' The young officer took the card, looked at it briefly, then turned back to his screen.

Megan walked out of the echoey brown-tiled foyer into the crisp mid-morning air. It had been a bit of a long shot that the police would give her any information, but the two hippies had proven quite useful. Now she had an exact date and time Penny was seen arguing with Stan.

*   *   *

The map on her phone showed the car park was about a twenty-minute drive from her motel, so Megan gathered her camera and an extra notebook and added them to her bag before setting off.

The drive through the tall eucalypts on both sides of the road was typical of country driving through this part of New South Wales; tall, thick, pale trunks disappearing into deep olive-green canopies overhead, the forest floor covered in green bracken and crispy brown fallen leaves. She parked in the Banksia Picnic area, close to the main road so she could get a good view of the area first, though there were no others in the car park.

The car park was next to a covered seating area, with a couple of large picnic tables, wood-fired barbeques, a water tank, and a couple of bins. Beside the seating were several signs with tourist information, maps of the walking tracks, and brightly coloured images of the local flora and fauna. The trail up to the waterfalls was a nearly two-kilometre loop and was marked as a track of medium difficulty, though Megan was sceptical whether it was truly for that level.

She looked at the photo River had sent her and tried to figure out the vantage point from which it had been taken, and from that, where the van was parked. She spun around a couple of times where she was and decided it was probably taken from the picnic area, facing back to the road in. The van was on the right, and she now saw that the entrance to the "Cabbage Tree Track" would have been covered by the van in the photo.

Of course they parked near the hardest track. Megan walked over to the head of the trail, in the hope there would be some piece of evidence left there even after a month had gone by. She found a couple of sun-bleached packets of chips, a blue plastic bottle cap, a circle of metal which might have been part of a button, and seventeen cigarette butts in the couple of square metres where the van would have been. For each piece of detritus, Megan photographed it in situ, put down her scale marker and photographed it a second time, before collecting them into individual plastic snap-lock bags. She marked each with the date, time, and location. They were probably meaningless and unrelated, but it felt good to be doing something other than waiting for Louise to show up.

The Cabbage Tree Track looked like she could walk it from where she stood in the car park, and Megan was unsure whether it was worth following it, looking for more evidence, or if she should wait for Louise and do it together.

Louise will be here tomorrow, it can wait until then, and we'll be able to put two sets of eyes on it. And if I fall down a ditch and break my ankle, she can go back for help.

As she was turning to head back to the car, her belly rumbled loudly, another reason to head back to town and consolidate.

*   *   *

Louise's flight landed at Kingsford Smith Airport in Sydney a little after nine the next morning. Megan was driving down to pick her up, and she texted as she waited at the baggage carousel.

> **Landed, waiting for bags. I'll meet you at the pick-up area.**

Since they didn't know how long they would be in Gosford or where else they might need to go for this case, she'd packed for at least a week. The weather was milder than Melbourne but still forecast to be chilly.

Outside the airport terminal, it was cool but muggy.

Damn Sydney weather. The pick-up rank was several small parking areas in front of the baggage collection hall. Louise walked up and down looking for Megan's little white car but couldn't see it. She checked her phone again; no message, so her sister was probably still driving.

Megan's car pulled up a little while later, and she threw her bags into the boot.

'How was your flight?' Megan asked as Louise settled herself in the passenger seat.

'You know, the seats are tiny, the air is recycled, and I didn't pay for food, so I could really do with a coffee and maybe a ham and cheese croissant.'

'Okay. Food. We can do that.' Megan pulled the car back into the stream of traffic leaving the airport. 'I'm a bit stuck on the case, to be honest.'

'Hold on, I'm looking for food joints around here.' Louise stared intently at her phone's map app, searching for somewhere in Marrickville or Newtown to stop on their way back to Gosford. Her hunger would be too distracting to focus properly on work until she addressed it. 'It was too early to eat before the flight, so now I'm all discombobulated.'

'I know what you're like. It's fine.'

Louise put her phone into the stand on the dashboard with the map to the café she'd chosen. It was only mildly hipster and seemed to have a decent menu. The sisters sat in comfortable silence as Megan drove, with Louise watching the streets go by.

When they arrived, the café looked swankier than she had anticipated. With pale dusky pink walls and gold and black accents, the frontage was narrow, and a line had formed for the coffee window. It didn't bode well, and Louise almost suggested going somewhere else until she saw the croissants in the display cabinet, which made it clear she couldn't leave without one.

There were very few seats inside, and the hostess seated them at bar stools along the high counter.

'I'll have a latte, and some fruit toast,' Megan said when the hostess came back to take their order.

'Can I get a latte too and a croissant?' Louise added. The hostess nodded and left them to it. 'You said you're stuck?'

'Yeah. I went to the cops yesterday, but they didn't want to talk to me—'

'Not a surprise.'

'No. Still annoying. I ran into these two hippies who had seen Penny and Stan on their last day together, they even had a photo near the forest where she disappeared. I was going to ask you to help me to look over the track I think they took. I wasn't keen to try it on my own.'

'Sounds like you've got a plan, and you're not actually stuck?'

'I guess not.'

Their coffees arrived, and Louise grabbed hers, inhaling the nutty, rich aroma greedily before taking a small sip. 'That's surprisingly good for Sydney coffee.'

'Don't say that too loudly, they might hear you.' Megan smiled and took a sip of her own drink. 'You're right, not bad.'

'Did you get the hippies' number?'

'Yeah, the woman, River, texted me the photo.'

'Can I see?'

Megan brought up the photo and handed her sister the phone. Louise examined it, zooming in and looking around the frame, though there wasn't much to be learned from the image itself, except that Penny and Stan were there. After sending herself the photo, Louise handed the phone back.

'Do you think they know more than they told you? Is it worth trying to meet up with them again?'

Their food arrived, and Megan looked thoughtful for a moment. 'Doubtful. This couple didn't run into them except for that one time, and apparently, Penny and Stan were fighting loudly.'

'Did they say what about?' Louise took a bite of her croissant, its crisp, flaky pastry crumbling in her mouth, the juicy ham and melted cheese covering her tongue— exactly what she'd been craving.

'Are you listening?' Megan asked, her fruit toast poised in front of her mouth.

'Sorry, I missed that last part.'

'Yeah, you may as well have been fucking that croissant.' She laughed. 'I said, no, I didn't ask what the fight was about. We could try to meet up with them later today, but first we should check out the trail. Did you bring sturdy shoes?' Megan's eyes travelled down to Louise's pristine grey suede runners.

'I only brought these and some nice Chelsea boots in case we have to look corporate.'

Megan grumbled in her throat. 'I should have told you to bring shoes that could get dirty.'

'Might have been nice, seeing as this is your plan.'

'You know fashion isn't my forte.'

Louise raised an eyebrow but said nothing. Their tastes in clothing differed significantly, and it was only ever an issue if they needed to blend into an office environment—Megan's wardrobe was squarely at the casual end of business casual.

'Why don't you text the hippies and see if they're around to meet up—'

'They're working on a local farm,' Megan interrupted.

'Right, see if they're free today, anytime, and we can look into the forest trail in the meantime.'

'Cool. Hey, can you drive back to Gosford? I'm a bit over it.'

Louise chuckled. 'I can imagine. You were the one who couldn't wait till I could share the driving.'

'But you're here now, so can you drive?'

'Yeah, okay.'

*　　　*　　　*

They arrived in Gosford a little before noon, the traffic had been unpleasant getting out of the Sydney metro area. Megan hadn't heard back from the hippies, so they went straight to the Banksia Picnic area to start on the Cabbage Tree Track.

The smell of eucalyptus hit Louise hard when she stepped out of the car; the air was crisp and clean, with a hint of mud and decaying vegetation beneath the eucalyptus scent. Birds were calling, and the midday sun streamed through the leafy canopy.

'It's a lovely spot,' she said.

'I can see why people like it,' Megan replied. 'I picked up a bunch of litter from here yesterday, it's in baggies in the motel.'

'Have you got more baggies and markers for the trail?'

'Of course,' she said, pulling her work bag out from the back seat and digging around in it for the items. 'Here, I have more if we need.'

'Thanks.' Louise could count on Megan to have a stocked backpack.

The trail stretched out in front of them, and what she could see was gravelled which boded well.

Maybe my shoes will be safe after all.

'I'll do photos, and I'll look to the left of the path. If you wanna take any notes and cover the right of the path, that should be pretty good coverage, yeah?' Megan said, slipping the camera strap around her neck.

'Sounds good.'

It didn't take long for the track to go from over a metre wide, and gravelled, to less than half that and packed mud. Vegetation on both sides crowded the path, and while Megan had set off quickly, Louise had chosen to walk slowly, methodically looking for discarded items that would give them an idea about what had happened to Penny.

About twenty minutes into the walk, Louise caught a whiff of something unpleasant. She couldn't quite put her finger on what it was, and then the smell was gone. The Cabbage Tree Track was a loop, and she found herself back at the car park about an hour after they started.

Megan was sitting on a post, waiting. 'Did you see anything useful? Collect any bits?'

'I picked up a couple of bits, probably just rubbish though.'

'Same.' Megan waved a couple of baggies. 'We'll have to do the loop the other way, to be sure.'

'That makes sense. If we don't find anything, we'll have to go over the other tracks too.' Louise paused for a moment. 'But maybe not today. Did those hippies get in touch?'

'Reception out here is spotty, but I'll check.' She put her baggies into her backpack and pulled out her phone, briefly flicking her fingertips over the screen.

'Anything?'

'Hmm? Sorry, I forgot what I was looking for. Nothing yet.'

'Okay.' Louise turned back to the track. She walked slightly faster this time, taking only fifty minutes to get back to the car park. She didn't smell anything weird this time and wondered if she'd imagined it. She paused briefly where she thought the smell had been and took a couple of photos in case she needed to find the spot again.

It's probably nothing, but it won't hurt to know for later.

They both picked up another couple of items: a chip wrapper, a beer-bottle top, and a cigarette butt or two.

'Hand over your evidence,' Megan said. Louise passed over her bags, unlocked the car, and got in. The early morning to get to the airport had caught up with her, and she wanted a nap. Sometimes she wondered if she was part cat, needing to sleep in sunbeams and working best at night.

She drove back to the motel in town, where they bought some sandwiches for a late lunch from a café around the corner. After moving her stuff into the room with her sister, Louise started grilling her on what evidence they had and what their next steps should be.

'Do we know where Stan is now?' she asked, after an hour or so of mostly unproductive conversation.

Megan frowned. 'I haven't looked…'

'Has he posted anything recently?'

'You're on the computer; why don't you look?'

Louise sighed. She should have thought to do that herself instead of asking Megan, *though if she'd already done the work, it would have saved me doing it again.* The VanLyfDiaries YouTube channel had much less frequent uploads in the weeks since Penny had disappeared. There were many reasons that might be the case, not least of which was Stan having to do all the work himself. What had been content most days had slowed to a post or two per week. The most recent of these was a video titled "Taking a Break in Port Macquarie", a town about three hours north up the coast. It had only a few hundred views; his numbers had been declining since Penny left, from a couple of thousand at their peak. Louise clicked on the video.

'Hey, all of you lovely people. It's been a bit of a tough slog the last few weeks, without Pen. She was—' he looked away from the camera, as though fighting back emotion, 'she was a really important part of my life, and to say that I'm feeling pretty devastated without her really doesn't give you the full picture. This vlog, this trip, was our dream together, and now to be doing it without her is such a gut punch.' Stan put his hand to his mouth and stared off to the side of the camera for an uncomfortably long time before continuing.

'I'm going to have to leave this project for a while. My money situation—well suffice it to say that I need to get a job and work for a little bit before continuing the tour, if I even keep going.'

'He's so full of shit.' Megan had come around to watch the video, hovering behind Louise's shoulder as she sat on the bed.

'Mmm,' Louise said, waving her hand to stop Megan from interrupting.

'I'm going to stay in Port Macquarie for a while,' Stan said, 'if I can get some work, and I hope to use that time to reevaluate my goals. I've had a really great time so far, and all of you, my loyal viewers, have really been my rock. I hope you'll all keep me in your hearts, and I'll see you all soon.'

'Vomit,' Megan said.

'Yeah, he gives me the creeps too. Although maybe it's just because we think he murdered his girlfriend.'

'Don't say that.'

'Why not?'

'Because we want to find her alive, isn't that why we're here?'

Louise closed the laptop lid and turned to look her sister in the eyes. 'It's been over a month. No contact.

Not much in the way of leads. If she was okay, I would expect her to have shown up again by now.'

'No, we can't think like that.' Megan's eyes were wet, and her nostrils flared in distress.

'I'm sorry to be a pessimist, but I will be truly shocked if she's not dead in that forest somewhere.'

They sat in awkward silence for a long time. Louise wasn't sure if she should try to comfort her sister, put her hand on her knee or something, but Megan had never been much of a touchy-feely type.

A short buzz sounded as someone's phone got a notification. Megan picked up hers and read the message preview on the screen. 'River says she can meet tomorrow, about ten.'

'Great. Excellent.' Louise nodded to emphasise the good news, though she suspected it wouldn't ever make up for the bubble of hope she'd just destroyed in her sister's heart.

Chapter 6

The next morning, Louise and Megan woke at nine, just enough time for both of them to shower and get ready to meet River and Harry for a brunch meeting at the local café.

They walked a couple of hundred metres down the road, following the curve of the shore of Brisbane Water, a body that looked like a lake from where they were staying, but curved around to join the South Pacific Ocean a town or two away. They turned off at the wharf, and the café was a few doors down, away from the shore. They arrived a few minutes before the meeting time.

'They here yet?' Louise asked.

'Don't think so.' Megan scanned the tables as they entered. The décor was odd, at least by Melbourne standards; the chairs were an assortment of blocky pine and vinyl, the tables covered in thick plastic tablecloths, and each table had a sprig of something in a small vase, along with the usual salt, pepper, sugar, and serviettes. A server waved them to sit anywhere, and when Louise sat at a four-seater table by the window, she noticed the sprigs of flowers were plastic, and slightly dusty. The whole place looked like a holdover from the eighties, though well maintained.

'I'm starving. Should we wait to order?' Louise asked.

'Nah, I have no idea what sort of timekeeping these two have; may as well eat while we wait.' Megan picked up the menu on the table in front of her; a laminatedA3 sized sheet.

'At least the prices match the furniture,' Louise said.

When the server, a plump older woman in all black with short, tightly curled salt-and-pepper hair, made her way over to them, they had decided.

They ordered, and as the server walked away, Louise glanced at the clock: ten past ten.

I'll give it till half past, then we can call them, although they don't have to talk to us.

'I wouldn't be surprised if they show up late. They seem to be a bit free with square stuff like timeliness.' Megan drummed her fingers on the table, a habit Louise really wished she would curb, especially pre-caffeine.

'No doubt.'

The drinks arrived a few minutes later, and their breakfasts came a little while after that, but still there was no sign of their guests.

'Have you checked your phone, in case they're lost or something?' Louise asked, loading her fork with egg and bacon.

'I've been keeping an eye on it; nothing to report,' Megan said without looking. 'Oh, I see them down the street.' She waved and knocked on the café window. When they entered the shop, they sat at the table, and Megan introduced everyone. The woman, River, looked like she had just woken, her eyes were puffy and slightly bloodshot, and her hair made a messy bun look like a sleek updo. The man, Harry, was slightly more alert and was wearing a knitted slouchy hat, so she couldn't assess his hair. They both smelled strongly of marijuana and incense.

'Thanks for coming.'

'You said you were buying breakfast, so we figured why not?' River smiled; her very straight teeth were yellowed, possibly from smoking.

'Yeah, we'll shout, of course,' Megan said.

Good thing it was one of the cheaper places in town, Louise thought, though it was all on Sue's account, so it didn't cost them one way or the other. River and Harry ordered their meals, and a couple more coffees and told them about life on the farm where they were living.

'It's pretty chill, really. We don't get paid much, but we don't pay rent or for meals on the farm. We have to do twenty-five hours work a week, so we just do a couple of hours a day and then we explore, or read, or whatever the rest of the time,' Harry said.

'Sounds like you have a good set-up,' Megan said.

'How long have you been up here?'

'A while… six weeks, maybe longer; I lose track,' River said, grinning. 'We'll stay here for a bit, then keep travelling north. The lifestyle suits us.'

'Do you have any plans to go back to—where did you say you were from originally?' Louise asked.

'I'm from Auckland originally,' River said, 'and I met Harry in a hostel in Melbourne, but he's from Adelaide.'

'Yeah, I was doing the whole solo travel around Australia thing, but when I hooked up with River, it really made everything way more fun.' He grinned at her and squeezed her hand. They seemed very much in love, despite their unusual lifestyle and their apparent lack of direction in life.

'So, you said you never met Penny and Stan?'

'No, just saw them in the car park, like I said at the police station,' River said, her eyes drawn to the server who was bustling over with their enormous plates of food.

'You said you could hear them arguing. Did you hear what they were saying?' Megan asked.

'Mmm,' Harry started with a mouthful of food. 'They were going on for a while; we were there chilling, having some food and whatever, and at first, they were just, like, being tense, you know, the kind of whispered argument you have when you're trying not to let people around hear.'

'I know the type,' Louise said, making a note in her notebook.

'But then the guy—you said his name was Stan? Well, he was saying she needed to do her part and that she couldn't let the team down, and he was doing all the work—'

'I've heard that sort of shit before, though,' River interrupted. 'Dudes who insist they're the most important thing, and the woman has to do whatever they say, like cook and clean and run around so that he can be free to do the good stuff.'

'Yeah, sounded like he was just berating her. I didn't hear any specifics, more generally "you're not supporting me",' Harry said.

'Were they were escalating?' Louise asked.

'Kind of. The guy was getting louder, but I couldn't hear what the woman was saying. He was flailing his hands around, but it seemed more like he was having a tantrum than a situation where she was in danger.' Harry frowned. 'Maybe I was wrong, since you said she's missing.'

'You couldn't have known how things would turn out,' Megan said. They were all silent for a while, River and Harry still mowing through their piles of food.

Louise rubbed her fingertip over her eyebrow, pondering what should happen next in the investigation. Their leads in Gosford were almost used up, though Megan said she had attempted to get information out of the police; it could be worth trying a second time. They hadn't walked the other two tracks in the national park, and she was curious if she could try to find the bad smell again. Not that she wanted to be morbid, but there was a distinct possibility Stan had murdered Penny and dumped her in the forest.

'Is there anything else you can tell us?' Megan asked after a long pause. Louise shook her head a little and brought her mind back to the conversation. The two young hippy types in front of them hadn't provided much in the way of new information, though they did confirm that Stan was being an angry douchebag leading up to Penny's disappearance.

'I don't think so. We walked down one of the tracks, and when we got back to the car park the van was gone. I didn't think about them again until we ran into you in the police station.'

'Of course. You have Megan's number; here is my business card as well. If you think of anything, or if you run into Stan or Penny again, please give us a call,' Louise said.

'We will. We'll stay here a little longer, then continue on our way up the coast.' River smiled and pushed the last morsel of toast into her mouth. Louise was slightly surprised that she'd managed to get through the whole portion, especially for such a slim woman, but perhaps they weren't used to being able to order whatever they wanted. The couple seemed happy, but it wasn't a lifestyle Louise had any interest in trying. Agricultural work sounded backbreaking—literally.

Louise stood and went to the front counter to pay, putting the whole meal onto the business account and getting a receipt for the records. River and Harry seemed settled, so she raised her eyebrows at Megan and inclined her head to the door.

'We'd better get going. No need for you to hurry out on account of us; the bill is all settled,' Louise said, picking up her bag.

'Thank you for breakfast; we don't often eat out, so it was a real treat. I hope you find Penny, and she's alright,' Harry said.

The Carter sisters walked out of the café in silence and stayed quiet until they were well away from the café—a habit they had established long ago to prevent any possible overhearing of comments about cases by people they'd just interviewed.

'That was a bust. Now what?' Megan said quietly.

'Not a total bust, my breakfast was very nice, and we confirmed Penny and Stan were fighting.'

'Some help that is.' Megan shoved her hands into the pockets of her jeans and hunched her shoulders; she looked like a cartoon character of disappointment.

'I think we try to get the police to give us something one more time, then go check out the rest of those trails. Did I tell you about the funny smell?'

'Yeah, you mentioned it. It's probably nothing, but since we're here, we may as well check back.' Megan slowed her walk. 'I'm pretty sure the police station is the other way.'

'Right.' Louise came to a stop. 'Lead on then.'

*   *   *

The police station was as grey and dreary as it had been the day before. Its brutalist concrete exterior, combined with the lack of activity in the street, made it look abandoned. Inside, the brown tiles and plastic chairs were depressing, though there were several people in the waiting area.

'The guy at the desk has changed; I hope that's a positive sign,' Megan said. They walked up to the window to address the officer standing at the desk behind it. He was in his late twenties or early thirties, with dark hair, and a prominent five o'clock shadow under puffy, tired-looking eyes. 'Hi, I came in the other day to ask about a missing person, Penelope Bean.'

The officer looked up; his eyes moved slowly over the two sisters before he responded. 'What's your relationship to the case?'

'We're investigators; we've been asked to look into it by the family,' Louise said.

'I see. Name?'

'I'm Louise, and this is Megan. The surname is Carter.'

The officer looked back to his computer and typed in a few things, reading the screen carefully. 'You're up from Melbourne then? Where Ms Bean was from?'

'Yes.' Megan frowned.

'I looked you up. It's not rocket science.' The officer's slow gaze returned to them. 'I can't tell you anything officially. It's a privacy thing, you see—'

'Could we get consent from the family? You know, authority to act on their behalf or something?' Megan interrupted.

'You could.' The officer leaned closer to the glass wall separating them, lowering his voice. Louise and Megan both leaned in closer. 'I wouldn't bother though; the file is pretty much empty. The boyfriend was interviewed, and there wasn't much of interest there. Her phone and finances are inactive.'

'Isn't that suspicious? Doesn't that prompt you lot to look into it further?' Megan said, trying to keep her voice level despite her inner rage.

'It might be, but that's out of my hands.' The officer's eyes slid back to the computer. 'I wish you all the best.'

'Let's go,' Louise said, pulling on Megan's arm. She didn't want to leave, but the police had batted away their request for information twice now, and though this officer had given them something, it wasn't what she had hoped for.

Megan was seething when they walked out into the chilly autumn air, the bright sunlight making her squint but doing nothing to warm her. They walked back to the motel without speaking.

In the room, Megan flopped onto the bed face down, groaning.

'What's wrong with you?' Louise asked.

'The cops are so useless.'

'That's not new.'

'Why didn't they do something? She'd only been gone a few days when Kate reported her missing, and they just sat on it.'

'They interviewed Stan.'

'So they say.' Megan rolled onto her side and struggled to take her backpack off without sitting up, causing her arms to flail inelegantly and adding to her frustration.

'I know you think cops are lazy, but we can't just go around assuming they can't or won't do their job. Just because Stan said the last place he saw Penny was that forest doesn't mean it's true. He could have left her anywhere and kept her phone.'

'That's a joyful thought,' Megan said gloomily. 'Not only are our leads here drying up, but they might not even relate to the timeline.'

'Are you up for a bushwalk then?'

'No,' Megan said into the bedcovers.

'Okay. I'm going to the toilet, and then I'm going up there. You should come. It'll make you feel better to be doing something rather than sitting here stewing in how little we have to go on.'

Megan sighed. 'Alright.'

*   *   *

Louise drove up to the Banksia Picnic area, trying to take in any nuances of the surroundings that she might have missed on her first trip up there, though she didn't see much new.

'We gonna go down to the waterfall this time?'

The three tracks heading out from the car park were all equally likely to have been used by Penny and Stan, and they had already tried one.

'I want to go over the track we did yesterday first. I thought I smelled something off, and I want to see if I can find it. It wasn't far in, so we probably don't have to do the whole track.'

Megan sighed. 'Okay.'

Louise headed off, leaving most of her investigation tools in the car, while Megan trudged along behind, with a few plastic bags in hand.

They walked slowly, and Louise paused frequently to sniff the air like an ineffectual bloodhound, though she didn't smell anything other than the expected forest scents. After about twenty minutes of slow walking, Louise looked around. She pulled out her phone to look at the photo she took of the spot where she had noticed the smell last time.

'I think we passed it.' Her voice felt flat; she'd been sure there was something in that smell. 'Let's head back and do the waterfall track.'

Megan turned and marched back to the car, as though glad to be done with the wild goose chase portion of the day. Louise continued to walk back to the car park carefully, checking for smells or spots that looked like the photo.

'Megan, come back, I think I found something,' Louise yelled as she walked past a fallen tree fern that looked familiar. There was a definite rank undertone to the forest scent in that spot. It was hard to tell which way the smell came from, but she decided to try the left of the track since the hill wasn't as steep in that direction. If she were burying a body, she wouldn't have dragged it anywhere with really difficult terrain.

We're not going to find a body, she told herself, though it didn't do much good.

'Where've you gone?' Megan yelled from the track.

'Down here. Come carefully; we don't want to step on evidence.'

Megan started crashing through the scrubby bracken down the hill. When she caught up to Louise, she fell into step behind her. Louise put her arm out to signal to stay behind.

They walked quietly and deliberately through the undergrowth for about fifty metres. The forest floor looked a little disturbed, but it could have been from animals or birds. Just as Louise thought it, she came across some square wombat droppings and stepped around them.

As they walked, the scent grew stronger in her nostrils. 'You smell that, right?'

'Yeah, it's not good. What do you think it is?' Megan asked.

'A dead thing. Not sure what, though.'

Following her nose turned out to be much harder than Louise had initially expected, and after another ten minutes, she started to think the smell was fading. 'Did we pass it again?' she wondered aloud.

'Maybe. Let's go back a bit and try up that way.' Megan headed off towards the track but to the right of where they had just been. Louise followed, taking a line between their original trail and Megan's heading, catching the smell sporadically.

'Oh shit,' Megan said, stopping suddenly.

'Did you find something?' Louise called from her position.

'You better come have a look.'

As Louise made her way over to where Megan was standing, still within view of the main trail but behind a small stand of straggly eucalypt saplings, she couldn't make out what Megan was referring to, then she saw blue fabric, just poking out from under some of the bracken.

'It smells bad over here,' Louise said.

'I think it's this.' Megan pointed to the fabric with her foot. 'Should we look under it?'

'I think we have to.'

'You do it.'

'No, you do it.'

'You're the older sister,' Megan said.

'You found it.'

'We could call the cops.'

'And tell them we found some highly suspicious stinky fabric in the bush? No, we have to look.'

Megan sighed and shifted her weight from one foot to the other. She wouldn't be the one to look. Louise looked around for a stick or something to pull the fabric up.

If I'm doing this, I'm not touching anything with my bare hands. A couple of steps away she found a sturdy-looking branch, about as wide as her thumb and the length of her forearm, perfect for poking things that smelled bad.

Louise approached the trees sideways, taking care not to step on anything that looked important.

'We should have brought the camera,' Megan said.

'Did you bring your phone?'

'Oh, yeah. Hang on, I'll film it.' Megan stuffed the plastic evidence bags into her jeans pocket and pulled out her mobile phone. 'Okay, I'm recording.'

'This is Louise Carter; it's twelve minutes past one o'clock on the ninth of May. With me is Megan Carter, filming. We're in the Strickland State Forest, near Gosford, New South Wales, and we've found a suspicious pile of discarded fabric. The smell around the site is pungent, indicative of animal decay. We're going to pull the fabric away and see what's under there.' Louise took a deep, shaky breath before hooking the stick under the corner of the fabric nearest to her and lifting. It was stuck fast and didn't pull off whatever was underneath it. Louise repositioned her hand and pushed the stick upwards, flicking the fabric away from her. As she did, the smell became significantly stronger.

'Oh God,' she said, holding her other hand over her nose and mouth. Behind the phone, Megan was trying not to dry retch.

'I don't see anything yet. I'm going in further.' Louise pushed the fabric up more and she saw a glint of silver. As she moved her eye upwards, she saw movement as small white worms squirmed over the flesh of a human foot.

'Is that a foot? Oh God.' Megan made a heaving sound as though she would be sick.

'Don't vomit on the evidence!'

'I'm okay.' Megan swallowed loudly. 'Wait, that foot is really small.'

Louise pulled the blue fabric up, revealing more of the body. There were no clothes visible; the flesh was in an advanced stage of decay. The skin had discoloured, and maggots and flies were crawling all over it. The body was small, likely a child, definitely human.

'Let's get out of here. We need to call the cops.' Megan's face was pale, and she looked as though she might throw up at any moment.

'You're right.' Louise dropped the stick and let the fabric fall back over the upper legs. 'I think I'd better stay here, make sure nothing happens to it before the cops arrive, and you call them.'

Megan fiddled with her phone. 'I don't have reception. I'll have to go back to the car park.'

'Okay. I'll wait… over here.' Louise pointed to a patch a little way away from the body that she hoped would be less upsetting and less odorous.

Chapter 7

Megan tried to slow her breathing and not think about the child's body they'd just found. When she reached the main path, she looked around for something to signal where to turn when she came back, but nothing seemed to fit. She mentally scanned the contents of her pockets, and still nothing useful came to mind. Just as she was about to start back to the car, she saw a long piece of eucalyptus bark. She pulled it off and laid it in an arrow shape across the dirt path.

Her stomach was roiling and queasy, but with some distance from the smell, she hoped it would settle a little.

One foot in front of the other. She concentrated on her feet as she walked, until she was back at the car park. Pulling out her phone, she hoped there was enough reception.

Is this an emergency call? Or do I just call the local station? Megan hesitated with triple zero keyed into her phone. In the end, she decided it was worth a call to the emergency number, and they could tell her off if it wasn't.

'Triple-oh, do you need police, fire, or ambulance?' a young man's voice answered the call.

'Police, please.' Megan's voice was unsteady; she swallowed and took a deep breath while the operator put her through.

'What state are you located in?'

'New South Wales.'

'Thank you, connecting you now.'

'Police, what's your emergency?' a no-nonsense woman's voice answered.

'Uh—' Megan coughed a little, licked her lips, and started again. 'I think I've found a body.'

'You think?'

'I'm pretty sure it's a human corpse, probably a child by the size.'

'I see. What's the address?'

'It's in a state forest. I'm calling from the Banksia Picnic area, near Strickland Falls in Gosford.'

'Okay, I'm just putting that into the system; the local police will be notified. While they're on the way, I'll get a few more details from you.' The woman went through a series of questions about Megan, name, date of birth, and usual address.

'That's all I need from you at the moment. The responding officers will be with you shortly.'

'Do you have any idea how long they'll be?' Megan had started pacing along the edge of the car park.

'I don't know. It shouldn't be too long; this is a priority response issue.'

'Okay, thanks.'

'Just stay where you are and wait for the officers.' The woman hung up.

Megan looked around, as though she had been seeing without comprehending until then. There were no other cars in the area, and she hoped it would stay that way. She dreaded having to tell some bushwalker or tourist that they couldn't go down that track, not that she could enforce it if they decided to dismiss her.

How long has that body been there? Megan wondered to herself. She tapped her phone against her hip as she paced.

After a minute or two of this, she unlocked her phone and started a search for local missing children. Her stomach had settled after the shock, and the smell had dissipated, and her PI brain had kicked into gear.

Judging by the size of the foot, the child was between five and ten years old; too small to be a teen, but too big for a toddler. The lack of clothes made it hard to determine the gender from what she'd seen. She scrolled through the National Missing Persons database, but it was confusing and difficult to use on her mobile. Nonetheless, it provided a distraction to scroll through the thousands of missing persons listed there.

Most of them had been gone for decades. Megan didn't think that a child in that state of decomposition had been dead for very long—months perhaps, not years. Not that she was an expert on that sort of thing, but the fleshy parts wouldn't last too long out in the open, even wrapped in the blue fabric.

What if the kid wasn't reported missing? Or if they didn't list every missing person on that website? Megan's mind was working overtime, probably full of adrenaline from finding something so disturbing. At that moment, she heard a crunch of gravel as a police vehicle pulled up in the carpark.

I must have been really absorbed to have missed them approaching.

She watched the two officers; one was the young man she'd seen behind the desk on that first day still looking largely uninterested, and the other, who had been driving, was an older man who looked like he'd had his fill of bullshit for the year.

'You Megan Carter?' the older one said gruffly.

'Yeah.'

'You called triple-oh about a body?'

'Yeah.'

The officer nodded. 'I'm Sergeant Burt Collins, this is Constable Tony Jennings. You'll need to take us to the suspected body.'

'Sure, yes, okay. It's down this track, and then off the path a bit.' Megan set her shoulders back in the hopes of seeming confident, though she didn't feel it, Collins' stare was very off-putting. She turned and started off towards where Louise was waiting.

'And how did you come across it, if it's a way off the path?' Collins asked, falling into step a little behind her, while Jennings trailed along at the rear.

'My sister—she's currently waiting with the body so we remember where it is. She thought she smelled something funky, so we uh… she went looking for the smell.'

Collins made a grunting sound, then continued to follow in silence. Occasionally his radio would crackle with instructions from other officers, but neither of the cops paid any mind to it. The walk back to her strategically placed piece of bark seemed much longer this time, and Megan started to doubt that she'd marked the spot.

'Oh, good, that's the marker,' she said aloud when she saw it. 'It's over here to the left.' Megan turned at the bark and started to head into the trees, trying to follow the slightly flattened bracken on the path she had made earlier.

'Lou? Where are you?' she yelled, then waited a while for a response. 'Lou? I've got the police,' she said louder this time.

'Over here.' Louise's voice came from the left, and Megan adjusted her track towards her. Megan didn't dare look back at the cops; she was sure they thought she was an idiot. A few metres later, she caught a whiff of that scent of decay again. Her steps faltered and Collins nearly collided with her back.

'Sorry,' she mumbled.

'God. I just got a face full of that smell. That's a dead thing alright,' Collins said.

A few steps further, and Megan spotted the group of trees where the body was hidden.

'We lifted the fabric to see what was under it. I'm sorry about that, Officers,' Louise said.

Collins introduced them both again, before starting his questions. 'You said you touched the fabric, with your hands or something else?'

'With a stick, that one.' Louise pointed.

'Did you do anything else?'

'No. We—I lifted the fabric, then I saw that there was what looked like a nude human foot and leg, and I let the fabric fall back to where it was, and Megan came up to call you.'

'You've touched nothing else? You're not in trouble, but we do need to know.'

'No. We're both private investigators, so we knew to preserve the scene as much as possible once we'd established a potential crime.'

'To be honest, I didn't want to have anything to do with the… uh, deceased after I realised what it was. I was quite happy to be up in the car park waiting for you fellas,' Megan said.

Jennings had started to look very green in the face.

'You alright, Constable? You need to get away from the scene if you're going to vomit.' Collins glared at the younger man, but his voice was softer than his face suggested.

'No, sir. I'm alright.' Jennings swallowed and averted his eyes. Collins stepped towards the fabric, his face set into a grimace, while pulling on a pair of blue nitrile gloves. He picked up the edge of the fabric between forefinger and thumb and carefully raised it to look for himself.

'That's human alright.' He replaced the fabric, removed his gloves, and stepped a few paces back.

'We'll have to do a proper cordon and the lot,' Collins said, largely to himself. 'Jennings, go back to the car, get the tape, and radio the station to have them send out the forensics blokes. We'll be here all day till they get here. I'll speak to these two and get some details and a preliminary statement.'

Jennings nodded, looking relieved to be away from the smell. 'Right away, sir.'

'Tell me again how you came across these remains?'

'We're here on a job; we've come up from Melbourne, looking for a missing person last seen in this area. We did a walk of the track yesterday to look for potential indications of where our missing person might have been and where they might be going,' Louise said.

'"We" is the two of you? I'll need your names, addresses, and contact information.'

They provided their details to Collins, and he wrote them in his little black notebook.

'Who's the missing person, then?' Collins asked.

'Penny—Penelope Bean. Last seen in the Banksia car park with her boyfriend, about five weeks ago.'

'You were in the station asking about that the other day; I think Jennings mentioned it.'

'That was me, actually,' Megan said. 'Louise only arrived yesterday.'

'Any luck finding Ms Bean?'

'Not really.' Louise bit her lip. 'When I walked along here yesterday, I caught a whiff that I thought was decomposition, and today I wanted to find that smell. I expected it to be Penny. I was pretty sure her boyfriend murdered her, but those remains are too small to be Penny. She was a slight woman, but that seems to be a child.'

'I'd agree with you there,' Collins said, scribbling a note. 'You just followed your nose?'

'Yeah, I thought I might be crazy, and I'm sure my sister thought it was a total waste of time, but here we are.'

'Doesn't help your case, though,' Collins said.

'No,' Megan replied. The three of them were quiet for a moment, punctuated by some indistinct burbling from the police radio.

'Can you tell us anything about the Penny Bean case?' Megan asked.

'Officially, I can't comment, even if there was any information to share.' Collins paused. 'Which there isn't. There are two main theories around the station: one Stan offed her; or two, she's run off and doesn't want to be found.'

'I considered that she didn't want to be found. She comes from a good family, she was having a burst of rebellion, sure, but her mother and aunt are beside themselves. If she just left Stan and wanted to go off on her own, why not say something?' Louise said.

Collins shrugged. 'People do some very odd things. In my line of work, I've seen a lot of really crazy shenanigans, and the one thing I can tell you is that you almost never know what someone is going through, or why they get up and leave their life.'

'Sergeant Collins, come in.' A voice crackled over the radio.

'Collins here.'

'The forensic team from Sydney won't be here for at least four hours, and by then we'll have lost the light. They'll be out first thing in the morning.'

Collins muttered something colourful under his breath, but not loud enough for Megan to hear.

'We'll have to stay here on the scene until they get here; that what you're telling me?'

'That's about the extent of it,' the voice on the radio said.

'Righto. Get someone to come and relieve us in a few then.' Collins turned to the two Carter sisters. 'Me and the lad will be tied up here for a while. Are you staying in town?'

'Yeah, we're in the motel,' Louise said.

'I know the one. How long will you be staying?'

'I'm not sure. A day or two longer, probably. There's not much to go on.'

'You'll both need to come into the station first thing tomorrow to give a full statement.'

'Of course. You have our details if you have questions in the meantime.'

'Sorry about having to stand out here till forensics get here,' Megan said.

Collins shrugged. 'Part of the job. Usually, it's natural causes or road fatalities. At least this one is outside. With this level of decomp, inside a house, the stink is really unbearable.'

Megan started up the hill back to the path, and Louise fell into step behind her. They were silent all the way to the car park, where they saw Jennings standing next to the police car on the phone. Megan waved to him, and he nodded. The surly, unhelpful man from behind the desk seemed completely different now outside; maybe he hated paperwork.

They got into the car and Louise started to drive back to the motel. When they'd pulled back onto the highway, she broke the silence.

'That was fucked.'

'Yeah. A kid.'

'We're no closer to finding Penny, and now we're embroiled in some other suspicious death.'

'We just found it. It's way too decomposed for either of us to have killed them.'

Louise said nothing.

'Stan and Penny might have killed a kid,' Megan said, the idea suddenly coming to her.

'I hadn't thought of that. It would make sense why Penny isn't talking to anyone. But I don't see her as a child killer.'

'Me either. And as much of a creep as Stan is, we don't have any evidence he'd do something like that.'

'Now what do we do? We haven't searched all the tracks, but I'm starting to doubt that after over a month there will be anything to find. Plus, I'm a bit… I don't really want to go poking around that forest anymore.' Louise was pale and had been rubbing her eyebrow non-stop since they got in the car.

'Let's spend the rest of today double-checking everything—online banking, phone activity, social media, the lot. Once we've spoken to the police tomorrow, we can assess whether we should try to chase down Stan and talk to him.'

Megan had looked through the vlogs from Stan since he'd been on his own already. He had kept travelling up the coast and had stopped in Port Macquarie. He had taken a job doing construction; maybe the vlog wasn't generating as much income as he'd hoped.

Sue had access to Penny's online banking, and for the purposes of checking if there had been any movement, she would have to call. Once they were back in the motel Megan called her.

'Hello, Sue Ingles speaking.'

'Hi Sue, it's Megan.'

'Megan, I'm so relieved to hear from you. Have you got any news?'

Of course, she wanted an update; they had been working on the case for a few days and hadn't done much to keep her informed. 'We've been very busy yes. As for news, I don't have much to tell you.'

Sue sighed heavily.

'Louise and I are in Gosford just now, following up on where Penny was last seen. It's been slow going, unfortunately.'

'I'll bet. I can't believe we let the police sit on this for weeks before acting. I'm sorry to have such a cold trail to give you.'

Megan swallowed. 'It's alright.' They were both silent for an awkwardly long time.

'Did you say you'd made some progress, though?'

'We haven't found much of Penny, except a couple of itinerant farm workers who said they'd seen her and Stan up in the forest on the day she disappeared.'

'That's something, I suppose.' Sue blew her breath out in a gust. 'Was there something I can help you with?'

'Yes, sorry, I've been a bit rattled today.'

'Why? What's happened?' Sue sounded very interested, as though she were leaning forward to hear the gossip.

'We found a body while looking for clues up at the forest.'

'What do you mean a body?'

'Human remains.'

'Oh my God. Oh, my God, Penny's dead.' Sue started to wail.

'No, no, no. I'm so sorry, I should have said first off, it's not Penny. The remains were much too small.' Megan took a breath. Why was she saying all of this? 'We think it's a child. Unrelated by the look of things.'

'I see. I know I shouldn't be relieved, but I am. As long as it's not our girl, there's still hope she'll come back to us.'

'There's always hope. What I was calling for was I wondered if you could recheck Penny's bank account and let me know if there has been any activity.'

'Okay, let me just—' There was a burst of scratchy sounds down the phone line as though Sue had put the phone in her pocket. 'I'll have to get the laptop open. Shouldn't take too long.'

While Megan was waiting, Louise watched on, perhaps interested to hear any developments. There were various sounds down the line, tapping and Sue muttering under her breath—though Megan was sure there was no expectation to chat while this was happening. She scrolled through Stan's uploads; he wasn't very good at updating since he and Penny had gone their separate ways, which didn't help them at all. Megan clicked to subscribe to the channel and get notifications any time he posted new content.

'Alright, it's just loading up her accounts,' Sue said after several minutes.

'Fantastic.'

'No, the last transaction is in April. I mean, there are a few automatic payments, but I don't think she would have had to do anything for them to come out.'

'What payments?' Megan didn't think it was relevant, but it was a lead to run down until they had something better to chase.

'Umm, looks like she's still paying for a gym membership every week and her mobile that's once a month. Oh, and one of the streaming services.'

I bet Stan's still using her account, Megan thought bitterly. 'You're right; doesn't sound like anything she would need to be actively engaged in. That being said, I might call the gym and see whether she's been in in the last month, and if we can suspend payments for the time being. Do you have her streaming password? Could be worth suspending that too.'

'I don't know, but Kate might have the details.'

'Can you send me her bank records? I'll have a look through them.'

'Of course.'

'I'm sorry I don't have better news. It's turning out to be a particularly difficult case.'

Sue sighed again. 'I know. I hope something turns up soon. I'd better get going.'

Chapter 8

The morning was cold and foggy, as though it were foreboding something, but Louise couldn't decide what. She and Megan had agreed to go down to the police station to give statements about the body they'd discovered in the forest the day before—a process that was largely redundant in her opinion, given they'd told the cops everything they knew yesterday—but she supposed they needed to follow procedure, do it formally, and probably sign something.

'Get up; we said we'd be there at nine,' Louise said, nudging the Megan-shaped lump in the bed with her sock-clad foot.

'They won't let us give statements together; you may as well go and I'll come in half an hour,' Megan muttered from under the bedclothes.

Louise sighed. 'Fine.' Sometimes, it felt like Megan wasn't cut out to be an investigator, since she preferred staying in bed to getting on with crucial tasks. However, Louise also admitted to herself that it wasn't crucial to their case, and she was probably right that they'd be interviewed separately. Besides Megan was better at staying up late for surveillance.

I hope I get the Sergeant, he seemed competent, the young fellow was a bit green for a possible homicide. Louise shrugged on her black jacket and walked out into the chill air.

The station was a couple of minutes' walk away, and she got herself a coffee and a muffin on the way. She would be there on time, but there was no telling whether the police would be running on time, so she prepared to wait.

Inside the police station foyer, with its ugly brown colour palette, no other people were waiting. It was a relief in a way; Louise could have her breakfast and maybe look through some emails while she was there. After only three or four minutes, the burly Sergeant Collins came out from a door next to the hole in the wall reception area.

'Good morning, Sergeant.' Louise stood and shoved the rest of the half-eaten muffin into her bag.

'Ms Carter. Is your sister joining us?'

'She'll be along a bit later; we thought you'd want to talk to us individually.'

'Mmm.' Collins ran his eyes up and down her body, taking everything in. She was sure he was going to make some sort of comment. 'No doubt you expected a longer wait, but I've been on shift since yesterday and would as soon get this over with.'

'Of course.' She wondered how he had known; perhaps he was better at his job than she had given him credit for.

'Follow me.' Collins led her back through the station's dull grey interior corridors to an interview room that had seen better days. There was a large, faded stain on the wall that Louise hoped was coffee, a strangely narrow wood-laminate interview table, and a couple of hard plastic chairs in the same brown as those in the waiting room.

'Take a seat. I'll be taking notes, but we're not recording this chat.' Collins sat heavily in the seat nearest to the door. 'I'll try to make this efficient, but there are protocols to get through.'

'Of course.' Louise sat down on the surprisingly uncomfortable chair. *I'd be surly too if I had to conduct my work in these chairs every day.* 'Did you get any sleep at all?'

'I had a couple of hours in the on-call room, but with a small crew like we have up here, something big happens and we're all hands on deck.'

Louise nodded, waiting for the Sergeant to direct the conversation. He sighed and rubbed his hand over his salt-and-pepper five o'clock shadow.

'We got the basics from you yesterday, so I'll go back over those briefly.'

Louise nodded again, and they went over the details of finding the body yesterday.

'Did you get any info on who it might be?' Louise asked as Collins made a couple of notes on his tiny notepad.

'I can't really say.'

'Of course. I had a bit of a look at the missing persons website, but I'm sure there are people who aren't listed. I thought it must have been a child, based on the size, but there weren't any children who matched the age range.'

'There have been a few kids go missing along the coast that could match the general description and date range.'

'How long would you say the body was out in the elements?'

'I'm not a pathologist.'

'I realise that, but you'd have a ballpark guess, wouldn't you?' Louise was pressing her luck, but it was worth a try. Perhaps, in his sleep-deprived state, Collins would give her more information than he intended to.

'Assuming the body was dumped where it was found, and was killed near enough to that time, I reckon two weeks, possibly a bit longer, given it's been chilly lately.'

Louise nodded. Collins held his pencil above the notepad as though he was about to write something and then seemed to hover there, as though he was paused mid-thought.

'Is there anything else you need for the statement?' Louise prompted after a long minute.

'Uh, no.' Collins seemed to come back to himself and sat up a little straighter. 'I'll have one of the fellas type this up, and you'll need to sign it. If you'd wait in the reception area while that happens, I can get on to speaking to your sister.'

Louise looked at her watch; they'd been a little over half an hour. She hoped Megan was there already. 'Happy to.'

Megan was waiting on the brown plastic chairs in reception when Louise came back out, and she exhaled her relief. 'Your turn,' she said.

'Megan Carter?' Collins looked at Megan, and she stood up. 'Follow me.'

If there had been time, Louise might have warned her that he was struggling after the long night, but it seemed rude to do so in front of the Sergeant. Louise waited, finishing the rest of her muffin and starting on her emails. Megan came out after another half hour or so.

'Did you get anything out of him?' Megan said, her voice low as she sat down.

'He said the body might have been there two weeks, possibly three. Not much more than that.'

Megan nodded. 'Collins mumbled something about poor Heather, which I had to assume was the mother of some missing child, or possibly a child they think might be the body.'

Louise shivered. 'It's awful.'

'Yeah.'

They sat in silence for a while before Jennings, the young constable from the day before, called them over to the window.

'I've got your statements here. You need to read over them, then bring them back to me before you sign. I have to witness you signing it,' he said, handing over two typed documents. Both Carters took the statements back to their seats to read over the content carefully before signing them.

'Seems like it's all in order,' Louise said after reading hers.

'Same here.'

They took their statements back to the window to sign. Jennings with deep purple rings under his eyes, paired with his pale skin and red hair, looked exhausted.

'Did you get any sleep?' Megan asked.

'Not enough,' he said, taking their statements back. 'I'll make copies for you, and then you're good to go.'

'Do we need to stay in Gosford? Or can we head off?' Megan asked. Louise turned to look at her sister, but she waved her hand in a 'we'll talk about it later' fashion.

'We've got your contact details, so you're fine to head off. I don't think either of you did the deed, so we probably won't need to talk to you again, but never say never. Especially once it gets to court… if it gets to court.'

'Thank you, Constable.'

Jennings shuffled over to a photocopier that Louise couldn't see but could hear before coming back with their copies. It was all very official, but she couldn't help feeling bad for the long hours, probably standing out in the cold forest all night.

The sisters walked back to the motel in silence.

'What now?' Louise said as she closed the motel room door.

'I'm done with Gosford,' Megan said with a sigh.

'I agree; we've exhausted the leads we had here.'

'There's been no more activity on Penny's finances or her social media. I think we need to talk to Stan.'

'Didn't Sue say something about the gym membership?'

'Oh yeah; she said it was still coming out of Penny's account, but that doesn't mean much.'

'We could call them and pretend to be her? See if they'd let us have any details.'

'Couldn't hurt to try, unless someone dobs us in for impersonating Penny.' Megan gave a lopsided smile.

'Sue's given us Penny's email logins, so if they need a one-time code, we can have it sent to the email. Let's see what we can get.' Louise pulled up the gym website and called the phone number. She had already logged into Penny's emails and had them up in a separate window.

'Hello, you've called Get Fit. If you would like to enquire about a new membership, press one, if you have questions about an existing membership, press two. If you're a trainer, press three—'

Louise put the call on speaker so they could both listen and pressed two. She was put through to some soft jazz hold music.

'Hi, you're speaking with Daniella. How can I help you today?' Daniella seemed very young and perky, probably a requirement for a person working at a gym.

'Hi Daniella, I'm hoping you can help me. I can't seem to find my dongle thing to get in. Are you able to let me know the last club I was in, in case I left it there? Or possibly send me a replacement?'

'Sure, that should be fine. Is this the number you're registered under?'

'Oh no, this is my friend's phone; mine doesn't have credit.' Louise gave Daniella Penny's number.

'Okay, can you confirm your full name?'

'Penelope Bean.'

'And date of birth?'

Louise gave the date of birth.

'And the last thing, we'll need to send a one-time code to your mobile or email—'

'Email, please,' Louise interrupted.

'Of course, just a moment.' Daniella tapped some keys in the background.

Louise refreshed the email account and waited for the code to come through. 'It's thinking.'

'Yeah, it can take a few moments.' Daniella seemed unfazed.

'Oh, here it is,' Louise gave the six-digit code.

'Great, thanks Penelope. We've confirmed your identity… I can see the last club you were in was Hornsby, on the twentieth of March.'

'Oh, I have been slack. I didn't realise it was so long ago,' Louise said with a laugh she hoped sounded self-deprecating.

'We don't judge.' Daniella was tapping away. 'I had a look in the club database, and it doesn't seem like they've picked up a dongle. You could pop in to check; otherwise, they can set you up with a replacement too.'

'Great, thank you. I'll go in and chat with them. You've been a great help.' Louise wrapped up the call as quickly as she could, not wanting to maintain the act longer than necessary.

'Well, I suppose that proves she hasn't been to the gym since she disappeared, which supports the other evidence that she's not doing anything we can trace.' Megan bit her lip.

'It doesn't give us any new information.'

'Wanna go find Stan?'

'I don't know. I was ready to be down on the cops for doing a bad job, but we're not doing any better. Apart from finding an unrelated corpse, we haven't gotten any further than they did.'

'We haven't interviewed Stan…' Megan said.

'Stan probably won't give us anything useful. If he killed her, he's not likely to say, "Oh yeah, I forgot to mention I murdered her."'

'But what if he didn't do anything to her? What if she's been in touch?'

'Wouldn't he have told someone? He must know that her family are going out of their minds, and the police think he's hurt her.'

'If I was Stan, I don't think I'd want to be helpful.'

Louise ran her finger over her eyebrow, thinking for a moment. Maybe her sister was right. 'I think it's worth talking to him, regardless. But if you don't think so, what other leads do we have?'

Megan sighed. 'Well, none. I don't think we can do anything else. I know I complained about the jobs looking for evidence of cheating or faked injuries, but they were way less complicated and stressful. I'm out of my depth, and I think we should stop spending Sue's money and tell her we've done all we can.'

If you decide to go to Port Macquarie to find Stan, read on.

If you decide to admit defeat and go back to Melbourne, go to <u>Chapter 18</u> *on page 299.*

Chapter 9

You go to Port Macquarie to find Stan.

'Port Macquarie isn't that far, is it?' Louise said, pulling out her phone and opening the map app. 'Three hours; we could get there by tonight and speak to Stan in the morning. What did you say he was doing?'

'Construction or something. He had a video of himself on a job site; I'm sure I would be able to find it if I had another look. He's not very good at protecting his privacy in his videos.'

'I guess that's more of a female trait—being paranoid that someone will find you from social media. A man like Stan doesn't have to worry about that sort of thing.'

Megan shrugged. 'I guess not.'

'Anyway, I think it's worth another day or two, just so we can say we've turned over every stone, you know?'

'Alright. We'll talk to Stan, and then, if and when he's not much help, we can call Sue and tell her we're stuck.'

They packed up their things and shoved them into the car, and within half an hour they were on the road again—up the Pacific Highway, stopping at Bulahdelah for a snack and a stretch, and arriving at a lodge five minutes from the centre of town.

The lodge, more of a glorified motel, was a two-storey pale beige brick veneer building, with a white sloping roof and white railings on the upper floor. Next door was the huge base hospital, probably the only one for a few hundred kilometres around.

The lodge office on the ground floor was greyer than the rest, the walls painted cinderblocks instead of bricks, but it was clean.

Louise got them a twin room on the ground floor; it didn't look like much in the dark of evening. There were several handrails bolted to the wall in the bathroom, and the couch was covered in vinyl—both reminded her of an aged care home more than a motel.

Perhaps it's an indication of their usual clientele, or maybe it's for people who aren't sick enough for the hospital but still need some extra facilities.

On the way there, when she wasn't driving, Louise had spent her time rewatching Stan's vlogs. He was dry and didn't have a good presence on camera, especially not in comparison to the content he made with Penny, but he had been posting semi-consistently even in her absence. She had to give him that. There were a few videos that could have been made during his lunch hour—five-minute snippets where he tried to come up with something interesting to say about being an itinerant labourer. If it were up to her, Louise would have advised him to save posting for when he had something to say, but apparently, the internet didn't work like that.

The job site he was working on would eventually be a leisure centre or something; vast steel girders loomed high above the ground over what she assumed would be a pool. To the side there were several smaller structures that might have been gym or function rooms. It was big enough that they would recognise it if they went past.

'Did you check the geotags on his Insta?' Megan said, stepping out of the oddly spacious bathroom.

'What?'

'Geotags. It'll show you on a map where the photo was taken if he's geotagged it.'

'Oh.' Louise hadn't checked, and she pulled out her phone to look at Stan's Instagram content. She struggled to keep the different social media channels and their respective functions straight in her head. Perhaps it was because she wasn't really interested, or more likely, that there were too many of them and they blurred together.

'That one.' Megan leaned over her shoulder and pointed at a photo of the construction site tagged at the Rosendahl Reservoir. 'You can see the reservoir in the background, so it must be there.' Megan tapped the tag, and a map showed them where the reservoir was, and by extension, the half-built recreation centre not far from it.

'We'll go tomorrow. See if we can spot Stan and follow him home, or to wherever the van is parked at the moment. Better not try to approach him at work.'

'No, too many people trying to find out what he's up to. Although whenever I see people on construction sites, they don't seem to be doing much.'

Louise made a sound of agreement, thinking of all the times she'd seen people in high-vis vests watching others holding stop signs.

*   *   *

Megan slept badly, whether it was the new motel bed, the lack of progress, or the thought of having to confront Stan in the morning she couldn't be sure, but she had lain there staring at the darkness for most of the night. She dozed off a couple of times, but when the alarm went off at seven o'clock, she pulled the covers over her face and hid.

'We need to get there early; construction has weird hours, and we don't want to miss Stan because we're too busy snoozing.' Louise looked almost chipper, which seemed very unfair.

'Sleep alright then?' Megan asked.

'Surprisingly well, actually. I don't mind a firmer mattress.'

Megan stayed under the covers and said nothing.

'Looks like they don't do breakfast here; we'll have to get something on the way.'

'You go ahead, and I'll meet you there for the second shift.'

'And how are you going to get to the site if I have the car?' Louise said, pulling the bedclothes off Megan's face.

'I'll walk.'

'It'd take you an hour. Just get up; you can nap in the car.'

Megan pushed herself out of bed. She'd never been an early riser, and even at the best of times she liked to have time in the morning to brood over her coffee before having to function. Being rushed along by her older sister brought back memories of when they were kids, and both her parents and Louise would form a procession to try to get her up for school. She forced herself into a seated position before shuffling to the bathroom.

In ten minutes, with a lot of ineffectual hurrying from Louise, they were on the way, with a short detour to a servo for some borderline drinkable coffee and sandwiches that were probably made days ago.

They parked across the road from the exposed metal monstrosity and settled in to watch. Louise had cruised up and down the street before they stopped, keeping an eye out for the van, but they saw no sign of it. Maybe Stan got a lift from someone.

Megan finished her coffee and closed her eyes. 'Wake me in two hours, and I'll take over.'

*   *   *

Watching and waiting were not her favourite parts of the job; Louise preferred ferreting around in people's files and social media. She surveyed the building site entrances, though she couldn't see much from their parking spot. Reaching into the back seat for her work bag, she pulled out a small pair of binoculars. She didn't like to use them too much as it made it obvious that she was watching something, but since she couldn't see the figures on the site clearly, she wanted to check whether Stan was in view, as he would have arrived before the sisters settled in.

Louise searched the visible parts of the building for five minutes before giving up. She hadn't found Stan and the only people she saw seemed to be standing around, and not doing much work.

It would have been ideal if she could read a book on surveillance, but that would mean taking her eyes off the subject too much. Louise had discovered an enjoyment of podcasts and audiobooks during her time as a PI, so she put her headphones in and started up her latest book, one of Dickens' longer works that she'd studied at uni but had never gotten around to finishing.

The sun shone down on the car, the skies were blue and clear, and after an hour, the car started to get hot inside. She wound down the window and took off her hoodie, but was still uncomfortably warm. Always a danger on a stake-out since warmth made her sleepy.

Too bad it's not Megan's turn yet. Louise pushed her fingers under her sunglasses and rubbed the bridge of her nose. As she let her hand fall back into her lap, she spotted a man in a hard hat, high-vis vest over a bulky dark hoodie, dark blue stubbie shorts, and tan-coloured work boots heading out of the main entrance with a lollipop stop/slow sign. She got the binoculars out again briefly to doublecheck, but it was definitely Stan.

He walked out into the road and held up his sign to stop the non-existent flow of traffic to let a huge concrete truck out of the building site. He waved to the driver and ambled back inside, out of view. At least she knew he was there. Louise made a note in her book of the time, what Stan was wearing, and what he'd been doing. Sometimes she needed to refer to these field notes, but even if she didn't, it was always useful to have contemporaneous documentation.

Megan stirred in the passenger seat beside her. Louise hoped she might wake up but she went back to the slow, shallow breathing of sleep.

At the three-hour mark, Louise tapped her sister on the shoulder. 'It's your turn. I need to stretch my legs and have a pee.'

Megan frowned and looked at her through narrowed eyes. 'Anything interesting happen?'

'I spotted Stan earlier; he escorted a truck out,' Louise then added a description of Stan's clothes. 'But nothing since then.'

'Are the guys worth watching?' Megan raised her eyebrows and gazed meaningfully at the binoculars.

'None I saw.'

'Disappointing.' Megan sat herself up and adjusted the passenger seat upright. 'I'll take over. You could do some foot recon while you're stretching your legs.'

'I could.' Louise wasn't keen to do more work on her break, but if she had been at home and on her own, there wouldn't have been another person to share the watching and waiting with.

Louise took her hoodie with her; after being in the warm car for so long, the outside temperature chilled her. She was sure she'd seen a little milk bar or convenience store not far away as they drove in, though the bathroom was a more urgent concern. She strolled away from the site and found a public toilet block about five minutes down the road. A little further on was the milk bar she'd seen, but it was closed. The windows were dirty, and the posters advertising flavoured milk and chocolate bars inside were faded and tatty. She would have guessed it was permanently closed if it weren't for the stock on the shelves she could just see through the grime.

There were no opening hours on the door, and Louise couldn't work out the business model of this store. Maybe it was only open for the after-school rush and weekends. It was the sort of place where a child might want to spend their pocket money, or where families who couldn't be bothered going into the supermarket could pick up bread and milk if they ran out.

After musing on the state of the small business convenience store economy, she turned around and headed back towards the car and the building site. She set her pace to a leisurely stroll, trying to look as though she belonged there but had nowhere in particular she needed to be. Attracting the attention of one of the construction workers by watching too closely would have been a mistake, and she hoped that the era of wolf-whistles and cat-calling passersby was over, though she was braced for it.

Close up, the site was full of activity and noise. She had headphones in her ears but had turned off the audiobook. At least one radio was blasting soft rock through the site, and men's voices yelled various commands. Everything was metal, with no insulation or walls yet, so the sound carried and echoed.

As Louise passed the site and headed out the other side, she made another note of the walk-by and that nothing of interest had been learned. She kept walking for another five minutes, then crossed the road and headed back to the car.

'No snacks?' Megan said as Louise slid back into the driver's seat.

'Nothing open.'

'Anything to report?'

'Seems like a standard site; terrible music and a bunch of shouting.'

Megan nodded.

'Anything of interest from here?'

'Nope, haven't spotted Stan.'

*   *   *

At a little before three o'clock, a steady stream of utes and cars started to leave the site. Louise was back on watch and elbowed Megan.

'We need to spot the car with Stan in it,' she said.

Megan used the binoculars to look into the cabins of the vehicles as they left the site, while Louise wrote down the number plates and a short description of each one.

'That's him, I'm pretty sure,' Megan said, pointing to a large orange and black ute. It had large black wheels, a double cab, and a big silver locked box in the tray. It was suspiciously clean for a tradie but Louise supposed that if you had a flashy vehicle like that, you would want to keep it pristine.

'I think you're right.' Louise had taken down the number plate, put her notebook away, and turned the engine on. 'Let's see where they go.'

Megan put the binoculars away and pulled out the camera with a long lens. She snapped a couple of shots of the ute as they turned around and followed it back towards the town centre. They passed an aged care centre, turned right, drove through a residential area, made a few more turns, and just as the beach came into view at the end of the road, the orange ute pulled over in front of the sign for the caravan park.

Louise kept driving towards the beach, hoping the ute driver hadn't noticed their dinky little hatchback following them for the ten-minute drive from the site to the caravan park.

'I suppose we should have known he'd be in a caravan park,' Louise said.

'He could have been parked in someone's driveway, like he did in Melbourne.'

'True.' Louise turned onto the beach road and parked. 'I guess we go back on foot to the caravan park and find the van then?'

'We could go in the car.'

'Is that more or less conspicuous? A car that follows you from work to home and then drives around looking for your van? Or two tourists having a stroll?'

'I guess you're right. We don't want him to clock the car.'

Louise thought Megan's attempt to walk casually was a bit over the top, she swung her arms too much, but otherwise they shouldn't raise anyone's suspicions. The caravan park was fairly small but still large enough that they needed to walk up and down several rows of caravans, tents, and empty lots before they found Stan's van.

It looked the same as it had in the videos and the photo the two hippies from Gosford showed them, though it could do with a wash; dust and dirt covered the exterior.

'Looks like he's been off-roading it,' Megan said when the van came into view around a corner.

'Or Penny was the one who kept it clean and now Stan doesn't bother.' Louise put her hand out to grab her sister's forearm.

'What?'

'Do we want to go talk to him now?'

'Why not?'

'What are we gonna say?'

Megan shrugs. 'The usual stuff, when did you last see Penny, what happened before she left.'

'And then what? He's not going to say he killed her.'

Megan bit her lower lip in thought. 'Back to the car to strategise?'

At that moment, Stan stepped out of the caravan and raised his chin in their direction, acknowledging them.

Louise raised her chin. 'G'day.'

'Why did you say that?' Megan whispered.

'I'm not going to ignore him. Anyway, the planning is moot; we'll have to go talk to him now, he's seen us.' Louise straightened her shoulders and walked towards Stan and his van, with Megan following a step or two behind.

'Are you Stan Warding?' Louise asked.

'Who's asking?' Stan frowned, folding his arms across his body.

'My name is Louise Carter, this is my sister Megan. We're private investigators. We've been employed to look into Penelope Bean's disappearance.'

Stan's mouth flattened into a line. 'And how did you find me?'

'That's not important right now. We were hoping you would give us a few minutes to talk about the last time you saw Penny.'

'I told all this to the police.'

'We're aware, but Penny's family are… sceptical of the amount of effort the police are putting into the case,' Megan said.

'Yeah, they're pretty useless.' Stan's eyes darted around, as though checking for anyone listening. 'You'd better come in. I don't want people to hear us.'

'After you,' Louise said.

The inside of the van was cramped with the three of them; the sisters sat together on a padded bench seat while Stan leaned against the sink. He held a cigarette in his fingers, twirling it absent-mindedly.

'You're welcome to smoke if you prefer. It's your house, er, van after all,' Megan said.

'I'm trying to give up. I keep them around for emergencies but still like to hold 'em.' Stan tapped the cigarette against the bench then tucked it behind one ear. 'So, what did you want to talk about?'

'I'm sure you went over everything with the police, but they're not exactly cooperative in sharing their notes, so if you could go over how you met Penny, how you ended up going around Australia, and of course we'll talk through the last time you saw her in due course.'

'Jeez, you want all that?' Stan rubbed his chin, his jaw rippling as he worked the muscles there. Louise was convinced he would clam up and ask them to leave right then.

'How we met isn't a very interesting story—I was at a party with a bunch of uni students. I prefer them to people my age, who tend to be boring and go to bed early. Anyway, we had a mutual friend, and I got chatting with Penny. She's a unique person, really passionate about the environment, studying engineering to please her parents—but she hated the boys' club mentality and all the maths, even though she could do it with her eyes closed.'

Louise hadn't brought a notebook with her; she looked over to Megan, who was also empty handed. 'Do you might if I record our conversation for my notes later?'

'No, I guess that's okay.'

Louise pulled out her phone and set up the voice recorder function. 'You were saying Penny wasn't enjoying her studies?'

'Nah, not really. It was all so dry and theoretical. Plus, she didn't really want to be an engineer. She wanted to be an influencer.'

'An influencer? What did that mean to her?'

'You know, she saw all these dynamic young women on social media making a living off vlogging and the rest. She was sure she would be able to do that, but knew her parents would hate the idea. I told her she needed to follow her heart. What else was she given all that natural intelligence for if not to try to make it on her own? Uni would always be there if she wanted to go back and finish her degree.'

'And were you dating by that stage?' Megan asked.

Stan chuckled. 'I tried to tell her I was too old, but she insisted we were a good match. I know what it looks like, hanging out with uni kids, dating a twenty-year-old, but she was very persuasive.'

I bet she was, Louise thought. 'I see.'

'We started dating, and as time went on, she was more and more convinced she should give travel vlogging a go. She'd always wanted to see Australia, and of course, I had the van. Penny's a doer, I've never been a person that gets things done, I usually just have ideas which float around for a while and then I forget them or move on to something else without achieving much.'

'She was the driving force behind the trip then?' Louise said.

'Yep. I had a good idea of where we should go, and I was good at driving; the rest was Penny.'

'And then what happened?'

'The first few weeks on the road were great. We were on a roll with content, and everything was going smoothly. I thought we were doing really good, but Penny always wanted more: more followers, more money…' Stan looked out of the window, apparently lost in thought. He pulled the cigarette from behind his ear and put it in his mouth before realising what he'd done and dropping it onto the bench top. 'We started fighting. She was so driven and she was getting sick of my "lazy" attitude.' He held up his hands up to indicate air quotes.

'What did she mean by lazy?'

'I wanted to spend more time at each stop, to take in the sights, you know, I didn't want it to be like, a grind every day. She said that was how you had to work to be an influencer. The laidback man she liked at the start seemed to be giving her the shits. I hadn't changed, and I guess neither had she, but over time, living in such close quarters, we started to drive each other crazy.'

'So, what happened in Gosford?' Megan asked after a lengthy pause.

'Nothing really. We fought again. We'd planned to go to the waterfalls. I didn't feel like going, but she said we needed content. I said she should just go on her own and she said I was a part of the channel and had to participate. I'd had enough, so I decided to leave. Penny said she was fine with it; she'd go to the waterfalls alone, and we'd meet up later.' Stan looked at the sisters in turn for a long moment before going on.

'I drove off; I probably shouldn't have since I was her ride. She had the little camera, but she'd left her phone in the van. I didn't realise till I was about half an hour away. I turned around to go back, thinking she'd want it, even if we weren't really speaking. When I got back to the picnic area, I couldn't find her, so I waited for a couple of hours, but she didn't come back.'

'And you didn't see her again after that?'

'Nope. Just disappeared. I probably should have tried harder to find her, but I assumed she was just punishing me and would come back when she thought I'd learned my lesson.'

'How long did you wait in Gosford?'

'A week or so. I started to think she'd gone back to her family in Melbourne and that I should just move on, but they called and said she wasn't with them. I guess her mum reported her missing. After that, I tried doing a bit of content on my own, but I'm not much chop at it, to be honest.'

'You didn't think it was weird she wasn't posting on social media?'

'What do you mean?'

'She hasn't posted anything on any of her social media, or used her bank accounts, or seen her family since that day.'

Stan stared hard at Megan for a moment before rapidly blinking. 'I thought she'd blocked me. Like I didn't see anything new, and I just thought she'd cut me off. I didn't realise she was, like, missing missing.'

Louise narrowed her eyes. 'You didn't think speaking to the police and her family was a bit of a red flag if she had just gone home?'

'I'm not proud of this, but I went through a pretty heavy drinking and smoking phase after Penny left. I didn't put two and two together. Part of me was pretending it was fine, and the other part of me didn't want to think about her. I really loved her, even though she was way outta my league.'

Megan looked at Louise and shrugged subtly. Louise had to agree; she couldn't think of anything else to ask.

'I think that's all we need from you at the moment. Thanks for chatting with us.' Louise stood up, digging in her pocket for a business card. 'If you think of anything that might help us locate Penny—and I need to stress that she is "missing missing", please give us a call.'

'Yeah. Thanks.'

Megan and Louise exited the van and walked back to the car in silence. They'd established early in their careers to make sure there was a good distance between themselves and a person of interest before they went over their impressions.

Back in the car, Louise sighed.

'What do you think?' Megan asked.

'I don't know. He seemed believable.'

'That's what I was going to say.'

They were silent for a few moments.

'Although if he's a psychopath, he's probably a really good liar.'

'True, but he played dumb really well. And not just dumb in the innocent way, dumb in ways that made him look bad, which a proper psychopath wouldn't,' Megan said.

'So, if we believe him, and I'm not saying we do, then what the fuck happened to Penny?'

If you think Stan is innocent, read on.

If you still think Stan has something to do with Penny's disappearance go to Chapter 12 *on page 160.*

Chapter 10

You think Stan is innocent.

'Did you ever see *Gone Girl*?' Megan asked.

Louise paused for a moment before answering. 'I don't think I did, but the basic premise is the woman set it up so that her husband would be blamed for her death, but faked it and ran off?'

'That's the gist.'

'You think Penny ran off?'

'It's possible. The way Stan was talking about her made it sound like she was in charge, and he was just along for the ride. Looking at his lifestyle and history, it makes sense. He seems like a total dropkick—I can imagine with someone who has the drive and discipline to actually do stuff, he might achieve something, but otherwise, he's a bit of a drifter.'

'I got that feeling too. He seems so… undirected, bumbling around, going from one entry-level job to another, partying a bit, and generally not making much of himself.' Louise was rubbing her eyebrow.

'He'd need to be a pretty good actor to fool us both.'

'We're not bad at knowing when someone is lying, but neither of us has ever met a real murderer before. Perhaps he's a skilled sociopath.'

Megan scrunched up her face. 'Seems unlikely.'

Louise looked out over the beach; Megan followed her gaze. The waves were coming in gently, leaving picturesque white froth on the shore that disappeared almost as soon as it arrived.

'Pity it's too cold to go for a swim,' Megan said.

'I didn't bring bathers; I hadn't imagined I'd need them for a work trip.' Louise chuckled. 'Should we go for a walk along the shore? We could get ice cream and think about what we do now.'

'Ice cream sounds good.'

They paid too much for their ice creams from a small kiosk on the waterfront, then walked along the chilly shore for a while. The sun was out, which was nice, but the weather was still cool, and the wind off the ocean had a bite.

'Not really ice cream weather,' Megan muttered as she licked the chocolate scoop. She was enjoying it despite the inappropriate climate.

'Not really, but it's nice here.'

They walked in silence for a while, Megan tried not to think about anything in particular, but her brain was running in overdrive. If Penny had orchestrated her own disappearance, how would they know? How could they prove that? She would have had to set up an alternative identity, which wouldn't have been easy. She'd need a phone, money, and transport. She wouldn't have stuck around Gosford; the local cops would have spotted her if Stan hadn't. Despite Megan's scepticism about the Gosford Police force, they would have looked in the local area.

'Do you remember if Sue has access to Penny's bank accounts?' Megan said.

'Yeah, we looked at her bank statements and whatnot at the start of the investigation. She hasn't used them.'

'I know she hasn't used them; I was going to look again for evidence she'd been siphoning off money to another account. If she faked her disappearance, then there must be some sort of paper trail.'

Louise paused walking for a moment, as though lost in thought. 'She'd probably need another phone, and some other stuff. I don't know how a person might go about getting false ID together but it couldn't be that hard, if you have money and know the right people.'

Megan's ice-cream was gone, and Louise had just popped the last bite of waffle cone in her mouth. 'Shall we go back to the motel, sorry the Lodge? Do some digging into Penny's financials?'

'Yeah. And let's look through the social media of her friends. Maybe she's made new profiles to keep in touch with some of them.'

'That would be risky,' Megan said as they headed back to the car.

'How many cases have we solved because people are idiots and can't keep a secret?'

'You make a good point.'

*　　*　　*

Back in the motel, both sisters were on their laptops, looking through various records. Louise had volunteered to start on the financials, copies of which she had stored in the agency's cloud storage, and Megan looked for social media links.

Penny had several social media accounts, the usual suspects: Facebook, though she didn't do much on it,

Instagram, TikTok, and Snapchat. Megan started with Facebook, thinking she might have befriended her mother or someone else close to her with a fake account to keep an eye on them. Kate Bean didn't seem to have added any new friends on Facebook, but she had a number of followers on Insta, some of whom were only new profiles. Being a woman of a certain age meant she was more likely to have scammers and bots trying to get her to give them money.

Megan sifted through followers for over an hour before taking a break to stand up and stretch her legs and neck. 'Any luck?'

'There are some weird transactions. Here, she withdraws a thousand dollars in cash, and then again two months later, which she could have used for anything—but the usual items—accommodation, supermarkets, takeaway food, phone bills—they're all coming out electronically.'

'Sounds sus.'

'Yeah. She also made a purchase at an electronics shop for a little under five hundred dollars, which could easily have been a phone, but it could have been something else.'

'If she bought an unlocked phone and a prepaid SIM with cash, we wouldn't know what network she was on.' Megan frowned.

'Even the supermarkets sell SIM cards these days, so it could be hiding in one of her grocery purchases.'

'And given how perceptive Stan seems to be, she could easily have been prepping and packing her little backpack with everything she needed to disappear. Get on a bus, or hitchhike to Sydney, and she'd be as good as gone.'

'Yeah.'

The sisters were quiet for a long time after this exchange. Megan felt as though a weight were sitting on her lungs. There was something they were missing, but what? Stan was a doofus, that was for sure, and he had seemed credible when they spoke to him earlier in the day, but was it merely a very crafty way to deflect attention?

'What do we know about Stan?' Megan said.

'Huh?'

'I was thinking about whether Stan could be faking being an idiot. It's a tried and tested method to get the cops, or in our case, PIs, off your trail to feign ignorance. I thought he was for real; you know he seemed genuinely dumb, but what if he wasn't?'

Louise closed the notebook she'd been jotting in. 'It's a good question. We looked into his background a little, but maybe it's worth another look.'

'Do we know where he's from?'

'I don't think so. Sue said he was a wastrel, from memory.'

'I'll have a look.' Megan opened her laptop and started searching for information on Stan Warding. They had been through his social media several times, but never went all the way back, or looked for his history. His Instagram account was a couple of years old, he had a lot of posts from the time he and Penny were travelling together, for traction she guessed, but before that and since Penny's disappearance, there was less content. She scrolled back to the beginning, in 2018 when he'd joined, and found some photos of him at Melbourne University. Perhaps he'd been a student there, and that's why he spent so much time hanging around at uni parties trying to pick up younger women.

His early posts didn't give her much context for his studies or his work, they were mostly selfies of him out and about holding a beer, or a cigarette, or both. In one photo, he looked to be at a nightclub, feeling the effects of at least one illicit substance.

One face popped up regularly on his nights out—a young man, clean-shaven, with floppy dark hair. Megan reviewed these posts carefully, trying to find a tag or a comment that told her who this man was.

'Have you come across this guy Chad?' Megan asked.

'It doesn't ring a bell. Who is he?'

'Looks like a uni friend. He's featured heavily in Stan's early Insta posts.'

'Hmm.'

'I might dig into it. If he knew Stan from before he met Penny, maybe he would be able to give us some insight into whether he's a crafty sociopath, a vacuous dropout, or something in between.'

'Sure. I've come up with a whole lot of nothing over here,' Louise said from behind her laptop.

Megan opened Chad's Insta profile and found his surname—Miller. She searched for Chad Miller and found a profile with his photo on it on a professional website. He was listed as Junior Counsel for a law firm.

'Damn. I think Chad is a lawyer.'

'He won't want to talk to us then,' Louise said.

'Probably not. Maybe I should tell him I'm a journalist.'

'Has that ever worked?'

'Just because it hasn't yet doesn't mean it's a bad line.'

'Be truthful and just say you're trying to get background on Stan for a family matter. If he's any good at law, he probably won't respond, but you never know, he might be dying to dish.'

Megan raised an eyebrow, but she opened an email to him anyway.

Dear Mr Miller,

You don't know me, but my name is Megan Carter, and I work with the Carter & Carter Detective Agency. We're currently looking into a family matter, and Stan Warding has come up as a person of interest.

Given your long-standing connection with Stan, we would appreciate having a conversation with you about his character and background.

Any information you share will be held in the strictest confidence.

She signed off with her contact details and sent it before she could think too hard about whether it was a good idea. Now all she had to do was wait for a reply.

'You've had no luck then?' Megan asked.

Louise looked up and rubbed her hand across her face. 'I've been combing through her finances. From what Sue was able to send over, there's nothing except those few cash withdrawals. She's still got nearly two grand sitting in the account. I would have thought if she were going to run away, she'd drain the account.'

'True. Although if she wanted to frame Stan for her murder, she would need to make it believable. Emptying the account isn't exactly innocent behaviour.'

'I hadn't thought of that.'

'Plus, they were probably doing cash-in-hand jobs along the journey, so maybe she'd been using Stan's money and her account for day-to-day expenses while pocketing the cash income.'

'You're making her sound like the sociopath now. Didn't Sue say she was a nice, naïve girl?'

Megan sighed. 'She did. I'm trying to justify my inclination to let Stan off the hook, but Occam's razor, eh?'

'Probably.'

Megan looked at the time; it was getting late in the evening, and her belly was starting to complain about not being fed. 'I'm going to get some dinner and give up on this for the night. You wanna come?'

'Yes. I'm reading the same lines over and over.'

Megan drove the two sisters the ten minutes or so into the town proper for a meal. She fancied something different from the fish and chip fare available around the motel. There were plenty of places along the water, though many of them looked too expensive to be reasonable on their per diem rate. It was one thing to have her friend paying for the investigation into her niece's disappearance, but it was another to expect Sue to pay for fine dining.

'What about this place, The Grill Hut?' Louise said.

'Grill sounds good, though "hut" makes it sound like a pizza chain.'

'Does it matter? It's just there, it's clean and doesn't look too busy… or suspiciously quiet.'

'Okay.' Megan glanced at the place as she found a spot to park. It was a two-storey building with a wraparound verandah on the first floor, giving it a Queenslander look. In the dark, the fairy lights along the railings were lit up and twinkled invitingly. It could have been tacky, but it managed to look quaint instead.

They were seated upstairs on the balcony, looking out over the wooden dock, and the small boats moored there. Some of the boats advertised tours and fishing charters along the river and out in the ocean.

'They have oysters,' Louise said, pointing to the menu.

'You don't like oysters.'

Louise looked up. 'No, *you* don't like oysters. I never eat them around you because you make that face.'

'We're billing all this to Sue.'

'I know, I won't get the oysters; I was just saying.'

Megan pressed her lips together. She wanted to tell her sister that oysters were filter feeders and should be avoided at all costs, especially raw. But she didn't.

'What are you getting then?' Megan asked.

'Probably a steak. Now that I'm here and I can smell the kitchen, it makes sense. No use going to a grill and getting a parma.'

'Well, I think I'll get the parma.'

'I'm starting to think we should stick to affairs and insurance,' Louise said after they had given their order to the waiter.

'Really?' Megan frowned.

'The stakes here are so high. If we don't find anything and Penny stays missing, then what? Maybe she's dead, and Stan killed her and got away with it. Maybe she's run off for reasons unknown… but it's a lot.'

'Trailing cheaters is pretty tawdry. Sometimes I wonder why we became investigators when that's all we do. But sorting stuff out is pretty fun.'

Louise shrugged, and the waiter came back with two glasses of house red wine. When he was out of earshot again, she replied, 'It feels like that to me too sometimes. I like being my own boss, I like the solitude, I like the puzzle of it, but having a person's life literally in my hands is a lot of pressure.'

'I've been feeling like that too. Especially after we met with Stan; he seemed so… not exactly normal, but I didn't get a murdery vibe off him.'

'Me neither.'

They sat quietly for a while, each staring out over the black surface of the water, listening to the low burble of the other diners' chat. A ute drove past, its windows down and its stereo blasting bass-heavy dance music. The driver was a young blonde man, his passenger had his head out the window, singing along loudly and offkey.

'Must be a lot of great things to do around Port Macquarie on a Thursday night,' Louise muttered.

'If that's their idea of a good time?'

'Yeah.'

'I don't think I'd want to live in a regional town. The chances of running into someone you've had a falling out with are so much higher.'

'I run into enough of my exes in Melbourne as it is,' Louise said quietly.

The waiter brought their meals, and when the smell of the fried food reached her nostrils, Megan's belly gurgled in anticipation.

'You don't have falling outs with people.' Louise spun her plate around so that her chips were closest.

'You don't know everything about me. I have people I don't want to see, and if they were always walking past in the supermarket or whatever, that would be super awkward.'

'Do they know you've had a falling out? Or do you just stop talking to them, these hypothetical people.'

'Most of the time, I just try to fade away, so I don't have to deal with conflict.'

Louise raised an eyebrow, but instead of responding, she put a piece of her steak in her mouth.

* * *

Louise drove them home—after Megan had had three glasses of wine with her meal, it seemed like the sensible idea. She was worried about her sister; the conversation about going back to cheaters and injuries had been intended to get her to open up about the case and maybe to air a concern that they should stop trying to do the cops' jobs without any training. But Megan hadn't taken it the way she'd hoped.

If the thing with Chad doesn't get anywhere tomorrow, I'll suggest we go home, Louise told herself. Megan was staring out the window into the dark. Roads in the country were so much darker than in the city, as though the night came down and smothered them. Even in the built-up areas, it was somehow smaller and quieter than Melbourne. She turned off the main road to the motel and parked.

They were quiet for the rest of the evening. Louise pulled out her tablet and started reading a book, while Megan lay on her bed and was soon snoring lightly. She was never much good at drinking wine.

In the morning, Louise woke up to her alarm at seven o'clock. She'd slept strangely in the unfamiliar bed, and the steak dinner, while delicious, had been a lot of red meat late at night— something she was learning her late-thirties digestive system couldn't deal with.

She pulled on her running gear and went out for a jog around the streets, hoping it would distract her from the standstill the case had reached. Louise jogged for an hour, her mind quiet as she focused on her feet landing on the footpath and her breath in and out.

When she arrived back at the motel, Megan was still asleep, though she woke as the door closed.

'You ran?'

'It seemed like a good idea.'

'I regret having wine with dinner. I'm old.'

'I'm older than you. But yes, wine on a school night is maybe something to be avoided.'

Megan grumbled and rolled over. Louise took a shower, enjoying the feeling of the clean water against her sweaty skin. The weather was stickier than in Melbourne, despite it being almost winter.

As she came back into the bedroom, Megan had roused herself from under the doona and was looking somewhat more awake.

'Anything from Chad?' It seemed unlikely, but she was curious.

'Nothing yet. But it's not even nine.' Megan shrugged and went into the bathroom. Louise read the news headlines and checked her emails, though none had come through since the night before other than spam and newsletters. She enjoyed running her own business, liked the freedom and even the responsibility of it, but sometimes the lack of structure made her anxious.

'Should we stick around here then? Do we want to talk to Stan again?' Megan asked when she came out of the bathroom. Her shoulder-length brown hair had disappeared under one towel, and another was wrapped around her body.

'I don't know what else we can get from him. He was fairly open with us, the cops never found anything on him, and unless we hear from Chad and there's something really concerning in his past, we've come to a dead end.'

Megan made a frustrated sound and flopped onto her bed. 'That's what I thought.'

Louise fussed with her hair, trying to get it to be not quite so flat.

Her mind turned back to the case. Stan had been their main suspect, the only person around at the time of the disappearance who really knew Penny, but he had seemed so guileless when they spoke to him. It was possible he was some sort of criminal mastermind, but that seemed very unlikely.

'Does Stan still have Penny's phone?' Louise said, the thought coming to her mind.

'Huh?' Megan had dressed, though instead of drying her hair she'd opted to just tie it up in a bun, wet, a bad habit but Louise said nothing. The last time she'd brought up hair with her sister, Megan had been depressed for days. Being stuck on a work trip in the middle of a bout of depression would be unpleasant.

'Penny's phone. Stan said it was in the van when she left and I'm trying to remember if he said he ever did anything with it.'

'Oh yeah.'

There was a long pause. Louise waited in case her sister was going to add anything further, but it seemed she wasn't. 'So do you reckon he still has it?'

'Probably. If he didn't give it to the cops or send it back to Sue, then I guess he's got it.'

It was unbelievable that he would hang onto his ex's phone for months, but at the same time, it fit with his affable yet dim persona. Maybe he'd forgotten he had it, tucked it away in a drawer waiting for her to come back from the huff she'd left in, and then when she didn't, he just moved on to other things. 'Stan will be at work, we could drop by later today to see if we can recover it. Do you think Sue or Kate have the PIN for it?'

'I could ask.' Megan moved to the table and chairs near the window of the motel room. It was a spacious room, with two queen-sized beds, a bench on which stood the TV and the kettle as well as tea and coffee, and a small circular table and two vinyl-covered conference chairs that were straight out of the nineties. She tapped away while Louise put on a little eye make-up and some tinted moisturiser-slash-sunscreen, ready to head out into the day, not that they had any leads to follow up until Stan got off work at two or three o'clock.

'I've emailed Sue about the phone. We'll see what she says,' Megan said, staring out the window at the car park and the street beyond. At that moment, Megan's phone, which lay ignored on one of the side tables, started to vibrate. Louise picked it up; it was a mobile number she didn't recognise, and not a contact in the phone.

'Hello, Carter and Carter Detective Agency, Louise speaking.'

'Uh, yes, I was looking for Megan Carter, please?' a smooth male voice said down the line.

'Sure, can I ask who's calling?'

'It's Chad Miller.'

Louise's eyes widened; she hadn't expected him to reply, let alone call them. She handed the phone to her sister, covering the microphone as she whispered; 'Put it on speaker.'

'Megan Carter speaking,' Megan said, placing the phone on the table between them. 'I'm putting you on speaker so you can speak to my colleague Louise and me at the same time.'

'Oh… okay.' Chad seemed hesitant.

'I'm so glad you contacted us. As I mentioned in my email, we're looking into Stan Warding. Are you able to have a chat about him now?' Megan had her professional voice on and looked very serious. She had also turned back to her laptop, presumably to take notes.

'Yeah, sure. I have to tell you I was surprised by your email. How did you find me?'

'We came across you on Stan's social media. It wasn't hard to get your email from there.'

'Right. Of course. What do you want to know?'

'Let's start with the nature of your relationship with Stan.'

Louise quietly grabbed her notebook and pen from next to the kettle.

'I was hoping that you might give me a bit more information on who you are and what you're investigating. I looked you up, and I confirmed that this phone number is listed on the website, but I don't really see why I should be giving you any information at all.'

Louise narrowed her eyes; what he said made sense, but he had also phoned them back when he was under no obligation to do so. 'We've been engaged by a family member to look into a missing persons case,' Louise said.

'Ah, shit. Well… to be honest, when I saw Penny wasn't in their videos anymore, I did a bit of digging. I assumed the two of them broke up. Are you saying she's incommunicado?'

'Yes, a police report was filed a few weeks ago, but that didn't get very far, so the family has asked us to look into it. It appears no one has seen or heard from Penny since early April,' Megan said.

'I see.'

'What we would really like to know is what Stan's character is like. We don't have many contacts who know him, and it's making it difficult to parse the information we have.'

'He's a flighty bastard, that's for sure.'

'Can you tell us more about that?'

'I met Stan at uni, we were at Melbourne, I was doing a double degree in Arts and Law, while he was just doing Arts. Anyway, we were in a couple of classes together in our first year, and we got on really well. He's great for a laugh, so when I wanted to move out of my parent's place at the end of first year, I asked if he wanted to join my share house.'

'I see,' Megan said, typing quietly as Chad spoke.

'It was me, Stan and another bloke I knew; we lived in a hovel in Carlton. It was pretty gross, three boys, you know what I mean? At the end of first semester in second year, Stan said he was dropping out. I thought that was a bad idea, but I also knew Stan wasn't much for sticking with things, so he stopped going to uni and started working more hours at his bar job. He really liked it.'

'And you continued with your studies?'

'Yeah, I moved into a better place in fourth year. Stan stayed in the Carlton place, but I still saw him around. He got invited to a lot of great parties; he's good at getting into groups.'

'What were your thoughts on his, uh, character during that period?' Louise asked.

'He was untidy, but not dirty; he didn't leave his dishes too long, and he cleaned the shower every so often. He was sometimes late with rent but would pay you back. I guess he was trustworthy but flaky. He used drugs a fair bit, but mostly soft stuff: weed and molly for a good time, not hard shit.'

'Were you ever concerned about his behaviour? Did he demonstrate any violent tendencies?'

'Stan?' Chad laughed. 'Hardly. He had his flaws, but he's a happy drunk and happy when he was high. He lived in his own world a bit and didn't always remember when he'd told you he'd do something, but nah, not violent.'

'Did it concern you that he was still hanging around at university parties even when he was older and not a student?' Megan asked.

'I can see how that might appear predatory, but Stan never seemed like that to me. He's pretty immature, so maybe it was more his crowd.'

Louise looked at her sister and shrugged. This wasn't the sort of information that incriminated Stan; it made him sound like a friendly idiot more than anything else, not a domestic abuser, and not a psychopathic murderer.

'How long ago did you last see Stan?' Megan asked.

'Must have been a little while before he and Penny left for their grand adventure. They had a get-together at a pub for a sort of farewell. I thought it was a great idea, going around Australia, vlogging and working on farms and stuff. If I'd taken a gap year like a lot of my friends did, I would have done something similar.'

'You weren't worried about the trip then?'

Chad hesitated. 'Well, I thought Penny would go nuts hanging around with Stan after a while. She seemed like a real girl boss, and he was not much good at finishing projects, let's say. I wasn't surprised that they split, but I was sorry Penny didn't continue the vlogs. She was good on camera.'

'Did Stan have any other long-term romances?' Louise asked.

'Not really. There was one girl he was seeing for a year or two, but she moved back to—let me think—must have been New Zealand when they broke up.'

'Was there anything suspicious about her departure?'

'No. She wasn't enjoying being in Australia; I think she missed her family, and when she dumped Stan, there wasn't much keeping her here.'

'You don't remember her name, do you?' It was a long shot, but Louise wanted to check her out.

'Hayley Reynolds, if memory serves.'

'I think that's all we need from you at the moment, Chad. Thank you so much for getting in touch. If we have any more questions, can we contact you at this number?' Megan said.

'Yeah, no worries. I don't know what else I might be able to tell you, but you never know.'

Megan wrapped up the conversation and hung up.

'What do you reckon?'

'I dunno,' Louise said, her fingers running over her eyebrow as she tried to process Chad's information.

'I'm not sure I completely buy the loveable doofus version of Stan,' Megan said after a long pause. 'The way he was in the videos made it seem like he was domineering and controlling. The way Sue and Kate describe him, he was the driving force behind the plan to go travelling.'

'Though would Sue and Kate have been able to cope with the idea of Penny running off like that? Maybe they didn't know her as well as they thought they did.'

'But if Stan is so innocent, what the hell happened to Penny?'

That is the question, Louise thought to herself. She opened up her laptop and started looking for Hayley Reynolds.

Chapter 11

Hayley Reynolds turned out to be a common enough name, and it took a while to find the right one on social media. At first, all there was, was information about her being missing, but after six months or so, the posts changed to in memoriam messages. Her family would post there regularly, trying to keep hope alive, but it had been nearly four years since Hayley had disappeared.

Louise didn't find anything in the official missing persons database, but that didn't mean anything; perhaps the family hadn't given consent for her name to be listed there. Hayley's social media presence was small. Louise found an Instagram account that had about three posts, and a defunct Twitter—she refused to call it X—account with only a couple of posts and followers. Both had photos of her smiling face pressed up against someone, though they were cropped out.

'Does this look like Stan to you?' Louise asked, showing the photo to her sister.

'Hard to tell, could be. Why?'

'This is Hayley Reynolds.'

'Who?'

'Stan's other ex who disappeared. It looks like Penny isn't the first one this has happened to.'

'No shit.'

'Did you miss that part of the conversation with Chad?'

'Clearly.' Megan's eyes were wide, as though the ticking of her brain were visible from the outside. 'One missing girlfriend is a tragedy, but two starts to look like a pattern.'

'Agreed.' Louise's stomach grumbled, and she looked at the time; it was after one in the afternoon. 'Let's get lunch, then wait for Stan to get off work and get the phone back.'

'You mean follow him from the site?'

'No, I thought we could just go to the caravan park… but now that you mention it, he could go anywhere after work. Better to get him on the way out and see where he goes.'

Megan agreed, and not long after, they were sitting in the car with sandwiches, parked across from the construction site. Forty-five minutes later, the same orange ute pulled out from the site with Stan in the passenger seat.

'That's them,' Louise said, pointing. Megan was in the driver's seat today. They followed at a discreet distance, knowing that where Stan lived meant they could be a little more relaxed in their pursuit, since he would eventually have to go back to the van if they lost him.

It turned out they needn't have worried; the ute stopped at the caravan park and let Stan out before driving off, giving the horn several long, loud blasts.

Megan pulled the car off the road and parked near the entrance to the caravan park, and they followed Stan in on foot.

'Let's wait till he's in the van, then knock on the door,' Louise said.

'Why?'

''Cause it feels less weird? Also, I don't want him to know we followed him from work.'

'He'll know if we arrive within five minutes of him getting in, though, so what's the difference?'

'I dunno, I'd rather not give the impression that we think he's a person of interest. Maybe let's say we're on the way out of town, and remembered he had the phone.'

'Alright,' Megan said with a shrug that Louise interpreted to mean, I don't think it's necessary but I'll go along with it. She squeezed her lips shut, supressing the urge to say something.

They approached the van, sitting on a bed of tanbark under the shade of a scraggly tea tree. 'Let me do the talking,' Louise said as she raised her hand to knock.

'I'm not home,' Stan yelled from inside the van.

Louise knocked again.

'It's you two.' Stan's face was cloudy, but he quickly plastered a good-natured grin on top of his frustration. 'I thought you asked all your questions yesterday.'

'We thought so too,' Louise said. 'We were on the way out of town, heading back to Melbourne, when we remembered you still have Penny's phone, and possibly other stuff, so we came back to ask for it. Her family would love to get back anything of hers, you know, in case she shows up in the future and wants it.' Louise smiled, though she didn't think it was very convincing. She wasn't much good at lying, though she was better than Megan.

'Oh.' Stan frowned briefly. 'Hold on.' He closed the door to the van, making no effort to let them inside this time. He clanked around in the van for a few minutes. Louise considered asking how he was going, but she didn't want to make him angry. He could always refuse to give them anything.

'What's he doing?' Megan said, her voice low.

'If I had to guess, I'd say he's trying to work out what he can give us of Penny's that won't make him look guilty. Either that, or the inside of the van is completely disorganised, and he's trying to find all her stuff that he's put somewhere safe. Given the state of it yesterday…'

Megan nodded; her eyes were troubled, and Louise internally agreed. The longer Stan banged around in the van, the more her gut said they needed to get out of there. She glanced at her watch. *I'll give him another three minutes.*

The three minutes seemed to take infinitely longer, just as Louise was about to knock again, the van went quiet. 'Stan? Are you alright in there?' she said.

'Maybe he thought we'd go away?' Megan said quietly.

At that moment, Stan burst out of the van, his face flushed and his ash-blonde hair now dishevelled. She didn't know what he'd been doing in there, but it seemed to have been hard work.

'This is all her shit.' Stan's voice was hard as he dropped a pile of clothing onto the tanbark ground in front of the van. 'I found her phone, but I think it's busted.' He dropped the phone on top of the pile before reaching back inside the van to pull out another pile of clothing, along with a selection of bathroom products.

'Thank you,' Louise said, bending to pick up the discarded items. She hadn't thought to bring a bag or anything with her.

'I'm not talking to you again. This is everything. I want nothing more to do with Penny Bean, her family, or any of her family's representatives,' Stan said before turning back into the van and slamming the door shut.

Megan picked up several of Penny's things, helping Louise with a few things that were escaping her grasp, and they managed to get the whole lot to the car without having to return for a second trip. They were silent until they had unloaded their arms into the boot of the car.

'What the hell was that?' Megan asked.

'I was about to ask the same thing. That's a very different person from the one we spoke to yesterday.'

Louise started to look through the assortment they'd collected, though it didn't seem to be anything significant. There was no journal or camera. They had a wallet and the phone, which was off and apparently out of battery, though that didn't seem strange after not being charged for over a month.

'Let's get out of here.' Megan looked around nervously.

'Yeah, he might decide to do something drastic.'

Louise plugged the phone into the car charger as they drove the ten minutes or so to the motel, but the phone still refused to turn on.

In the motel, they carried all of Penny's stuff into the room to look through it more carefully.

'See if you can do anything with this.' Louise handed the phone to Megan, as she laid out the first item of clothing on the bedspread.

The clothing, all of which seemed relatively clean, didn't give her much in the way of leads. There were no pieces of incriminating paper in the pockets, no suspicious stains or blood. The bathroom items didn't shed any light either; a tinted moisturiser, a lip gloss, a toothbrush, a face wash, and sunscreen, all inexpensive brands held together in a zip-lock bag.

'It's turned on,' Megan said, breaking into her thoughts.

'Is it locked?'

'Yeah.'

'What do we do now?'

'I'll call Sue.' Megan put Penny's phone down and picked up hers, tapping the screen a few times to get Sue's number up.

'Hello, Sue Ingles speaking.'

'Sue, it's Megan and Louise; we've got you on speaker. Do you have a moment?'

'Sure, I was beginning to wonder how it was all going but didn't like to interrupt.'

'The short rundown is that we followed Stan up to Port Macquarie, and we have Penny's phone, but we don't know the code. Do you have any ideas?'

'Brilliant work. How did you find Stan? Did you talk to him? I would have a few choice words to say if we ran into one another.'

'We can fill you in when we're back in Melbourne,' Louise interrupted. 'Right now, we're trying to get into Penny's phone. Do you know the code?'

'Let me think. Kate might have written it down for me.' There was a clunking sound, presumably Sue had put the phone down, followed by the rustling of papers and indistinct muttering. This went on for several minutes.

'I've found something that might be the phone code. Try five-zero-zero-five.'

Louise picked up the other phone and typed the numbers in. 'It needs to be six digits long.'

'Hmm.' More paper shuffling. 'Okay, try one-two-seven-one-seven-two.'

Louise typed them in. 'That didn't work. It says two chances remaining.'

'The last thing I can think to try is two-zero-zero-two-seven-seven, that's her birthday.'

Louise typed in the last number, and the screen unlocked. 'We're in, fantastic, thanks Sue.'

'We'll have to fill you in on the case progress another time; now we need to focus on the info we've just unlocked,' Megan said, her eyes staring hungrily at the phone.

'Okay. Sure. I'll let you go. Take care, girls.'

Megan disconnected the call and looked at Louise. 'Do you think there's anything useful in the phone?'

'Depends. If she ran off, it's unlikely she would have left anything on her phone that would link back to where she went, but if she met with foul play, then maybe there's something there.'

'What do you think happened to her?' Megan asked.

'I really don't know, but Stan is back to the top of my list. He was suspicious as hell when we saw him today, not to mention this is the second girlfriend who has gone missing—one is sad, but two is sus.'

'He could just be a shit boyfriend. Just because two women he's dated have fallen off the face of the earth doesn't mean he was responsible.'

'Yeah, well, I'll believe that when we have proof that he hasn't done something with Penny. Remember that staircase guy? He had two wives die by falling downstairs—that's a pattern and nothing you can say will make me believe otherwise.'

'Again, I would argue there are other things that could be going on,' Megan said as Louise pressed her lips together.

'It could mean he marries women with alcohol issues or lives in houses with dangerous stairs. Just because you think he's a creep doesn't make him a murderer.'

'It doesn't make him not a murderer either.' Even to herself, she sounded sulky. 'You want first go at looking through the phone?'

'If you want, I assumed you wanted to do it though.'

'I'm not in the mood for reading through a stranger's texts and whatever. You're always better at finding hidden or non-obvious stuff.'

'Okay.' Megan took the phone and lay on the bed, propped up on her elbows. It was a part of the job that continued to feel weird to Louise—looking through people's texts and emails. She should try to get over it;

she was looking for a killer, even in their normal cases, there was a good reason. Someone who was lying to hurt another party, either a spouse or less often, an insurance company, needed to have their lies uncovered.

They'd been following this trail for days with very little to show for it; she was frustrated, they both were, and making slow progress. Despite their best efforts, they were no closer to knowing where Penny was or whether Stan was involved, though he seemed to be putting on a good performance of innocence.

'I'm going for a walk.' Louise stood up, put her running shoes on for the second time that day, and left the motel room.

*   *   *

About an hour after Louise left for a walk, Megan started to worry she wouldn't find anything useful on the phone. All the usual social media apps were there, plus a couple of messaging apps. She had conversations with people that spanned several platforms—something Megan tried to avoid but usually failed at, especially if she was sharing content on one platform while the main conversation was on another. She had conversations with Stan on all her platforms, along with some friends, her mother, her aunt, and several others. Her Instagram had a few interactions that looked like fans of their vlogging activities—some she chatted with, but most didn't last very long.

There were no dating apps installed, which was a good start, though many people used social media to meet others, so it didn't mean much. The Snapchat was the hardest for her to investigate; with its disappearing messages and unfamiliar interface, Megan started to wonder if she was too old for this part of the job.

She read back over the conversations with Stan, though they weren't very interesting—mostly asking if he needed anything from the shops, or sending memes and reels. Since they were travelling together, it made sense that their digital interactions were limited. Megan searched through the other messages looking for evidence that Penny was complaining to friends about her boyfriend and only found the usual, innocuous stuff; leaving the toilet seat up in the van, being messy or smelly, or having spent too much on some item Penny thought was unnecessary. They appeared to be a normal couple, so how did one of them end up vanishing?

Louise walked back into the room looking flushed, her mouth set into a grim line. 'Did you find anything?'

'I haven't had long.'

'I know, sorry. Perhaps I should rephrase, did you find anything obviously sus? Anything that would encourage me to keep going with the investigation?'

'What do you mean?' Megan sat up on the bed and tossed the phone aside to look at her sister.

'I mean, we've been on this case for days, and we're getting nowhere. We're racking up expenses for Sue, leaving the cats with Jake. If there are no tangible leads by checkout time tomorrow, I think we need to call it and head back to Melbourne.'

Megan's brows drew together. Their neighbour Jake had looked after the cats before when they were away, but Louise had a point, they were usually only gone a day or two. 'But we've just got the phone. There could be all sorts of leads on it; we can't give up now. Have you spoken to Sue?'

'Not yet. And we can keep working the phone from Melbourne. I want to go home. This case is too different from our normal stuff, and we're not doing Sue any favours by both being up here.'

Megan was silent for a moment. On the one hand, it was ridiculous to want to chuck it in so soon after a big break. On the other hand, they weren't going to get much else from Stan, or from Port Macquarie. 'It'll take a couple of days to get back home. If we share the driving, it might be a bit shorter, though I can't do any work on the phone from the car—I'll be sick.'

'Yeah. It's probably a two-day drive back, maybe one if we left early and got back in the dark, but I don't know if that's such a great idea.'

Megan picked up her own phone and started looking up the online maps. 'About thirteen hours of driving, all up.'

'We could do it in a day, but it'd be tough.'

Evening had fallen, and her initial investigation of Penny's device hadn't brought anything to light that they didn't already know. 'I vote we leave at first light and drive hard to get home by tomorrow night. If we're going, I'd rather be in my own bed tomorrow.'

'Deal.'

The next morning, they were up at seven and out the door by half past. Not exactly first light, but they should be home before midnight if they kept a good pace and limited their rest stops. Megan had spent a little more time looking through Penny's phone but hadn't found anything of use.

'I'll take the first shift,' Louise said as she closed the boot on their luggage.

'Sure. Let's get Macca's for coffee and something to eat.' They hadn't had any breakfast, and the motel coffee was even worse than the McDonald's drive-through stuff.

'Okay.' Louise started the car, and Megan hopped into the passenger seat. Her sister was driving with a kind of laser focus that made it seem like she was mad about something. They passed a Macca's on their way out of town, but Megan held her protest in—there would be other places to stop, and it wasn't worth risking the ire of the driver.

They listened to the radio, though Megan would have preferred a podcast or audiobook; she might swap it over when it was her turn to drive. She watched the scenery— mostly trees, sometimes farmlands. It was greener up here than it was in Victoria; she assumed that the coastal areas had better rainfall. It would be drier as they went inland after Sydney. She tapped her fingers against her thighs; it had been almost an hour of driving, and Louise hadn't stopped for food or coffee.

To stop her fingers tapping, which she knew annoyed Louise, Megan pulled out her phone and started going through Stan's social media posts again. She took lots of breaks to stare out the window to stop herself getting motion sick, but just as they were pulling into a roadside service area, with a petrol station and a small café-diner attached, she came across a photo of Stan holding a large rifle. The caption read 'Awesome day of hunting out in the bush with my bro. Boar we got not pictured.'

Louise pulled the car into a spot in front of the café and turned off the engine. 'I'm going to pee and get something to eat. You good to take over the driving for the next bit?'

'Sure…' Megan hesitated; the photo didn't necessarily mean anything, but the gun was new information. 'I found this.' She held out the phone.

'Stan's a hunter? Did we know that?'

'No one mentioned it. This pic is from like seven years ago.'

Louise squinted at the phone, swiping at the screen to enlarge the photo. 'Doesn't say where it is, but I'm getting real farm boy vibes off that. Do you think he means his actual brother? Or just a dude he calls "bro"?' She handed the phone back and made her way inside.

'Hard to tell. Do you wanna have a bit more of a look for other gun stuff? Or for a brother while I'm driving?'

'I'll try. You know I'm not good at reading in a car.'

The café didn't have much in the way of variety, so they each got a ham and cheese croissant and a coffee. After a quick toilet break, they were back in the car, and Megan switched the sound play from her phone so she could listen to an audiobook.

Megan and Louise stopped in Yass, about halfway back to Melbourne, for lunch, and took half an hour to walk around and stretch their legs.

'I haven't found any other references to guns in Stan's stuff, nor to his family, so I'm guessing he wasn't using the term "bro" literally.'

'Another dead end,' Megan muttered, sliding back into the driver's seat.

It started to get dark as they drove through Benalla, and Megan hoped there wouldn't be any kangaroos or other animals on the roads, now that they were only a couple of hours from home. Louise was driving, and while she'd tried everything she could think of, given the limitations of her phone in the car on country roads, Megan hadn't been able to find anything that backed up the single photo with the rifle. It was as though Stan was a different person depending on who he was with— maybe he was. It wouldn't be the first time someone was a chameleon. Perhaps he was a sociopath and had done something to Penny, but they hadn't found any evidence to support that theory.

In spite of her general suspicion of the police and their possible lack of competence, the Carter & Carter Detective Agency had done no better.

Megan drove the last leg down the Hume Highway and into the northern suburbs; they pulled up at the office a little while after eleven o'clock that evening. As she turned off the car, she rested her head on the steering wheel. 'I'm never driving that far in a single day again.'

'Tell me about it. Let's only take local cases from now on.' Louise groaned as she stepped out of the car.

'And maybe stick with cheaters.'

'Dibs on first shower.'

Megan cursed inwardly; a shower, or even better, a bath would be just the ticket after all day in the car, but her sister had beaten her to it. They unloaded the bags in silence, and when they went into the office, the cats were distinctly aloof, as though punishing them for having been away for so long.

*　　　*　　　*

The next morning, when Louise woke up her body ached all over. Her forearms and shoulders were stiff from holding the wheel, and her legs and lower back were tight and bunched from all the sitting in one position for so long. Despite going to bed at nearly midnight, she was awake early again. She got up, dressed in her running clothes, and went for a jog.

The case had stagnated. Both agreed that now it was just about telling the client they had to give up. It wasn't the first case they'd had to end without getting the conclusion the client wanted, but it felt terrible. Their other cases were low stakes; at least when you compared them to losing a child. Divorces were messy, but by and large, the people involved came out physically unharmed. The kids were sometimes a little worse for wear psychologically, and the spouses would often take the opportunity to tear shreds off one another, but this was different. Sue had trusted them to find her niece, and they had failed.

She arrived back at the office, with the apartment they lived in above it, a little after eight o'clock. Louise's usual circuit had taken longer than normal; she put it down to travel fatigue but was glad she'd gotten out to use her body a little. Megan wasn't up, so Louise put on the coffee and hoped the smell would entice her sister out. Now that they were back home with no leads to speak of, she wanted to get the case off the books as quickly as possible. The guilt had started to gnaw at her stomach.

The coffee was cold by the time Megan shuffled out a bit before ten.

'Morning,' Louise said, raising an eyebrow.

Megan squinted against the bright daylight coming in through the windows. 'You're up early.'

'More like you slept in… but yes, I didn't sleep well.'

'The case?'

'Yeah.'

'That's why I slept in—couldn't get to sleep for ages, turning everything over in my mind.'

'Did you come to any conclusions?'

Megan poured the remaining coffee from the French press into a mug and stuck it in the microwave. 'The conclusion I came to is we've fucked it.'

'That's the conclusion I came to as well.' Louise looked down at the paperback she had been reading before Megan got up. There seemed to be nothing left to do. 'We'll have to tell Sue.'

'I know.' The microwave pinged, and Megan took her mug of reheated coffee to the couch and sat down heavily. 'I'm not looking forward to it.'

'I'm not either, but it's better to rip the Band-Aid off.'

Megan sipped her coffee and said nothing. She sometimes needed a while to fully wake up, and no doubt the last couple of days had been as draining for her as for Louise, who still felt a little like a zombie.

After coffee, Megan was moving a little more quickly, and they were in the car on the way to give Sue the news an hour or so later. Louise drove, though her body protested when she tried to fold herself into the driver's seat. Sue's expensive-looking house in the posh suburb of Kew was only twenty minutes away. The sisters were silent for a while when they parked along the kerb, not far from Sue's.

'Do you think she'll be home?'

'She's retired, or semi-retired. I expect she'll be here,' Megan said.

Louise was stalling. She stepped out of the car, her lower back protesting, squared her shoulders and walked towards Sue's front door. She didn't turn to see if Megan was following. She rang the bell; the chimes were not soothing this time. For a moment, nothing happened, and she started to think Sue must be out, but then there were footsteps in the hallway behind the door.

'Louise! Megan! Goodness, I wasn't expecting you today, was I?'

'Uh, no. We just wanted to drop by and update you,' Megan took the lead; they had agreed given that Sue was her friend, it would be best. 'Can we come in?'

'Yes, yes. Sorry.' Sue led them through to the enormous kitchen at the back of the house. Louise always felt it wasn't as cosy as it was supposed to be, despite the French farmhouse aesthetic.

'Can I make you a cup of tea or anything?'

'Sure, that would be nice,' Louise said. Megan plonked herself down in one of the pine dining chairs and stared hard at the tabletop. It was as though Sue could sense the tension; as she clanged around making tea in a giant ceramic teapot, none of them spoke.

'Tell me all about the trip.' Sue set down the teapot and joined them at the table.

'I'm afraid we have bad news,' Megan said, looking up briefly before turning back to look at the table.

'We weren't able to find much more in our search for Penny than the police did.' Louise said.

'I see.'

'We were able to recover Penny's phone from Stan, along with some of her personal items, clothing and the like,' Megan said.

'You saw him then? Met him?'

'Yes. We had a good chat with him.'

'What did you think? Slimy so-and-so.'

'I was suspicious of him from the start, but I admit we have no evidence to back that up,' Megan said.

'It's icky for sure. He seems to be a layabout, a perpetual child, and not at all suited to the sort of person Penny would have settled down with in the long term, in my opinion,' Louise said. 'But none of that points to his having had anything to do with her disappearance.'

'He gave you her phone then? No weirdness or defensiveness?' Sue asked.

'There was some hesitation, though I read that as him not wanting to be railroaded for killing her,' Megan said.

Sue made a distressed squeaking sound.

'There's also very little evidence to indicate that she's dead. Apart from the disappearing act, it's possible she's alive and having some sort of adventure or rebellious outburst.'

'Rebellious outburst? That doesn't sound like our Penny.'

'Neither did her running off to live in a van with a no-hoper, but she did that,' Louise said, trying to keep her tone kind.

'A lot of people disappear; most of the time they show up again. If she really wants to stay gone, she will, but don't lose hope. In six months, she might be sick of living in scummy flats and working in sweaty kitchens, and she'll turn up on her parents' doorstep as though nothing happened. As long as you don't close the door, there's always hope,' Megan said.

Louise looked up, Sue had started to cry, silently, while they'd been speaking.

'What are you saying to me?' Sue sniffed.

'We think we should close the file. We're out of leads, and it's not fair to keep the case open when there's not much more we can do.' Megan reached out to pat Sue's hand, but she flinched away.

'Nothing more you can do?'

'I mentioned to you when we took the case that it wasn't our usual thing. Taking your money when we know we're out of options isn't right.'

'I can't just give up on her,' Sue wailed.

'You don't have to give up. Keep looking for her on social media, pester the police, make your own enquiries.

If anything of interest comes up, send it over to us and we'll be happy to reopen the case…'

'But for now, we need to stop,' Louise said, hoping to make it clear that it wasn't a negotiation.

'Will you give me all your files? Everything you've found out? And her things?' Sue asked.

'We can prepare a bundle for you, of course.'

Sue stood up and paced back and forth in front of the windows for a few minutes. She had mostly stopped crying. 'I'll expect your final invoice, and the files and Penny's things by the end of the week. I'll make sure you're paid promptly. Thank you for all your help.'

Louise looked at Megan; Sue's tone had become oddly formal.

'Of course. We'll leave you to it. I'm sorry we don't have better news,' Megan said.

'So am I.' Sue looked over to them, her eyes still wet, but now there was anger in them too. 'You can see yourselves out.'

Megan and Louise left their half-drunk tea on the table and left. There was nothing more to say; Sue had clearly dismissed them.

'That was awful,' Megan said when they were back in the car.

'I vow to never take on another missing persons case again.' Louise started the car and they made the short trip back to the office.

You failed. Go back and try again.

Chapter 12

You still think Stan is had something to do with Penny's disappearance.

'I don't know what happened to Penny, but I say we stick to Stan's tail for the evening and see what he does,' Megan said, her anger rising along with the idea of him getting away with something.

'Did you see anything out of the ordinary in the van?'

'Like what?'

'I dunno. I was thinking blood stains or signs of a struggle, but now that I say it aloud, it seems ridiculous that they would still be here after more than a month.'

'I didn't see anything, but when I walked in, I thought I caught a whiff of antiseptic, maybe bleach. That's suspicious.'

'Or he's a germophobe.' Louise frowned. 'Though the van was messy, so bleach would seem unusual. Plus, they don't have a shower in the van, just a sink.'

'What does that mean then?'

'I don't know, but if we watch him for a bit longer, maybe he'll go out and one of us can take a look in the van while he's gone.'

It was a little after four in the afternoon; he might stay in for the rest of the night, but he might head into town for dinner. It didn't look like he did much cooking in the tiny van, Megan thought to herself.

'Alright. I'll park near the entrance of the caravan park and watch. You can come and relieve me in an hour.

Louise stepped out of the car, taking her laptop and bag with her, off to find a café with Wi-Fi to check her email. Megan reparked the car opposite the caravan park driveway, facing the beach, hoping that if nothing else, she'd get a nice sunset to watch while waiting for Stan to do something interesting.

Several people entered and exited the caravan park, mostly on foot, some in cars, and one teen boy on a bicycle. Megan wrote down a short description of each, along with the time, in her notebook.

At five-thirty, Louise walked up to the car and got in the passenger seat. 'Anything?'

'Nah.'

'The café closed, and my laptop needs to be plugged in, so I'm here to relieve you.'

'Thanks. I think I'll go for a walk. Let me know if he leaves.'

'Will do.'

Megan strolled to the foreshore and turned down the track towards a large rocky hill that appeared to have a nice view. It was chilly in the wind coming off the ocean, and she wished she'd brought a thicker jacket. She found a spot under a tree that was less windy and sat watching the waves on the sand. Louise texted her with an update.

He's walking out, maybe going for dinner. I'll follow on foot.

Now was her chance to get into the van and have a good look around. Megan hurried from her spot on the beach back to the caravan park. She spotted Stan in the distance turning north along Pacific Drive and hung back until Louise also passed her, giving her a nod as she went.

I hope she stays off his radar; she sometimes follows too closely on foot.

Darkness was falling over the streets and foreshore; dusk was a better time for creeping around the caravan park than daylight since human eyesight was at its worst at dawn and dusk, or so she'd been told once. People were wandering around the campsite, a few sat outside having a beer, at least one person was having a barbeque, judging by the scent of the smoke and grilling meats. Stan's van was surrounded by trees, and the sites on each side were conveniently vacant.

Megan looked around to double-check whether she was being observed, but no one was looking her way. She tried the sliding door of the van and was unsurprised to find it locked.

Worth a try. She pulled out her slim Jim, a piece of thin flexible metal useful in opening car doors. She pushed the slim Jim down beside the window of the passenger side door, fished around until she felt the mechanism inside, and carefully pulled it up.

Once inside, she used the small torch she'd brought with her rather than turning on the van's interior lights.

'If I were Stan, where would I have hidden the important stuff?' she muttered to herself. The glove box was an obvious choice; nothing of interest there, though she did find a scrap of what might have once been beef jerky. She moved into the back of the van and started looking through the drawers and cupboards.

It was messy and disorganised; she wasn't sure how he ever found anything he needed. In a drawer beneath the kitchen seating, she found a mobile phone, the battery dead. *It's probably Penny's*, she thought as she slipped it into her back pocket. Under the phone was a handbag—a small fabric cross-body bag, like the one that Penny had worn in some of her photos. She put the bag on the kitchen table and started to look through the contents.

The standard stuff was all there: wallet, chewing gum, three lip gloss sticks, some loose coins, a scrunched tissue, a mirror and some unused sanitary products. Inside the wallet, she found Penny's driver's licence, bank cards, Medicare and various other cards, along with about forty dollars in cash.

Why hadn't the police confiscated this? Or given it back to her parents? Megan put the dead phone into the handbag and zipped it closed. She slung the bag over her shoulder and closed the drawer. At that moment, she heard footsteps on the gravel outside.

She looked up and saw Stan approaching, his eyes fixed on the phone in his hand, a plastic bag containing what she assumed was his evening meal in the other.

Louise was supposed to text her when he was on the way back, but it was too late now. She couldn't get out of the van without him seeing her, so she straightened up and stepped out with what she hoped was a confident air.

Stan looked up as he pulled the keys from his pocket. 'What the fuck are you doing here?' His voice was cold and his face fierce.

'I found Penny's handbag. And her phone. Did you forget to mention those to the cops?'

'I'll ask one more time; what are you doing here?'

Megan shifted her weight on her feet, he looked as though he might attack her and any moment. 'I think you killed her. I think you dumped her body somewhere, and this playing dumb thing you're doing is all an act.'

Megan caught movement in the corner of her eye, over Stan's shoulder, but she didn't dare break eye contact to check if it was her sister.

'That's Penny's bag. I'm calling the cops, breaking in is against the law, even if you're a private investigator.'

'You'd have to tell the cops you were withholding evidence.'

'They didn't want her stuff. I told them she'd run off, showed 'em the handbag and the phone, but they said I could keep it.'

Megan took a step away from the van, Stan was coming towards her, but he bent to put the plastic bag on the ground and slid his keys back into his pocket. The anger in his eyes intensified.

'I'm putting the bag down, and I'm leaving. No need for anything drastic.' Megan's voice shook as she slipped the bag off her shoulder and placed it on the gravel. She broke eye contact with Stan briefly to look behind him, and at that moment, he lunged forward.

'I didn't fucking kill her,' he screamed as he tried to grab her. Megan twisted and attempted to get away, but she'd hesitated for a moment too long. Stan slammed his body into hers, and they both crashed down onto the tanbark in front of the van. He was kneeling on top of her, his hands gripping painfully onto her shoulders as he shook her violently. 'I didn't do anything!'

'Stan, stop!' Louise yelled from behind him. She grabbed one of his hands and tried to pull him away. Her other hand held her phone to her ear. 'Yes, I need the police.'

'Stan, the cops will be here any minute,' Megan said, still writhing under Stan's full body weight to get away while Louise tried to pull him off her and talk to the emergency services at the same time.

Just as abruptly as he'd lunged for her, he slumped, seeming to lose all the rage he'd held a moment before. His face fell, and he looked tired. Stan rolled off her, shuffled over to the van and leaned back against it. 'I'm having you charged with breaking in and burglary.'

'We don't seem to be in danger any longer, but we will still need police to attend,' Louise said to the operator, before turning to Megan and Stan. 'The cops will be here in five minutes.'

'We could just go,' Megan said.

'Yeah, you could, but that won't stop me telling them about how you broke in and stole what's rightfully mine.'

'It's not yours. It's Penny's,' Megan's anger was rising again now she was confident Stan wasn't going to strangle her.

'If and when Penny comes back, I'll give it to her. But it's not yours. This is my home. I've been cooperative, even though you don't have any standing, and I don't have to talk to you, but you've decided I did something to Penny and I deserve to be treated like a criminal. It's you who has broken the law.'

Louise was frowning at both of them. 'What were you doing?'

'We'll talk about it later.' Megan had been sure Louise knew she planned to search the van, but maybe she had taken it too far. It wasn't the first time she and the slim Jim had gotten into a vehicle and found compromising evidence. In their other cases, the target was too ashamed to go to the police; usually they were happy to just accept the less advantageous divorce settlement and leave the cops out of it, but she'd underestimated Stan.

They remained in strained silence until the police car arrived a few minutes later, lights flashing but no siren. A tall, slim man with greying hair stepped out of the car and looked over the scene. Megan still sat on the tanbark, Stan slumped against the van a little way off, and Louise hovered over them as though ready to step in if either of them made a move to attack again.

'I'm Senior Constable Martin Taylor. What seems to be the trouble?'

'This bitch broke into my van and tried to steal my stuff,' Stan started.

'He attacked me,' Megan said at the same time. The officer held up a hand to silence them all.

'Who called triple-oh?' he said.

'I did,' Louise answered. He took down her name into a tall, narrow notebook he had produced from one of his many pockets.

'And whose is this?' He waved his hand toward the van.

'It's mine.' Stan stayed seated on the ground, giving the officer his name as well.

'And you are?' His pointed gaze fell on Megan.

'Uh…'

'Name?'

'Megan Carter.'

'She's my sister,' Louise said.

'And what is your business here?'

'Well, we're investigating a missing person,' Louise replied.

'I'm speaking to Megan actually.' Taylor's jovial expression had turned steely.

'As Louise says, we're investigating the disappearance of Stan's girlfriend—former girlfriend, he was the last person to see her,' Megan replied.

'And how does that lead this man to accuse you of stealing?'

'I come home from getting a bit of tea and she's standing there, bold as brass, about to make off with my stuff,' Stan interjected.

'It's not your stuff, it's Penny's stuff.'

'Who is Penny?' Taylor asks.

'Penelope Bean is the missing person,' Louise said. Megan frowned, first at Stan and then at her sister. Why wasn't she defending her?

'Megan, were you in the van?'

'Yes, but I—'

'I don't need an explanation at this point. And you, Stan, did you attack Megan?'

'She was stealing my stuff, I was just trying to get it back. I might have overreacted.'

'I see.' Taylor took a moment to write a few things in his notebook. 'Stan, are you looking to press charges for the break in and the burglary?'

'Attempted, she gave the bag back,' Louise added, though Megan didn't think it was helpful and turned her glare back to her sister.

'Megan, are you injured?'

'I don't know.'

'You don't appear to have any significant injuries, but we can have a doctor look you over. Given this seems to be use of force in defence of property, it wouldn't seem necessary to charge you, Stan, however you will all need to come down to the station to make statements. Megan, you'll need to come with me.'

'Am I under arrest?'

'Not at the moment, but if I need to arrest you to get you to accompany me to the station, I will.'

Megan sighed. 'I see.' She allowed the officer to put her into the back of the police car, and though she wasn't handcuffed, she may as well have been; the doors didn't open from the inside.

From inside the police car, Megan saw Taylor take the handbag from Stan, and put it into a plastic evidence bag he'd retrieved from the boot.

The Port Macquarie Police Station looked smaller than the Gosford station. The exterior was brick veneer painted a bright white. Megan supposed that it would be a very brave vandal indeed to graffiti the cop shop, so maybe it wasn't a bad choice.

Night had fully fallen and the wind off the Hastings River across the road was chilly. Louise had followed in their car and was just arriving at the station as Megan was led inside.

The interior reminded Megan of the 1980s; although it had been repainted recently, the layout and popcorn ceiling were very retro. It seemed this police station didn't have the budget for interior renovations, but it smelled okay. Senior Constable Taylor nodded to the younger officer behind the glass at the reception desk and escorted Megan through a door marked 'Authorised Personnel Only' and into the back of the station. Taylor was mostly silent as they walked through an open-plan office area with four desks, past a tiny kitchenette and into an interview room that was so grey it was only the scrapes and scratches in the paintwork that made it feel real.

'Take a seat Ms Carter.' He pointed to a textured grey plastic bucket chair beside a wood-laminate table. He sat on a similar chair by the door, leaned back, and folded his arms. 'Tell me what happened.'

Megan swallowed hard; her mouth suddenly dry. 'Well—' she started, but her voice croaked and she swallowed again. 'My sister and I are private investigators. We have licenses in Victoria. We were engaged by Penny's aunt to look into her disappearance when it seemed that the police were moving on to other things.'

Taylor's eyebrow twitched up. 'Take a step back. Remind me who Penny is?'

'Penelope Bean, known as Penny, is a twenty-year-old Melbourne woman, last seen near Strickland Falls in Gosford on the fourth of April.'

'Go on.'

'She had been travelling with her boyfriend, Stan Warding. He's the last person to have seen her. He assisted the police for a while, but no arrests were made. Penny's aunt, Susan Ingles, was not satisfied with the investigation going cold and engaged Carter and Carter Detective Agency to look into the disappearance further.'

'Stan Warding, the same fellow whose van you were in?'

'Yes, same guy. We followed Penny to Gosford and found very little to help our investigation. We decided to come to Port Macquarie to speak to Stan ourselves, in case he had any information he hadn't shared with the police or if he had remembered anything since the interviews.'

'And perhaps to see whether he seemed dodgy for yourselves?'

'There was an element of that, yes. Given the number of women killed by their intimate partners every year, we felt it was our duty to meet him and see what sort of vibe he gave off.'

'What sort of *vibe* did you get from him?'

Megan paused; Taylor's face was unreadable, his arms remaining crossed over his chest. She couldn't tell if he was genuinely curious or trying to shame her. 'I admit that, at first, he seemed truthful—he and Penny fought, she stormed off and hadn't been in touch since then. But there were a couple of moments of… I don't know what to call it, inconsistency maybe? You know that feeling you get when people have dead shark eyes? He gave me the creeps.'

'So, you broke in?'

'No.'

'You didn't break into the van?' Taylor's eyebrows twitched up a little before falling back into their impassive position.

'I wanted to see if he had her phone and handbag.'

'You couldn't have asked him for them?'

'I probably could have.' Megan looked at the floor, mottled grey carpet tiles worn in places and stained with drips of what might have been coffee, and a large pale splash that might have been a bleach-based clean-up job. She shuddered to think what the stain might have been before it had been cleaned.

'Did he have Penny's personal items?'

'Yes, he had her mobile, and her handbag, and wallet—all her stuff was there, license, cards, the lot. If she'd left, as he claims, she would have needed all of that stuff.'

Taylor pulled on his earlobe, as though considering it. 'I would have thought so.'

'Before you arrived, Stan said that the police in Gosford weren't interested in Penny's belongings, but that doesn't sit right with me. Wouldn't they have taken it? If not for evidence, then for her family? I don't see why Stan should be holding onto that.'

'Irregardless of whether Penny's things were of use to the Gosford police, I'm still not clear why you illegally entered the van. It's a crime to do so, and your licence as an investigator is at stake if you were to be found guilty.'

'I know.' Megan's cheeks heated. It had been a dumb idea. Louise had told her so; every instinct in her body had warned her not to do it, but her anger at Stan getting away with doing something awful to Penny had clouded her judgement.

'Let me make a couple of calls, and then we'll continue this chat.' Taylor stood and went out of the interview room, leaving Megan alone with her thoughts and the various stains and marks on the walls and carpet.

If he called the Gosford police, and they were able to corroborate Stan's assertion that they didn't need the handbag and phone, she'd be in real trouble. She was likely to be charged with breaking and entering, her career ruined, and facing a possible prison sentence.

Megan's left leg jiggled up and down; her nerves were frayed, and the wait for Senior Constable Taylor to return to the interview room seemed interminable. She wondered where Louise was, probably sitting in the waiting room, asking herself why she'd allowed her sister to join the agency only to be its downfall. At least Louise could claim she wasn't involved in the break-in, and would be able to carry on, unless they were both tarnished by the scandal.

Round and round Megan's thoughts went; all dark, all disastrous. Taylor had confiscated her phone when she entered the police station, and as she didn't wear a watch so she had no idea how long she'd been sitting there when he walked back into the room, his face inscrutable as ever.

'I've spoken with Gosford,' he said, taking his seat again in the grey chair.

'Okay.'

'They were of the impression that Stan did not have any of Penny's property. His statements led them to believe that Penny had left of her own accord; however having now found her handbag and phone in his possession, they are inclined to re-examine the case.'

'What?' Megan was stunned, she'd been right all along, Stan was hiding things. 'They didn't search the van? The stuff wasn't hard to find.'

'They searched the van. They looked for signs of foul play, it would appear that Stan was rather better at hiding things from the Gosford police than he was at hiding them from you.'

'What does that mean for me then?'

'I'm going to recommend that we suspend any proceedings until Gosford can examine Penny's things and reinterview Stan. Given the items you were taking weren't Stan's, he isn't in a strong position to charge you with burglary though he would have a case for breaking.'

Megan looked down at her hands, they were clasped together so hard her knuckles had whitened.

'For the moment, it's best if you go back to Melbourne and leave this with us. We have your contact details, and if the matter is taken further—either by Gosford with Penny's disappearance, or by Stan, about damage to his van, then we'll send out a subpoena and you'll need to return to deal with that.'

'I see.' Megan sighed; it was about the best she could expect, really, having been caught in the act. What it would mean for her license, she had yet to properly think through, but she hoped, if there were no charges, she would be able to continue her work.

'I'll walk you out. I'll be checking in with the lodge tomorrow to make sure you've checked out, and I'll let the station in Northcote know to expect you to check in with them in the next day or so—'

Megan opened her mouth to interrupt.

'Something to add?'

'I drove up here, I might need a couple of days to get back.'

'I see.' Taylor pulled his earlobe. 'Within five days then.'

'Sure. I can do that.'

Taylor sighed heavily and took his time rearranging the papers in front of him before standing up. 'If you'll follow me, I believe your sister is waiting for you.'

'Thank you.'

Taylor mumbled something inaudible, though it might have been, 'don't thank me yet.'

Megan had caused the entire investigation to go sideways. Despite having found what could be circumstantially incriminating evidence in the van, she'd humiliated Stan and the Gosford police—something that could come back to bite her later. If the police were inclined to think she wasn't a suitable person to be a private investigator on those facts, they could pull her licence even if Stan didn't press charges. From what she remembered when she had applied, there was a "good character" clause in there somewhere, meaning the police, who issued PI licences, could take it away from her and probably her sister too for being associated with her, for any reason.

'There you are.' Louise's expression was pinched, as though the strain of having her sister interrogated weighed on her more than she might admit.

'Yeah, they're letting me out.' *For now.*

'Right.'

Taylor had come with her into the lobby area and now turned to Louise. 'You and your sister need to head straight back to Melbourne. Further actions are pending; in the meantime, go home and keep your head down.'

'Of course, thank you for your time,' Louise said, holding her hand out to shake his.

'Thank you,' Megan added. Taylor nodded and went back into the employees-only area without another word.

Louise grabbed Megan's arm, just above her elbow. 'Keep quiet 'till we get back to the car.'

Once in the car, Louise remained stonily silent. They drove the short distance to the lodge, and Megan followed her sister into their room.

'What the actual fuck?' Louise said, glowering and pacing between the beds.

'I'm sorry.'

'Sorry? Interesting. When were you going to tell me you were going to break in to get a look at Stan's stuff?'

'What did you think I was going to do?' Megan frowned; surely the plan had been clear.

'Look in the windows… I dunno, lurk?'

'We needed to search his stuff; the only way to do that was to be in the van, and he wasn't likely to agree to it, so I made an executive decision. Honestly, I thought you knew what I was going to do. That's why you were on Stan watch, to prevent this,' Megan gestured vaguely, 'from happening.'

'We're lucky they haven't run us out of business as well as out of town.'

'They still might.'

Louise stopped pacing. 'Yes. They still might.'

Most of the evening had passed, and the excitement and adrenaline of the day had started to wear off. Megan's belly rumbled loudly—they'd missed dinner— and she wanted very much to go to bed, though she expected sleep wouldn't come. She flopped onto the bed, staring at yet another popcorn ceiling.

'We'll leave first thing, take it in turns to drive, and we should be home in two days.' Louise seemed to be talking to herself more than to her sister. 'Sue will be furious. But hopefully the cats will be happy to see us.'

Megan didn't move her gaze from the ceiling as Louise banged around packing her bags. There was a definite passive-aggressive vibe to the amount of clomping and muttering going on. Her stomach rumbled again, and she looked at the clock—after ten o'clock. Megan sat up.

'I'm going to find something to eat.'

'Where?' Louise asked, not looking up from her bags.

'Everything is probably shut; maybe the servo is open. You want anything?'

'Corn chips. And a Coke… on second thoughts, make it a lemonade, I don't need caffeine right now.'

Megan nodded and headed out to the car. The servo wasn't far, but she didn't fancy walking around in an unfamiliar town, especially since the cops had told her to get out.

The service station around the corner was closed when she arrived. 'That's the perfect end to today.'

You failed, go back and try again.

Chapter 13

You agree with Louise's condition to go to the police if any evidence is found.

'Fine, we'll turn it all over as soon as we find something useful,' Megan said, though she planned to work on Louise to make that option less and less attractive. The police had been looking for weeks, and given they probably thought she'd just run away, she and Louise were bound to do better. On the other hand, if they did uncover some juicy evidence of a crime, something irrefutable, the police were the right people to go to. It wasn't as though the agency could make arrests.

'What's the next step? Sue's busy dealing with her sister. Can we do anything from here?'

'I'm not sure. Sue gave me a pretty thorough rundown, but we probably need some more info before we start digging around. Maybe we can get Sue to give us access to bank statements; Kate's a signatory for her daughter, and have a look at the transactions?'

Louise muttered something to herself, rubbing her left eyebrow as she had a habit of doing when she was considering something. After several minutes, she looked at her sister. 'Where did you say she lived?'

'Sue's in Kew, and Penny was doing the whole van life thing, so no fixed abode.'

'Mmm.'

Kew was full of rich folks in big houses, a suburb in the inner east of Melbourne, about a twenty-minute drive from their office in Northcote.

'Are you thinking of going over there?' Megan asked. 'Sue probably doesn't have any documentation.'

'And what's this missing girl's name?'

'Penny. Though her legal name is Penelope Bean.'

'Do you know where Kate lives?'

Megan thought about it for a moment. 'I'd have to ask Sue. Sorry. I should have got more details from her before we agreed to take the case. Though to be honest, I thought you would completely block the idea; I'm surprised you gave in so quickly.'

Maz wandered into the room at just that moment, pausing to stare accusingly at Quince before rubbing herself along Louise's legs.

'The divorce tango has been getting stale, it's true. If there's some proper investigating to do, I'm open to a change of pace.'

Despite her efforts not to, Megan was sure she looked smug.

'I guess we don't have much to do until Sue is more available then.'

'I'll text her, see if she's up for a visit.' Megan picked up her phone to compose the message.

Hi Sue, Louise and I have agreed to look into your case. No guarantees at this stage, but we would like to come for a chat to hash out some specifics. When is a good time?

Megan showed Louise the message before sending it off, and she nodded her approval.

'In the meantime, I suppose I'd better get all those surveillance photos logged for the Atkins case.' She briefly hoped Louise would volunteer to take the task off her hands, but instead she returned to her novel, while Maz sat on her lap looking haughty.

I guess that's my afternoon then.

*　　*　　*

They had no calls or texts for the next four hours. Louise looked up from her novel occasionally to check whether anything had come through. She'd been trying to train herself to focus on one thing at a time, whether it was work, reading, or something else, but her desire to remain plugged in to the goings-on of the world of social media was just as strong as it ever was. *So much for willpower.*

She would normally have been working when Megan was, but their office was on the ground floor and their tiny, shared apartment was upstairs, so it was much more comfortable to use the client armchairs for her leisure as well. They each had a bedroom, both small, a kitchen that might more accurately be called a kitchenette consisting of a mini-fridge, sink, microwave, two-burner cooktop (no oven), and a table big enough for two. The whole arrangement wasn't very user-friendly, and they tended to eat out or buy prepackaged meals rather than cook. There was no lounge room in the apartment, so if either of them wanted to watch TV or something on one of the streaming services, they did it from the bedroom.

Louise had considered watching TV shows down in the office but decided against it, especially during office hours, on the off chance a client came in.

Her first client, before Megan joined her, before there even was an agency, Roman, had been a friend of the family going through a messy divorce. Louise had been a copywriter for a large electrical goods retailer at the time. The job was soul-destroying, but the paycheque was steady, and she had thought that was worth sticking around for.

Roman and his husband Peter had been married in 2018, not long after same-sex marriages were legalised in Australia, but had been together five years before that. Unfortunately, with the stress of the pandemic, their relationship had developed some cracks. Roman found out when a text message came through to Peter's phone while he was using it to order food for the two of them. The message had been intimate enough to raise his suspicions, and he'd asked Louise to look into it since, he said, she was good at finding things out.

It had taken Louise about a week after work and on weekends, going through Peter's phone calls, text messages and other information—Roman provided all the details—before she found the paper trail.

'I don't believe it,' Roman had said when she presented her findings.

'You were the one who asked me to look into it. You know deep down what I'm saying is right. They've been seeing each other for two years, I'd say, perhaps only casually at first, but now at least once a week.'

'Motherfucker.' Roman massaged his temples and closed his eyes. 'And to think I've been worried about the overtime he's been doing lately and it's all for this boy toy.'

'I'm sorry.' Louise had felt guilty for confirming the betrayal, but she had always believed that lying in a relationship was the best way to kill it, and cheating was the ultimate lie. If it had been her, she would have wanted to know.

'I need proof. I want a picture of them together.'

'If that's what you want,' she said. *I have plenty of proof in their messages to one another, but if you want the pictures, I can do that too.*

'I do. I can pay you. I know you've done a lot of work on this already.'

'No, that's okay. I couldn't take your money; you're a friend. If I have any expenses, I'll let you know.' She didn't add that she wasn't sure if this was entirely legal if money changed hands. Something else to add to the list to research later.

Her day job was unusually slow at that time, and outside of the office, Louise used her days to read up on surveillance photography techniques. Online tutorials showed her how to set up a long-distance camera lens and how to maximise the shots if they were low light or through glass.

I can't believe you can learn this stuff by watching videos, Louise had thought to herself while taking notes in a little spiral-bound journal she'd brought for the purpose.

'Always have the right stationery for the job,' Louise had told herself many times, though she mostly used it as an excuse to buy cute notebooks and pens at the office supply place. Perhaps not the best use of her funds, but given Roman would be paying expenses, she thought it was probably fine.

Once she'd learned all she could from the tutorials, Louise needed to source a good quality digital SLR camera and a telephoto lens. This had been a more difficult prospect. Buying the required stuff would have been the easiest, but she couldn't justify stinging Roman a couple of grand for photography equipment. Megan had had a phase of being really into photography a few years prior and had some of what would be required lying around her apartment somewhere; the only problem with that was she'd have to tell her sister what she wanted to use the camera for.

'Hey Louise,' Megan sounded surprised to hear from her sister over the phone.

'Hey Megan...' Louise wasn't sure how to broach the topic.

'You rang?'

'Yeah. I, uh—are you free for dinner? We could go to that little Vietnamese place across from yours?'

'Sure. I don't have anything planned except leftover spag bol.' There was a beat of silence. 'Do you need money? Is that what this is about?'

Louise coughed out a laugh. 'Why would you ask that?'

'You're being super shady.'

'Oh.'

'That's not an answer. Seriously, are you okay?'

'Firstly, I don't need money, but I was going to ask you a favour at dinner. You'll probably have a bunch of follow-up questions, so maybe we can leave it till then?'

Megan sighed down the line. 'You're a terrible tease. But I suppose if you need a *favour,* I can wait until you buy me dinner.'

'Okay, great. I'll be 'round at seven.' Louise ended the call, marvelling at how quickly her sister had gone from asking if she needed money to accepting a free meal.

A couple of hours later, Louise was looking at herself in the rear-view mirror of her tiny pearl-blue hatchback, making sure her brightly coloured hair, pink at the time, was still looking good. Once satisfied that she was presentable, she stepped out of the car and buzzed Megan's apartment. The building was a converted warehouse; the severe red brick exterior had been heritage listed and couldn't be changed, but the rest of the building had been gutted and turned into tiny, overpriced apartments. The location was spectacular.

'I'll be right down,' Megan's voice crackled through the intercom. The night was humid despite the early autumn chill, and a sudden gust of wind whipped Louise's hair around her head. *So much for the last-minute adjustments.*

'You hungry?' Megan said, startling Louise out of her reverie.

'Always.'

The restaurant was across the street, directly in front of the warehouse-slash-apartment building. There were a couple of other patrons, but it was pretty dead. A cold drop of disappointment formed in Louise's belly. She hoped they had enough patrons to keep the shop running; their food was excellent.

Megan ordered for both of them; she ate there frequently and had narrowed down the best of the menu. 'And two beers,' she said just before the waiter left the table.

'If I'm paying, we'll have to keep the beers to one each,' Louise said.

'I suppose that's fair.'

As they waited for their food, Megan recounted her day. She was a graphic designer and content specialist for an adult education provider. It sounded fancy, but it seemed to be more of a sneaky way of getting her to do whatever needed doing, and while there was a Director of Marketing, Megan was the only other person in the team.

'I seem to have taken on moderating all the social media comments now, too. Up until last week they weren't keeping tabs on anything on the page or our posts, but then we had some jumped-up neo-Nazi telling everyone the Hebrew classes were Zionist propaganda and a few other less polite things, so now everything has to be checked.'

'Oh.' Louise took a sip of her beer, which had since arrived.

'Yeah, it's like Simon doesn't know I already do about four jobs. We're going to need to hire someone else.'

'Are you clocked off for the day then?'

'I have to get a couple of things done later, but mostly.'

'Drawback of working from home…'

'I know, gotta keep myself separate and not let them use up all my time, but I also can't leave them in the lurch.'

Louise frowned. 'If you ask me, they'll just keep asking you to do more work until the cracks start to show. Maybe you should be less good at your job if you want an assistant.'

Megan laughed. 'You reckon?'

She wants me to expand on that, but I don't want to get bogged down in her work drama, Louise thought.

'You wanted to ask a favour then?' Megan changed the subject after an uncomfortable pause.

'Yes.' Louise took another sip of beer, looking around for the waiter in case he was nearby to stall the conversation, but she couldn't see him. 'You remember Roman?'

'Dad's mate from the bank?'

'That's him.'

Their father had a long list of people he knew from various jobs. He could be very charming, and if one didn't get too close to him, he remained so.

'What's he up to?'

'He and Peter are on the verge of divorce.'

'That's terrible.' Megan's brows contracted in sympathy. 'They're such a cute couple.'

'They are. But Roman is sure Peter's cheating. There are suspicious texts and emails, but he wants proof.'

'The texts and emails aren't proof?'

Louise shrugged theatrically. 'I thought the same thing, but apparently no. Roman wants photos of the two of them together. He seems to think it will make all the difference in settling the divorce in his favour.'

'Wow, he's really going scorched earth.'

'Mmm.'

The waiter arrived with the *entrées*: spring rolls with lettuce and mint, grilled beef wrapped in betel leaf, and spring onion pancakes. Megan had gone heavy on ordering.

'That's so sad about Roman… but you haven't asked your favour yet,' Megan said around a mouthful of spring roll.

'I hoped you still had the DSLR camera; I wanted to borrow it.'

'Roman wants you to provide this pictorial evidence? I wasn't expecting that.'

Louise shrugged, chewing the beef and betel leaf morsel to buy some time. 'Yeah, I guess he thought I was nosey enough to want to follow his husband around?'

Megan frowned. 'Why didn't he ask me?'

'You'd have to ask him that. Perhaps your overly demanding day job was a factor.'

Megan mumbled something inaudible.

'Anyway. I'll have to hire a big lens unless you have one, but if you still have the camera, that'll help keep costs down.'

'You're not doing it for free, are you? Roman's loaded.'

'He may well be loaded, but I don't want to get caught impersonating a private investigator.'

Megan opened her mouth to reply but closed it again. 'That's a good point.'

'I'm charging expenses though.'

'You could always get a licence,' Megan said, apparently not hearing her last comment.

'What?'

'A PI licence. It wouldn't be that hard, surely.'

'I hadn't thought about it.'

'Well, you keep saying how much you hate your job and how you'd like to do something more exciting and independent. Maybe this is what you need.'

Louise rubbed her eyebrow. It wasn't something she'd ever considered, but if the job for Roman turned out to be interesting, or even fun, she would look into the requirements of becoming a private investigator. At least if she were working for herself, she wouldn't be contributing to the capitalist downfall of society in quite the same way as pushing the latest and greatest kettle (it comes in lavender too) onto unsuspecting suburban housewives.

'Earth to Louise?' Megan had obviously been saying something that she hadn't heard at all.

'Sorry… off with the fairies.'

Megan cocked her eyebrow in an amused way. 'I said, do you want to come up and get the camera after we finish here? I have a long lens, but maybe not long enough for covert surveillance. You're gonna look like a psycho paparazzo.' She grinned.

'Probably. As long as I don't get arrested, and Roman is still speaking to me after this, I'll consider that a win.'

The waiter returned to the table with the two enormous bowls of pho Megan had ordered, despite their having only eaten half the *entrées*.

'And are you gonna be a gumshoe?'

'I'm very tempted. Let me think about it for, I dunno, six months, and ask me again.'

*   *   *

After dinner, Louise picked up the camera equipment from Megan's apartment. With the camera and a 70-200mm lens, not the 300mm lens that her online searching had suggested was best, but close enough, she was all set to start following Peter in the hopes that he would do something worthy of photographing. Roman had supplied screenshots of Peter's calendar and his usual work schedule, so all Louise had to do was show up at his office at five o'clock for a few days and wait for him to go somewhere he shouldn't.

The next day was a Tuesday, according to Peter's calendar, he had a gym class, cycling, at six o'clock, and then no other entries. Louise texted Roman when she pulled up in front of Peter's office building a little after five that evening:

**Does Peter often go back to work
after the cycle class on a Tuesday?**

She had the camera out on the passenger seat, ready to get a shot of Peter leaving the office; it would timestamp

189

everything, though she also had her notepad to write down any pertinent details.

Depends; sometimes he's home by half past seven, other times, he doesn't get home until after nine.

Roman replied after a couple of minutes, though it didn't provide much insight. After another ten minutes, Louise put the radio on, her mind already wandering from the dull task of waiting for someone to leave a building. If he was going to the gym, which was only a few blocks away, he would likely stay at work until ten to six, at least that's what she would do. On the other hand, the cycling class could be a lie, and he might leave at any time.

Looks like being a PI involves a lot more waiting around than I had anticipated.

In the late autumn, the sky started to darken early, and with it the temperature dropped. Louise decided not to turn on the engine and let the heater run in case someone saw her. Sitting in a parked car was suspicious enough; she didn't need to run the engine as well.

As she had expected, at ten to six, Peter walked out of the glass doors of his building. He was wearing his suit, carrying a small duffel bag and a briefcase. He walked over to his car and got in, throwing the duffel and briefcase into the back seat.

Louise followed Peter's car, trying to stay at least one car behind without losing him. It occurred to her that she would need training in how to trail a vehicle inconspicuously if she was going to do this full time.

Peter drove several suburbs away to a residential street in Caulfield, before parking in front of a block of units. Louise drove past him before turning around to find a park. By the time she had done so, Peter had disappeared, probably into one of the units.

'Shit,' she said aloud. Without knowing where he'd gone, she would have trouble getting incriminating photos.

Time to settle in for another session of waiting around, I guess.

While she waited, she started looking up the addresses in the street in an online search, on the off chance she could find the names of owners or something useful, and to keep herself occupied. The housing prices in the street made her brain hurt; it was certainly a well-to-do suburb out of her reach, not that the housing market anywhere in Melbourne was much better.

The next time she saw Peter was nearly three hours later, when he stepped out of a small terrace house squeezed next to the block of units. A woman in her fifties followed him out; she was slim, wearing an expensive paisley silk dressing gown over a slim, shapely figure, her grey hair in an artfully dishevelled pile on her head. Grabbing the camera, Louise nearly dropped it. Her adrenaline spiked, her breathing was loud in her ears, and her hands shook.

She snapped a couple of photos of the two having a brief chat, the woman's hand lingering on Peter's elbow. Then they leaned in and kissed each other goodbye. Not the peck on the cheek of friends, nor the drawn-out pash of a new relationship, but the brief lip lock of the long-term romance. Louise snapped a few more photos, including the kiss, before stowing the camera away again lest Peter see a flash of light off the lens and spot her. She hadn't thought of a good reason she might happen to be in the same street as her father's good friend's husband on a Tuesday night.

Her heart sank, and her pulse returned to normal as Peter got into his car again and pulled out. Roman would be devastated, perhaps doubly so as his husband was having an affair with a woman. The messages and emails he had dismissed, but these photos, assuming they turned out okay, were damning.

Peter drove to his house in Hawthorn, an old-style Edwardian home with a wrap-around verandah and a beautiful garden that he and Roman had tended together. When she was parked a few doors down, Louise grabbed the camera and looked through the images she'd captured. There were a couple which were motion-blurred, and they were all a bit under-exposed, but they clearly showed Peter kissing someone who wasn't his husband.

> **I've just arrived in your street. I followed Peter from Caulfield. I have photos. What do you want to do?**

She hadn't thought through what to do with the photos once she had them. If Roman wanted to see them now, she would have to go into the house and lay out all the evidence while one or both men had an emotional breakdown.

Next time, I'll make an appointment to go over the evidence later.

It was exhilarating to follow people, and catch them doing something, though the waiting around was dull. It could be a nice change from sitting in her home office in her pyjamas all day and having meetings with clients who insist she couldn't use specific words, like "fresh", "lit", or "baller", or going into the office where other people wanted to talk to her all the time. The income would be more variable, and she could end up with nothing, and possibly a bunch of very unhappy customers, but the allure of exposing a mystery was strong. Then her phone pinged.

> **Make me copies, I'll pick them up
> from you later.**

An enormous weight left her chest, and she started the car to head home.

*   *   *

Louise arranged to meet Roman the following Saturday, at the coffee shop around the corner from his and Peter's home. Louise had never been there, it looked much like any swanky suburban café: dark wood tables and wainscotting, sculptural wire mesh chairs, dark blue walls with huge prints of flowers. The flowers seemed a little sexualised to Louise, but she couldn't say exactly how.

Roman wasn't there yet, so she sat at a table towards the back; if there was a commotion when Roman was presented with the photos, she wanted to be away from the windows. Not that she expected him to have a full meltdown. She wasn't sure what he might do, but he seemed a stiff-upper-lip type.

He waltzed in the door five minutes after their agreed time, looking surprisingly upbeat, freshly shaved and slightly flushed in the cheeks as though he'd been exercising in the chilly morning.

'Louise, you're here already,' he said, holding out his hand for her to shake. It seemed oddly formal for someone she'd known most of her life, but perhaps formal made him feel more comfortable.

'Hey,' she said.

'Sorry I'm late.' Roman sat on the chair beside her, instead of the one opposite, as she had expected. 'I walked around the block four times before I could get up the courage to come in.'

'Ah.' Louise nodded, waiting for him to continue.

'I'm sure you've got bad news for me. I don't know what I thought I would get from photos that I didn't already know from the texts and emails, alas, I'm a romantic fool.'

'You're not a fool.'

'I've been behaving like one. I haven't even seen a divorce lawyer yet, though I guess that's where this is headed.'

A waitress approached the table and handed them menus. 'Can I get you any coffee to start?'

'I'll have a weak soy latte,' Roman said.

'And an English breakfast tea for me,' Louise said, the waitress nodded and left them.

'You take after your father, then.'

'Pardon?'

'He's a tea drinker too.'

'Oh, yes. Megan loves coffee, maybe a bit too much, but it doesn't always agree with me.' Louise touched her eyebrow.

'Do you have the photos?' Roman said after a long pause.

'They're on my tablet.' She reached into her bag for the tablet before flipping it open to show him.

'I waited at Peter's office after work on Tuesday, he left a little before six,' she flipped to the photo of him leaving, with the time stamp in the bottom left corner. 'From there I followed him to Caulfield. To this house.' Again, she flicked the image to show the front verandah. Roman scratched his nose but said nothing.

'I was there until he left, about nine. This woman appears to be the resident of the house.' She showed the photo of Peter and the woman leaving, pre-kiss. 'Do you know her?'

'This is who he was visiting?' Roman asked, his voice strained.

'Yeah. Who is she?'

Roman sighed. 'That's his ex-wife.'

'Oh.'

'There's more then?'

'One more.' She slid her finger across the screen to the *coup de grâce*, the photo of Roman's husband kissing his ex.

'I should have known. He said they were *just friends*, that he wasn't into women anymore. The lady doth protest too much, methinks.'

'Huh?' Louise frowned.

'It's from Hamlet.'

'I knew that much.'

'I should have known he was up to something when he kept insisting he was gay.' Roman closed his eyes and rubbed his hand over his face.

'Weak soy latte.' The waitress had reappeared with their drinks. 'And an English Breakfast tea.'

'Thank you,' Louise said, mostly so that she would leave.

'Were you after anything to eat?'

'We'll need a bit longer, thanks.' *Go away.*

'Wave me over when you're ready.'

'Will do.' Louise waited until the waitress was out of earshot again before she spoke quietly to Roman. 'I'm sorry it turned out like this.'

'It's not your fault.'

'Still.'

'Put them away.'

Louise closed the tablet case and slipped it back into her bag.

'Even the coffee tastes like ashes today. I wonder how long it will be until I feel joy again.'

Louise wasn't sure what to say; she'd never known Roman to be melodramatic, but heartbreak does funny things to a person.

'You'll have to email that last one to me. I'll show Peter and then ask him to stay elsewhere for a while.'

'Will you separate? Divorce?'

'I haven't decided. I have to work out whether I can ever trust him again, and whether I love him enough to believe he won't do it again.'

'I'm sorry.'

Roman downed the remainder of his coffee in one swig and stood up. 'Thank you, sincerely, for getting me the truth. I appreciate it. I need to go for a long walk now, and when I get home, Peter and I will have a talk.' He pulled a fifty-dollar note from his wallet and laid it on the table. 'Have some brunch, on me. I'll be in touch.'

Louise watched him go, shoulders drooping—certainly not the same swagger he came in with. She poured herself some tea and looked over the breakfast menu. The tea was hot but flavourless, and her appetite had disappeared, so she paid at the counter and went home. Roman had known, deep down, that things weren't right between them, but having it confirmed, and Peter going back to his ex-wife, must have been a blow. In her apartment, she gathered the most damning half-dozen photos and emailed them.

> **Hi Roman**
>
> **As discussed, please find attached photos of Peter taken last Tuesday.**
>
> **Let me know if you have any further queries.**
>
> **Kind regards.**

Louise used her official work tone, on the off chance it was brought into divorce proceedings. The last thing she wanted was for someone to grill her about why she was taking photos of her friend's husband with a long lens, but the reason why was immaterial. What mattered was that he was having an affair, and Roman deserved to know.

*   *   *

Roman went radio silent after that. Louise assumed they had had the talk and had decided to stick it out, at least for the time being, though there was another possibility: Roman hadn't said anything. A couple of weeks after their meeting, on a day when she'd chosen to go into the office, Louise's mobile phone rang. She didn't recognise the number.

'Hey, Louise,' a man's voice said.

'Who's this, please?'

'It's Peter. Roman's husband.'

'Peter… I wasn't expecting a call from you.'

'I got your number out of Roman's phone. Sorry for calling out of the blue.'

'Okay.' Louise waited, unwilling to give anything away in case Peter wasn't aware of the photos or that she'd taken them.

'Look, I'll get to the point. I'm concerned about Roman. Ever since he met you for brunch, he's been very cold and distant. He's been working long hours, and when we manage to be home at the same time, he doesn't seem interested in talking to me, let alone anything intimate.'

'Okay,' Louise said again.

'I was wondering, did he say anything to you that would account for how he's been? I've tried asking him, and he just clamps his mouth shut and goes into the study. It's not like him, my thoughts started spiralling, and I'm worried he's got cancer or something.'

'I see.' Louise took a deep breath. It wasn't really her place to say anything, but Peter sounded so upset. 'He and I did discuss something, uh, upsetting, at brunch, but I really don't think it's my place to say what.'

'I knew it. He's been so strange. You have to tell me. I deserve to know what's going on.'

'I agree. You do, but I really don't think I should say.'

'Was it about his health?'

'No.'

'His family?'

Louise hesitated. *I need to shut this down.* 'I really can't say.'

'Oh no, was it about me? Is he leaving me? Oh God, I can't live without him.' Peter started to ramble, words falling over one another about how much Roman meant to him. Anger started to rise in Louise's belly. It might be that Roman was too scared to say something to Peter, but this over-the-top display of love stuck in her craw.

'He knows you're fucking your ex-wife,' she said, breaking into his stream of consciousness and stopping him dead.

'What?'

'Roman asked me to follow you; he knew you weren't going to the gym after work, so he wanted to know where you went. I have photos of you going into a woman's house, spending a couple of hours there, and then kissing her on the doorstep. A lover's kiss, not a friend's.'

'You've got this all wrong—'

'Roman told me it was your ex. Shame on you for lying to him and for coming to me to work out what's wrong. He should have told you himself, but clearly, he loves you more than that.'

'Lindsey and I aren't lovers.'

'I'm not the one you need to convince. Roman has the photos. He's the one who's been betrayed. And even if you're not lovers, why are you lying to your husband about where you're going? Just because you're not cheating with your dick doesn't mean you aren't cheating with your heart or your words.'

'You have to believe me; I didn't do anything wrong.' Peter was sniffling down the phone line. *Crocodile tears, or tears for himself.*

'I'm hanging up. Talk to your husband and make it right or grow up and leave him if you can't be faithful.' Louise ended the call. Her hands were shaking, and she wasn't sure how she would be able to get back to her work tasks with all the adrenaline and anger coursing through her.

'I'm going for a little walk,' she said to her boss, Vicky.

'Are you okay? Was that call bad news?' Vicky asked.

'Sort of. It's nothing serious, but I'm a bit shaken and need to take a minute to get my head back into work. You want me to grab you a coffee or something while I'm out?'

'No, I'm okay. See you in a few.'

Louise walked down the block from her office and stopped at the coffee place she often visited. It was closed, since it was after three, but the short walk helped get her feelings under control.

Poor Roman, he'd sat on that news for weeks, and Peter thinking he wasn't the cause of the change between them. He might have been innocent, maybe he did just kiss his exes on the mouth, while they wore silky dressing gowns, but it didn't change the fact he'd lied. She hoped they would get it all out in the open so they could deal with it properly, whether they split up or not; in the end the lies and unhappiness needed to end.

Back at the office, Vicky frowned at her as Louise sat back at her desk. Her task list wasn't super long; they'd been having a slow patch for a couple of weeks, so it wasn't late work that caused Vicky to make that face. *She can't think I'm slacking, I'm ahead of all the deadlines, maybe it's a concerned frown.*

It didn't take long for Louise's questions to be answered. A little later, just before the end of the day, Vicky asked her to step into a meeting room.

'Have a seat,' Vicky said, her eyebrows drawn and her mouth compressed into a thin line.

'Okay.' Louise's stomach fluttered; she hadn't expected two challenging conversations in one day, but everything about Vicky's body language said bad news.

'I'm sorry to have to do this on the day you had a difficult phone call.'

'Do what, exactly?'

'I'm sorry, let me start again. You know that we've been slow for the last few weeks.'

'Yes.'

'It's looking like that isn't going to change. Management and I have had a conversation, and we'll have to make your position redundant.'

'What?' Louise had expected something bad, but this was worse than she'd imagined.

'We need to make budget cuts. Your position can be most easily redistributed to others in the team. I'm sorry; you're being let go.'

Louise tried to form her thoughts into speech, but instead her mouth just flapped up and down.

'I've been authorised to give you eight weeks' pay, in addition to any annual leave you have accrued, as a severance package. You won't be needed in the office after Friday.'

It was Wednesday. 'Two days? You're giving me two days' notice?'

'The eight weeks' pay is partly to compensate you for that. It's been a very difficult decision to make. We all feel terrible.'

'Who is we? How many people know?'

'Myself and the management team. None of your peers have been informed; obviously, we wanted to give you the news first.'

'I see.' Louise's mind was working a million miles an hour, but nothing seemed to be coming out the other side. 'I'm going home. I'll see you tomorrow.'

'Of course.'

Louise left the meeting room, collected her things, and went home.

It didn't hit her until she was about to walk into the office on Thursday morning that she'd been fired. Yes, they said redundant, and it was true; it probably wasn't about the quality of her work, but she couldn't help feeling as though it was a reflection on her abilities. She stood in front of the building, mind spinning again, trying to decide if she wanted to go in or needed a bit longer. She turned around and walked down to the café—so what if she was late? What were they going to do? Fire her?

Louise ordered English breakfast tea, in a pot, and sat at one of the tiny tables to drink it. She was going to take her time. She wanted to talk to someone about it, and while all of her friends would be at work as well, she knew Megan would answer her call.

'Hey, Megan.'

'Hey, Louise. What's up? I'm just getting stuck into work.'

'I need to tell you something, and I guess I wanted to vent a little bit before I go into the office today.'

'Uh…' Megan hesitated. 'Sure, I can give you ten minutes.'

'Thanks.' Louise sighed. 'How's work going for you?'

'I thought you needed to tell me something. I can make time for something urgent, but if you just want to chat, I might need to get back to it.'

'Yeah. Sorry. It's hard to say out loud.'

'Oh God. That sounds ominous.' Megan's voice rose as though she was excited by the concept.

'Yesterday, at about four thirty, Vicky pulled me into a meeting and told me my position was redundant.'

'Fuck. No way.'

'And that I won't need to come into the office after Friday.'

'No way!' Megan repeated. 'What did you do?'

'I didn't do much. I packed up my shit and went home. But all last night I kind of pretended it wasn't really happening, so now I have to face going in and telling everyone.'

'Damn. How long have you been there now?'

'Three years, almost.'

'And there was no warning?'

'Well…' Louise's tea arrived and she nodded thanks to the waiter. 'It's been quiet for a couple of months. I guess I hadn't really been paying attention. After the hectic pace they'd always set before then, I was glad of the break. I probably should have been more curious. Maybe if I'd been more on the pulse, I wouldn't have been so blindsided.'

'Maybe. Sometimes management don't really say much, don't wanna give away any trade secrets or whatever. Is anyone else going?'

'I have no idea. I was too furious yesterday to ask any useful questions—'

'Sometimes when they make people redundant, they do last in, first out, but didn't you say there were new people at the beginning of the year?'

'Yeah. There are a couple of new juniors, but they won't cost as much as I do. They're probably going to keep most of the grads.'

'Phew, what a gut punch,' Megan said.

'Are you still there?' Louise said after several long beats of silence.

'Sorry, I just saw a bunch of emails come in, kind of urgent. I should probably get onto that. Sucks about your job. What will you do now?'

'Do you remember I did a favour for Roman?'

'A couple of weeks ago?'

'That's right, got pictures of his husband with a woman. Anyway, I've been thinking about whether I should go into business on my own. Maybe freelance, maybe get into investigations. It was kind of awful, but it was also exhilarating—actually, it was mostly awful because I know Roman and Peter personally. If they weren't friends, I think it would be less upsetting.'

'You wanna be a private investigator?'

'You were the one who suggested it, but I think I'd be good at it. And I'm kind of sick of being in a job where I sit behind a desk all day. It'd be good to work for myself.'

'It's a big change. I guess take some time to really look through the options, y'know. Maybe do some temp work, or freelance stuff, in the interim, and see how you feel.'

'I wasn't expecting you to be so pragmatic.'

'Sometimes I can still be surprising. Hey, I really should get to work. Will you be alright?'

'Yeah. Fuck 'em. I don't need to work for people who don't have work for me or think I'm not worth the salary they pay me. Maybe I'll suggest they keep me on their freelance list in case they get an influx of work the grads can't manage, then they can pay me triple what they pay now for the same work.'

'That would be fun. I'll call you later, yeah, maybe come over and we can drink wine and look at job ads?'

'Okay, thank you.'

'No worries. And don't work too hard. Just the bare minimum to get through today and tomorrow.' Megan ended the call.

Louise drank her tea slowly and looked at private investigator courses online. The ones she could see were about a year long, so she'd need to do something else while that came through. Maybe she could do some little low-key jobs, people Roman knew or something, so when she was licensed, there was a bit of word of mouth already. Plus, she was a copywriter, she knew how to sell other people's crap, why not sell herself?

Chapter 14

Back in the armchair in the Carter & Carter Detective Agency, Louise turned her mind to the case they'd landed in the here and now: Sue's missing niece. Megan had gone to the initial client meeting alone, and when she'd returned, the details were thin, at best. Penelope Bean, known as Penny, was twenty years old and had dropped out of university last year to drive around Australia in a van with her boyfriend, Stan Warding, twenty-seven. He seemed to be a run-of-the-mill skeeze bucket who hung around younger women and was a chronic drifter. They'd last been seen in Gosford, a town a couple of hours north of Sydney, and had been making video diaries and doing cash-in-hand jobs to fill in their time and supplement their incomes. Louise didn't imagine vlogging would be particularly lucrative.

'So where do we start with this investigation?' Louise said after Megan had given her the rundown.

'I think we need to go up to Gosford; it's where she was last seen. See if the local cops will talk to us, most likely not, but we should still try. We might even be able to find some people who saw her there and could give us some info on what she was up to.'

'Sounds reasonable. How would we get there?'

'With the two of us, it's probably more cost-effective if we drive up; then we have the car while we're there instead of hiring one.'

Louise pursed her lips; the idea of a road trip beyond Sydney was not her idea of a good time. 'I suppose that makes sense. We'll have to do some online research before we set off first thing tomorrow.'

'I'll start with her social media; we also have some of her banking information; Sue sent over copies of her statements.'

'I'll start on the bank statements then. If I get through the bank stuff, I'll look for somewhere to stay in Gosford tomorrow night.'

Megan nodded and settled herself on the couch in their downstairs office. Louise retreated to the armchair to go through the documents. There wasn't much of interest in the banking, a few recurring payments for a gym membership and phone, which still continued to be drawn from her account after her disappearance, but no other transactions.

She hadn't made many deposits in the last several months, except small amounts of revenue from the vlogs, though she had appeared to be covering most of her day-to-day expenses from the account. There were charges for grocery stores and service stations regularly, but it appeared she was living within her means. It was possible she used income from the cash-in-hand work to buy frivolous things, clothing or meals out, since it wouldn't show up on the statement.

It's a shame we don't have Stan's financial records as well. They would have given a much more complete picture of how they were living.

Louise leaned back, rubbing her hand over her face. There wasn't anything in the bank statements that would lead her to a useful conclusion.

'Any luck?' Megan asked after a few hours.

'A bit. You?'

'Some. Tell me about your bit.'

'Most of the stuff here is straightforward, but there are some weird transactions. Here, she withdraws a thousand dollars in cash, and then again two months later. Most of the usual items are covered electronically, food, petrol, etc, so it's unclear what the cash was for, especially since Sue said they were getting cash jobs, and her income is all small payments.'

'Sounds sus.'

'She also made a purchase at an electronics place for a little under five hundred dollars, which could easily have been an unlocked phone, but it could have been almost anything as well. Given they were vlogging, it would make sense if they needed more, or better, recording equipment.'

'She left her phone with Stan,' Megan said, 'Sue was sure of it. Maybe she bought a backup phone and cash, and just left of her own accord.'

'Is that something Sue thought was likely?'

Megan frowned for a moment, thinking. 'Sue said she was a good girl who didn't get into trouble, but how often are people actually as above board as their parents, or aunts, think they are?'

'Very true. Did you get any weird vibes from Sue about the family situation?'

Megan shrugged. 'She was the same as she always is—a highly strung, rich, upper-middle-class lady. She doesn't work much because she doesn't have to. The vibe I got was out of touch.'

'And have you met the mother?'

'No, never met Kate. I would expect her to be similar, except with a child.'

'Penny was her only child? Any other siblings of Sue's?'

'I don't think so. What are you thinking?'

'I don't know yet, but an only child of a rich, distant family, the possibility of her having done a runner seems more likely.'

Megan held up her index finger. 'Well, just hold that thought.' She moved to a chair at the desk usually reserved for clients. 'I've been looking through the vlogs, and there are some weird bits.'

Louise spread her hands, inviting her sister to continue.

'This one, from a few months ago, Stan is in the background driving, but Penny comes up and tries to be funny with the camera, and he's really angry, just for a moment, before they cut away.' She showed Louise the scene; it was subtle, but the look was definitely there.

'Any others?'

'Yeah, there are a few more. It's more of a vibe than anything specific. Stan's not much use on camera, so it's mostly Penny talking, and him in the background. Occasionally, he pitches in, but she's clearly the star. I've even had a brief look at the stuff that Stan's been posting since she left.'

'Anything interesting?'

'Hard to say; there's only a handful of videos, but I dunno, I would have thought after your girlfriend disappears mysteriously, you might take a break from vlogging, but he never did.'

'That's so weird. Is he posting to their couple channel?'

'No, the couple channel went quiet after Penny's disappearance. Stan has his own channel, which he's had for several years, and he's been doing short vlogs every week or so for that without many gaps.'

Louise chewed her lower lip for a moment, giving herself some time to consider the new information. 'That's a bit odd.'

'Yeah, but it could be socially awkward odd, not "I murdered my girlfriend" odd.'

'You're right. We'll have to speak to Stan at some point.'

Megan nodded. 'I'm about ready to give it away for the day. I don't have any more brain capacity, especially since we're driving all day tomorrow. I'm going to order Vietnamese; do you want some?'

'Yes, please. I'd better give this up for the night and think about packing.'

*　　　*　　　*

Megan took the first shift driving. They left a little after seven o'clock, as it was a ten-hour drive, plus stops. Louise hooked her phone up to the car's Bluetooth and went through some more of Penny and Stan's vlogs as they drove. When it was Louise's turn to drive, and therefore Megan's turn to program the stereo after they swapped drivers, she opted for nineties club bangers.

'We're not gonna keep going through the vlogs?' Louise asked, her eyes on the open highway in front of them.

'I can't listen to any more of Stan's voice right now. I had hours of it yesterday and this morning. He's so grating.'

'I know what you mean. Like, is he really that dumb, or is it an act? And why would a girl like Penny—part way through a uni degree, good family, all her options in front of her—hook up with him?'

'I don't see the attraction.'

'Me neither.'

Megan stared ahead, quietly singing along to the songs that reminded her of high school fun. She'd joined the detective agency officially about a year after Louise got her private investigator's licence. She'd had a few clients and occasionally had asked Megan to do a favour here or there. It was much more fun than working for the adult education institute and the associated expectations to work after hours without overtime pay or appreciation. With the odd jobs she was doing for Louise, she'd cut back on her extra hours, and the bosses had started to get snarky.

'I can't help it if you have too much work for the hours you pay me for. I was able to do extra hours for a while there, but my life outside of work has become more demanding, and I can't do unpaid overtime anymore,' she'd told Simon, her manager.

Louise wasn't paying her much to do these little jobs, but it was the principle. Megan knew they didn't have a budget to pay her for the extra time and would have to swallow her objections. Maybe it would even mean reallocating some of the workload, or working on setting up better automation and systems so their double handling was reduced.

'We need to get through the backlog. Megan, you're our best worker.'

'I'm aware. I also know I get through more than anyone else would in my role, and you've benefited from that for a couple of years now. I'm sorry I can't keep working for free. I'll do what I can to get through as much work as possible, as I always do, but I won't be able to work out of hours.'

Her boss had frowned; it seemed the idea of her refusing hadn't crossed her mind. 'Management is starting to doubt your commitment to your job.'

'I'm sorry to hear that. My commitment hasn't changed.' Megan had stood up and walked out of the meeting room. It was too much to sit there and be criticised for not working fifty or sixty-hour weeks. Since she'd discovered things to do in her evenings and weekends, things that were fun and independent, her perspective had changed. Several weeks later, when she was complaining to Louise about management continuing to try to get free work out of her, Louise had asked if she wanted to join the Carter Detective Agency officially.

'It's not secure income; some weeks we'll be really flush, other times we might struggle, but I've never been happier than working for myself—doing hours when it suits me and the client, and not having to deal with middle management.'

'But I don't have a licence.'

'You can get one, and I'll make sure you only do the stuff that doesn't need one to start. If you want to stick with it, then we can look into getting you into the course; otherwise, you'll be able to get another job.'

Megan hadn't thought about leaving; she'd just been letting off steam, but now the idea was in her head. She mulled it over for a week or two, considering how it might be to have different hours, to get out from behind a computer and be out in the field. In the end, she'd joined the agency, first as an assistant, then, when she'd finished her qualification, as a partner. They'd changed the name to Carter & Carter Detective Agency, which had quite a good sound to it.

Megan looked back at Louise in the driver's seat. It was strange that Penny had run off with an apparent no-hoper like Stan but, more often than not, people uprooted their lives for a good reason, not just on a whim. She pulled out her phone and started scrolling through Penny's social media accounts again.

'You onto something?' Louise's voice broke into her thoughts sometime later.

'Huh?'

'You stopped singing along about half an hour ago. I thought you must have had a brainwave.'

'Oh.' Megan looked up; the landscape had changed, and it was later in the day than she'd realised. 'I was looking for hints Penny's home life wasn't so rosy, something that might give us an idea of why she left with Stan. He's cute, I'll give him that, but most people have warning signs before they leave like that—often only realised in hindsight, but even so.'

'Did you find anything?'

'Not really. A couple of mentions of big nights out and party favours, which suggests she was trying some substances.'

'Is that important?'

'Sue insisted she wasn't into drugs. She thought it was all Stan's influence, but there are some very questionable selfies from months before she even met Stan that point to her having been experimenting without him.'

'Perhaps the innocent girl her family saw wasn't the whole picture.' They drove past a sign for roadside services: food and petrol in five kilometres. 'Let's stop for lunch, then it's your turn to drive again.' Louise had been driving for nearly two hours.

'Alright. I need to pee as well.'

They had sandwiches and coffee from the café attached to the service station, which was less terrible and fresher than Megan had expected, but still not great. While they ate, Megan looked for Penny's friends on her social media. A woman called Belinda commented on most of Penny's content and seemed like a good place to start.

'Do you think we could get in touch with one of Penny's girlfriends? This Belinda person is pretty active on the socials and appears in a few of the posts.' Megan showed the phone to her sister.

'Sure. How are you gonna do that? Just DM her?'

'I guess.' Megan put the last of her tuna and salad sandwich in her mouth. 'I'll send her a message.'

> **Hi Belinda,**
>
> **You don't know me, but I'm looking into Penny's disappearance on behalf of her family. It looks like you were close. I wonder if you could give me a call when you have a moment. It would be great to get some info from you.**

'What do you think?' Megan showed the message to Louise before adding her phone number and pressing send.

'Looks good. I wonder if she'll reply.'

Megan shrugged and sent the message. 'Can't hurt to try.'

'I'll have a look for some others who come up multiple times. We should be able to get at least one friend interested, if they're concerned about her welfare, that is, and haven't forgotten about her.'

Megan frowned. 'Why would they forget about their friend who might be dead?'

Louise shrugged. 'I dunno; some young people seem really uncaring like that.'

It didn't seem like the sort of thing a friend would do in Megan's opinion, but at the same time, there were no posts looking for Penny, no Facebook groups set up to find her; it could have been because they weren't that worried. 'Maybe they know something we don't—like she's off living somewhere and doesn't want to be found.'

Louise stood up, her hands massaging her lower back. 'Alright, let's get this show on the road.'

*　　*　　*

They arrived in Gosford a little before eight that evening; over twelve hours of travel. Louise's brain was completely fried, and her body was aching. The motel they stopped at was on the main street approaching Gosford's central business district, if you could call it that.

'I'm going to have a bath,' she announced once they were settled in the room. She'd only been in the water about five minutes when there was a vigorous pounding on the door.

'Go away, I'm not done,' she shouted.

Megan opened the door and put her head into the bathroom, her eyes closed. 'Belinda's on the phone. If you want to talk to her, get out.'

Louise scrambled out of the bath quickly, wrapping herself in a towel without bothering to dry herself off properly.

'So, when did you meet Penny?' Megan was asking as she came into the room, seated in a chair at the small

217

table. Megan had the phone on speaker and was taking notes with a pad and pen.

'We're friends from high school. I guess it would be more accurate to say we were friendly in high school, but we've been closer since we started studying engineering together—there are a lot of boys in the classes, and us girls gotta stick together.'

'Of course.' Megan put her finger to her lips. 'My colleague, Louise, is going to join the call; is that okay?'

'Yeah, fine.' Belinda sounded young and vaguely uninterested.

'When was the last time you saw Penny?'

'She had a leaving party in, like, January, I guess, so it would have been about then.'

'What was the party like?'

'It was great; hectic for sure.'

'What do you mean by hectic?' Louise asked.

'Umm, we all got pretty wasted. Penny was—wait, is this going to get back to her parents?'

'We have to report on our progress to the family, but we don't need to give specific details of anything, especially if it turns out to have nothing to do with her going missing.'

'Okay, well, don't tell her mum, but Penny always had a good supply of party drugs, coke mainly, but some other stuff like benzos, MDMA, and Ritalin. I dunno how she got it, but it was good quality.'

'And she supplied people at the party?'

'People knew she had access to good stuff; they would go to her to get it. She wasn't, like, addicted or anything, more like she knew people who knew people who could get what you wanted.'

'Interesting.' Megan wrote this down. They'd need to look into the possibility of Penny dealing drugs, even if just to her friends. 'Anything else of note from the farewell?'

'I mean, not much.'

'Belinda, this is Louise, Megan's colleague. Did you ever meet Stan?' Louise asked.

'Yeah, he was alright. Hot but a bit of a stoner; not much ambition. I didn't know what she saw in him, to be honest, but Penny was totally in love.'

'You don't think he was pressuring her? Influencing her to leave?'

'No way—if anything, it was Penny who wanted to do the van life thing. She had all the motivation; Stan was more of a come along for the ride kinda guy. You know?'

'I know what you mean. And when was the last time you heard from Penny?'

'Umm,' Belinda paused, as though considering the question. 'Easter, I guess, maybe the start of April?'

'Close to when she disappeared?'

'Must have been. We weren't, like, chatting all the time or anything, but I would send her memes and reels and stuff, and she would send stuff back. And I watched her videos; some of them were really fun. The ones with Stan in them a lot weren't as good.'

'Are you worried about her?'

'She can take care of herself. If she wanted to disappear, she could.'

'You don't think Stan could have hurt her?' Louise asked.

'Hurt her? I don't think so. She was tough, and he was a puppy as far as I could tell. Real golden retriever energy. Followed her around everywhere; it was kinda sad, to be honest.'

'And you haven't heard from her since April? She hasn't created separate accounts? Gotten a new phone to hide from her family or something?'

'If she did, I don't know about that.'

'You're not concerned then?' Megan asked.

'Not really; I'm sure she'll turn up sometime, when she's finished whatever side quest she's doing.' Belinda laughed a little, clearly amused by the idea.

Louise looked at her sister, unsure how to proceed with the interview.

'I'm glad you're not concerned, but her family are. Is there anyone else you think we should talk to? Anyone who might have been in contact with her since her disappearance? That way we could reassure the family that she isn't in any danger.'

'Hmm.' Belinda paused. 'You could try Yolanda? Yolanda Petrakis. They were tight and hung out more than she and I did. If Pen's pulling a shifty to punish her parentals or something shady like that, Yolanda would know.'

'Do you have contact details for her?'

'Yeah, I'll send you her phone number.'

'That'd be great, thank you.' Megan paused, giving Louise a little shrug. Louise returned the gesture. 'I think that's all for the moment. Can we give you a call back if we think of anything else?'

'Sure. You have my number now.'

'Thanks again.' Megan wrapped up the call and hung up. 'What do you reckon?'

Louise had started to get cold sitting in her towel. 'I need to dry off properly. But it puts the whole thing in rather a different light than what Sue said. With young people, there's always the possibility that their family don't know them very well. Especially where they think the sun shines out of their arse, like Penny's family do.'

'You can't blame them—on paper, Penny is the perfect daughter: good school results, got into a good course at a good uni, and then meets this older flake of a guy and goes off on an adventure.'

'That's what I was thinking. It's time to dig a bit more into Penny. You can go back to the bath, though, unless it's gone cold.'

Louise went back into the bathroom, and while the bath water was still quite warm, her desire to lounge in it had passed. She finished her ablutions and dried herself off properly before returning. Megan was busy on her laptop, and Louise changed into her deep purple flannelette pyjamas and climbed into bed. *I'll just read a little bit.*

*   *   *

Louise woke early the next morning without any memory of having fallen asleep. Her book was on the nightstand next to her, but her phone was almost out of charge. She plugged it in and rolled over, trying to get back to sleep.

Unfortunately, it wasn't possible to get back into a comfortable position with the stiffness in her body from driving all day. She got up quietly, went into the bathroom, and got dressed. She left her phone on charge but took her wallet and keys and went out for a walk.

Maybe I'll be able to find the local coffee shop while I'm out.

The local area was beautiful; the sun hung low and golden over a large lake directly across from the motel. She turned left down the highway, the direction to go further into town, and headed off in the crisp late autumn air. She crossed over some railway lines, walked through the park and stopped at a swish-looking café.

It had a very minimalist, white interior, with long, weathered wood tables down both sides of the room. It wouldn't have looked out of place in Melbourne, except for the *Live, Laugh, Love* sign.

Louise ordered two coffees and two muffins and took them back to the motel. Her coffee was finished by the time she got back. No doubt Megan's coffee would be cold, but even cold barista coffee was significantly better than the instant sachet and UHT milk pod provided by the motel.

'You awake?' Louise said as she let herself into the motel room. Megan was sprawled over the bed, her blankets askew, apparently unconscious. It was just after eight o'clock, and they would need to get started on their plan for the day. When they were travelling on the client's money, she wanted to get the most out of the time.

'No.' Megan's muffled voice came from the pile of bedclothes.

'In that case, I'll leave the coffee and muffin here for you; you can have them later.'

'You got coffee?'

'Yeah, it's surprisingly good for a town this size. I haven't tried the muffin; I predict it's from a pre-made mix, but it'll be tasty enough, I'm sure.'

Megan mumbled something inaudible and levered herself out of bed. The muffin was quite good in the end, and Louise made a mental note to go back to that café the next day.

'What are we going to do while we're here? We want to talk to the cops, not that they're likely to tell us anything, and perhaps ask around, see if anyone saw Penny and Stan?'

'Yeah, both of those. I'll try Yolanda too, maybe a little later; it's too early to call a uni student. I was also thinking about tracking down Stan.'

'Yeah, I was thinking about that too. Do you have any ideas where he is?'

'I haven't watched all his latest vlogs, but he was headed further north the last I saw.'

Louise thought for a moment. 'I say we go to the police first, see what they'll tell us, then fill in the gaps with other people as needed.'

'Alright.'

They left the motel a little after nine, then walked the short distance to the Gosford Police Station. It was a blocky, brutalist building; all yellow brick veneer and pale concrete stained grey with rain. At three stories, it was a large station for a regional town.

Perhaps they were a hub for some of the surrounding areas as well, Louise thought.

The sisters entered through brown-tinted automatic sliding glass doors into the main reception area. The dated seventies exterior continued inside; the foyer floor was tiled with shiny, dark brown tiles, and the rows of middle-brown plastic bucket seats seemed to be original, though some were bleached and stained, possibly from where they had tried to remove graffiti. There were two other people already seated: an older, scruffy-looking fellow who was nodding off in his chair, and a young woman with dreadlocks.

A young male officer stood behind a glass screen, clicking around and occasionally typing something into the computer terminal. He didn't quite look bored, nor did he look enthused. His light brown hair was trimmed short and styled neatly away from his face, and though he had pleasing symmetrical features and clear, pale blue eyes, he was not handsome.

'Can I help you?' He briefly looked away from the screen to notice their approach.

'We're here to ask about a missing person, Penelope Bean,' Louise said.

'What's your relationship to Ms Bean?' The young man typed a few things into the computer, continuing not to look at them.

'We're looking into her disappearance on behalf of the family.'

The cop frowned, his eyes tracking slowly over to meet Louise's gaze. 'Private investigator? Or enthusiastic amateur?'

'I have a Victorian Investigative Services licence—'

'Have you got a New South Wales licence?'

'No, we don't usually work in New South Wales and have come up expressly to look into Ms Bean's case.'

'Your names?'

'I'm Louise Carter; this is my sister Megan Carter.'

'I'll have to speak to a supervisor. Take a seat.' The young man waved towards the rows of seats and turned back to his screen. Louise and Megan sat down, facing the window behind which the young man was working, though he didn't seem to have called a supervisor, and Louise was suspicious that he had any intention to do so.

'Not a promising start,' Megan muttered.

'I know what you mean.' Louise stared out the window; at least it smelled normal in the waiting room, and they hadn't been turned away outright—both were positive signs. 'Let's give it ten minutes, maybe fifteen, and if nothing has happened, we'll ask again.'

Louise looked over the woman with the dreadlocks and wondered whether she was a good prospect to have information about Penny. It seemed unlikely, given the time that had passed, and the fact Penny wasn't local, but it was worth a try, and there was nothing better to do while she waited. Louise stood up and took a seat next to the young woman.

'Hi,' she said cautiously.

'Uh, hello.' The woman frowned at her but returned the greeting.

'I wonder if you might be able to help me. Are you a local?'

'I guess so. Depends who you ask.'

'That's great. My sister and I are here looking for a young woman, about your age, actually, who went missing from here a month or so ago. Penny or Penelope Bean, do you know her?'

'Penelope? You don't hear that name much anymore.'

'You're right; her parents are a bit traditional. I believe it's all the rage at the moment to use old-style names, though.'

The woman raised an eyebrow at her. 'Why would I know her?'

'It's a long shot, I just wondered, while we're waiting for the police to speak to us… I'm sorry to have bothered you.' Louise stood and started to walk back to Megan on the other side of the reception area.

'You don't have to go.'

'I'm Louise Carter, that's my sister Megan.' She pointed to where Megan sat, looking decidedly confused. 'What's your name?'

'I'm Cindy, Cindy Archer.'

'Do you live around here, Cindy?' Louise pulled out her notebook, the trusted tool of the intrepid PI.

'Yeah, I live out on the farm commune a little bit out of town.'

'Very nice. How do you find it?' Louise hoped the conversation would lead to rapport and possibly some useful information, but on the other hand, it was a pleasant enough way to fill in time.

'It's okay. The farm is hard work, but I get a share of the profits, you know, so that's nice.'

'That sounds like a good system.'

'I think there was a Penny on the farm for a while.'

Louise tried not to get too excited; there was still every possibility that the information wouldn't go anywhere. 'Did you ever meet her?'

'Umm…' Cindy looked off into the middle distance, perhaps considering. 'Yeah, once or twice.'

'Do you remember what she looked like? Or when this was?'

'She was young, very pretty, with brown hair and a tan. I wasn't really sure why she would be working on the farm.'

'What do you mean?' Louise made a note to herself to find this farm.

'Most of the people on the farm are like, locals, or backpackers, or no-hopers who can't get a real job. I guess I'm a combination of all of them.' She smiled, her eyes had a far-away look that made Louise wonder if she'd taken something recreational.

'And when did you think you might have seen Penny?'

'A while ago, a couple of weeks maybe?'

'So two weeks?'

'Could have been longer. I'm not great with time, and y'know, we didn't really chat too much.'

'Of course. What was the name of the farm again?'

'Blue Granite Farm. It's like a twenty-minute drive out of town. If you put it into the maps, it'll come up.'

'That's fantastic, thank you—'

'Louise and Megan Carter?' An older male officer had appeared at the door next to the glass screen where the young officer was studiously watching his screen. He was balding, with ruddy skin from too much sun, and maybe too much beer with it. He wore a neat uniform and had a small protrusion of belly over his belt.

'Here,' Louise said, raising her hand. She hurried over to the officer, as though her speed would determine how much information he was willing to impart. Megan followed, a little slower.

'Follow me.' The officer led them through the station's dull grey-on-grey interior corridors to an equally grey interview room that had seen better days. There was a large, faded splatter on the wall Louise hoped was coffee, a strangely narrow wood laminate interview table, and three hard plastic chairs in the same deep brown as those in the waiting room.

'Have a seat.' He indicated to the chairs and took the one closest to the door, probably a tactical decision; no doubt they were trained not to be blocked in. 'I'm Sergeant Burt Collins. I understand you've come to ask about Penelope Bean?'

'Yes, we have.' Megan leaned forward in her chair.

'We hoped you might be able to give us some information. We've been retained by the family in Victoria to do a bit of investigating,' Louise said.

'There won't be much I can tell you; it's an open case and there are privacy concerns.'

'Of course. Any help at all will be greatly appreciated.' Louise pulled out her trusty notebook. 'Why don't you tell us what you can, and we'll follow up with any clarification questions.'

Collins sighed. 'There's not much to tell. Missing person's report came in from the mother, a couple of days after she left her boyfriend up in the forest. We looked into the situation and found, well, bugger all really.'

'I see. Was Stan investigated?'

'I can't tell you specifically. However, in cases of this nature, the partner or spouse is frequently to blame, so it is procedure to investigate them.'

Louise made a note. 'Thank you. It would appear there wasn't much in the way of evidence against Stan, given he wasn't charged or arrested.'

'I couldn't possibly comment,' Collins said, nodding.

'We haven't found much else to go on. We'll have a look at the site, up at Strickland Falls, but with so much time gone past, we wouldn't expect we would find much,' Megan said.

'A search of the area at the time didn't turn up much either,' Collins said.

Louise added go to Strickland Falls to her notepad. 'Do you know anything about Blue Granite Farm?'

Megan frowned and looked at her sister; Collins also let a look of surprise briefly cross his face before he forced it back to neutral.

'Blue Granite Farm? How would that be relevant?'

'I was speaking to a source who said Penny might have been seen there a few weeks ago.'

Collins raised an eyebrow. 'I can't tell you anything about the farm, officially, though the locals aren't keen; it has a reputation for being full of drugs and ne'er-do-wells.'

'Ne'er do wells?' Louise asked.

'Stories of unwashed backpackers who come into town trying to scam something or have sticky fingers. The farm has been there about ten years, and it's been a thorn in the side of certain people for a while. Who mentioned it?'

'I'm not sure we should reveal a source, though if we go out there and find anything of use to the police, we'll be sure to share that with you,' Megan said.

Collins frowned, then leaned back in his chair. 'This is the attitude you take when you want the police to be open with you, is it?'

'Uh…' Megan's face reddened slightly.

'We wouldn't want to waste police resources on something that's effectively hearsay; as Megan says, we'll be sure to pass on anything that is of actual use in the investigation.'

'It would be best if you did. You wouldn't want to obstruct us by withholding anything.'

'No, quite right, Sergeant.'

'Did the police collect any of Penny's things from Stan? We're looking for anything that might need to be returned to the family, or might be relevant to finding Penny, like her phone or cards,' Louise said.

'I don't believe anything was taken into evidence.' Collins paused to rifle through a manila folder, presumably holding the case information. 'The notes state that Stan didn't have any of Penny's personal items—phone, wallet, that sort of thing.'

Louise frowned. 'That's strange; the family said Penny left her handbag in the van. That's why he came back to the forest for her. He realised she couldn't even call him to apologise or whatever, since he had her phone.'

Collins' eyebrows moved upwards. 'I need to check something with my colleagues, if you wouldn't mind waiting here.' He left the room, and Louise and Megan looked at one another.

'You think Stan lied and said he didn't have her stuff?' Megan said, her voice low.

'I'd guess so, based on our friend's hasty exit. Could mean they didn't look as hard at Stan as perhaps they should have.'

'Yeah. What's Blue Granite Farm?'

'The woman with the dreadlocks said she saw Penny there two weeks ago. Obviously big if true, but she seemed a bit stoned, so I'm not sure her experience of time passing is the same as ours. Even so, if Penny was out there, and as Collins says, the locals are up in arms, it could mean there are dodgy people out there doing dodgy things, and they could have done something to Penny.'

'I see why you didn't want to give her name to him—not exactly reliable. Maybe they're a cult and Penny's run off to be with them.' Megan laughed.

'I'm not discounting anything at this stage. We need to check it out either way.'

Sergeant Collins burst back into the room, opening the door with a little too much force. 'Thank you for waiting. I've conferred with my colleague, and we'd like to take your details down for the file, if we could.'

'Of course, Sergeant. Is there anything you want to share with us about that chat?'

Collins' face was a little more ruddy than it had been previously, and she suspected he'd just told someone just how royally they'd screwed up not getting the phone from Stan. 'No, I can't share details of an ongoing investigation. If I could get your contact details…'

Megan gave him their phone numbers, the email address of the agency, and the physical address in Northcote, which he wrote on a form and slid into the manila folder.

'I'll have to get on with my work; thank you for coming in.' Collins stood up and opened the investigation room door.

'Thank you for speaking to us,' Louise said, offering her hand for him to shake.

'If you'll follow me.' Collins led them back out through the oppressively grey corridors into the brown foyer.

'Interesting,' Megan said.

'Very. Let's talk about it outside.'

They walked back to the motel via the café Louise had found. Sipping her English breakfast tea, the idea of Penny having joined a cult seemed ridiculous, but it wasn't any good to discount things until you've thoroughly investigated them, even the far-fetched ideas.

'Are we going to the farm or the falls first?' Megan asked.

'Good question.'

If you decide to go to the farm first, keep reading.

If you decide to check out the Strickland State Forest first, go to Chapter 16 *on page 257.*

Chapter 15

You decide to go to the farm first.

'We know the cops checked out the national park; that's where Penny was last seen, so I reckon we try the farm first, yeah?' Megan said. If she'd been murdered by Stan and dumped in the forest, the police would have found her—at least she hoped so.

'Alright, let's go check out the cultists.' Louise finished her tea and tossed the empty paper cup into the bin. 'Ready to go?'

'I'll just find it on the map.' Megan pulled out her phone and searched for Blue Granite Farm. The map app showed it was about twenty-five minutes' drive away, to the north of the town.

'Look, we go right past the falls to get there. That doesn't seem like a coincidence.' Megan showed her sister the route.

'It's suspicious to say the least.'

Louise drove, following the directions on Megan's phone, which she attached to the dashboard mount. While they drove, Megan used Louise's phone to look at information on the farm.

'There's not much online about the farm. Just a terrible website; no social media or anything.'

'Interesting. Does it say what they grow?'

Megan scrolled around the website, which looked like it had been developed in the late 2000s, and was very busy and hard to navigate. 'I don't see anything. There's a section about how they offer spiritual retreats, which sounds super culty, but otherwise doesn't say what they grow or sell.'

'Say she did go to the farm; what's the attraction? She seems like a wholesome young woman, not someone I would expect to get sucked into a cult. And despite her dabbling in party favours, I wouldn't expect her to be wrapped up in drug production or growing, given the implication of the Sergeant.'

Louise shrugged. 'We don't know much about Penny, to be honest. Only what her family told us, and that could be wrong. Maybe she's got a secret double life we don't know about.'

'Maybe.'

Blue Granite Farm was about ten minutes further along the highway from the forest. The road had transitioned from being surrounded by tall eucalypt forest to open brown paddocks abruptly, and as they approached the place on the map, it looked like any other farm. At the driveway were two large, blue fabric flags, which had become tattered at the edges after flapping in the wind for a long time. A hand-painted sign with 'Welcome to Blue Granite Farm' written on it was attached to the fence; both were also a little worse for wear. A roadside stall, consisting of a large wooden table with a little peaked roof, where Megan assumed they would put produce for sale, stood empty.

'It doesn't look very lived in. More like kind of abandoned,' Megan said.

'Despite the sign, I don't think they want us to come in.' Louise slowed down and turned up the rough gravel driveway. They kept along the drive for a hundred metres or so, going slowly and attempting to avoid a couple of large potholes.

As they crested a rise, a collection of squat, haphazardly-arranged mudbrick buildings came into view. The largest of them looked to be a farmhouse, and the surrounding buildings were more like tiny homes or storage sheds. Louise parked the car and stepped out; Megan followed.

Further down the drive, to the left, stood an enormous metal packing shed and several low greenhouses. 'Maybe they do grow something after all,' Megan said, inclining her head towards the greenhouses.

'Could be vegies, or flowers… or weed.'

A crunch of gravel behind them made both sisters turn around abruptly.

'Help you?' The man had long hair tied in a ponytail at the nape, a large untidy beard, and could have been in his late forties, though it was hard to tell. He was remarkably handsome, even in his unkempt state, and she could easily imagine he would be a magnet for young people.

'Is this Blue Granite Farm?' Megan said.

'Sure is. Can I help you with something?' the man asked again.

'I'm Megan Carter; this is my sister Louise. We think someone we know might be living out here and we wanted to say hi.'

The man raised an eyebrow and crossed his arms across his chest. 'Who you been talking to that said you might find your friend here?'

'Uh, well, I didn't quite catch her name. We're looking for Penelope Bean, you might know her as Penny.'

'Nope.'

'What was your name?' Louise asked, putting out her hand to shake his.

'Allan King. This is my farm, and I know everyone here. We don't have anyone called Penelope or Penny.' Allan's arms remained folded, and Louise dropped her hand. Megan looked over to her sister, unsure how to break through the gruff, hostile exterior.

'I'm sorry to have arrived unannounced; I'm sure you're very busy. What are you farming?'

Allan sniffed and looked briefly at the greenhouses. 'We grow organic vegetables and herbs.'

'How's it going?'

'Are you really interested?'

'Uh…' Megan was surprised by the aggressive tone he had taken, and asking about his business hadn't helped. 'We're just looking for someone; her family hasn't heard from her in a while, and they are worried. If I show you a picture, perhaps you might know her by a different name?'

Allan said nothing, so Megan pulled out her phone and brought up the photo of Penny. She was dressed in black slacks and a white shirt, ready for a catering job she'd had for a while before she left on her van life adventure. Allan took Megan's phone and looked at the photo for a while. Megan looked around at the other buildings but saw no other people. If it was a working farm, she would have expected to see more activity.

'Nope, I don't know her by any name. Who told you she might be here?'

'Local gossip. We're clutching at straws, really, it's likely her boyfriend has done something unspeakable to her, we were just… hoping perhaps she'd lost her phone and started working on a farm rather than being murdered.' Louise laughed nervously. 'We'll be on our way. Thank you for the chat.'

'Righto.' Allan stood and watched them get back in the car, execute a three-point turn, and head back down the driveway. Megan's stomach hadn't stopped churning since he'd shown up.

'He's awful,' Megan said.

'You can say that again. I don't know why anyone would work for him if he's that curt to potential workers.'

'He probably isn't like that to lost, skinny twenty-something year-olds looking for an adventure. He'll turn on the charm when he needs to, and I'm sure when he's not scowling, he'd be hot.'

'Yeah, it's weird how he was both attractive and terrifying at the same time.' Louise paused at the end of the driveway. 'Where to now?'

'Check out the forest?'

Louise shrugged. 'It's on the way I guess.'

On the ten-minute drive from the farm, Megan watched the fields and farmland transition back into towering forest. The trees were beautiful, but with the context they took on a sinister aspect. She'd seen enough Australian bush horror movies to know better than to expect the forest to always be friendly and innocent.

They pulled into a car park, the sign read "Banksia Picnic Area", a large flat clearing in the middle of the eucalyptus forest. The gravel was unmarked, and Louise stopped in front of a large wooden information sign. A couple of trails headed off from points around the car park, and there was a small, covered area with a couple of picnic tables, some wood-fired barbeques that had seen better days, and a dingy-looking toilet block.

'You want to go down a couple of the trails?' Megan asked, closing the car door and looking around.

'I guess so. We aren't likely to find anything, but we've come all this way.'

Megan looked down at her sneakers and wished the terrain didn't look quite so muddy. 'I really thought she'd joined the commune. I know Allan said he didn't know Penny, but do you believe him?'

'I have no idea. I can't tell if he's a creep or a lying creep, you know what I mean?'

Megan nodded. It was hard to know if the aggressive stance and evasive answers meant he was hiding Penny, or that his farming operation wasn't entirely legit, or nothing at all.

Louise was reading the information board, and Megan joined her. 'There are three main trails; we can do two of them at the same time, and then the third after we get back here. They don't look too difficult, but I expect they'll each take half an hour, maybe an hour.'

Megan looked at her watch. 'You're buying lunch after then.'

Louise rolled her eyes and headed toward the start of Cabbage Tree track. Megan trailed along behind her sister, who had always been more inclined towards physical activity. The tracks were called medium grade on the information board, but Megan was struggling soon after they started; the humidity in the forest made her sweat, and she panted along behind her sister for the three-and-a-half-kilometre track without really taking in any of the surrounds.

When they got back to the car park, she perched on the car bonnet and flopped back onto the car. 'How are you not dying?' she asked, her eyes closed.

'I like running, you don't.'

'That must be it.'

'Come on, we need to get the other track done.'

Megan lifted her head and forced herself to stand up, at which moment her legs seemed to turn to jelly and she had to sit down again. 'I don't think I can.'

Louise rolled her eyes, then looked at Megan's left leg, which had started twitching, and her face softened. 'I can do this one on my own. We don't want you falling on your face halfway round.'

You'll probably get through quicker without me anyway, Megan thought. She had lain back on the bonnet but pushed herself up again to sit in the car, only to discover Louise still had the car keys.

She eyed off the picnic tables and decided she could lie down on one of the benches and see whether she fell asleep. Louise would wake her when she got back.

*　　*　　*

When Louise got to the waterfall, she was a little underwhelmed. Not that they weren't beautiful, but they weren't what she had expected when she thought of waterfalls. The water cascaded in an unimpressive series of trickles over a boulder into a small pond at the bottom. She sat down, looking at the falls. In spite of her statement that she was fitter than Megan, the tracks were hard going.

Louise had seen a bunch of litter scattered along the trail, but nothing that would lead her to think it had any bearing on Penny's disappearance. From Sue's story, it didn't seem like Penny was in the forest long enough to have seen the falls before she disappeared. She had hoped the farm would produce a stronger lead, something concrete that would indicate whether Penny had been there, but the fact that the one guy they saw there was a bit of a creep wasn't enough to come to any conclusions.

She sighed and stood up; the longer she took getting back to the carpark the later lunch would be and her stomach had started making noises.

At the end of the trail, Louise looked to the car and couldn't see Megan, either sitting on the bonnet or inside, and for a moment she worried her sister had wandered off. Then she saw the bottom of Megan's shoes poking out from the end of a picnic table.

'See anything useful?' Megan said, sitting up from where she had been lying on a bench.

'Nah. The falls are pretty but not exactly Niagara.'

Megan nodded.

'I thought you'd be in the car.'

'I would have been, except you have the keys.'

'Oh.' Louise patted her jeans pocket. 'Sorry.'

'You're buying lunch already, but if you weren't, I'd make you buy lunch to compensate.'

'Fair enough. You wanna drive back to town?'

'Sure.'

As they drove back to Gosford, to the café where they'd got muffins earlier that day, Louise looked online for any mention of Allan King. The only thing she found was a business registration for the Blue Granite Farm seven years ago, and the website they'd looked at earlier; otherwise, it was as though he didn't exist.

They went inside the café in silence, Louise was mulling over their next move, and Megan seemed almost asleep standing up. The specialty of the house was toasted sandwiches served with tomato soup, so they both ordered that.

'There's something wholesome about country cafés, don't you think?' Louise said.

'Mmm.' Megan nodded.

'Do you think Allan King is his real name?'

Megan looked up, suddenly more alert. 'What makes you think that?'

'A hunch? I don't know. He seems shady, and while we were on the way here, I couldn't find much on him online.'

'He's a hippy; possibly he doesn't have an online presence or paper trail because of that. He's probably a sovereign citizen as well as a cult leader.' Megan laughed.

'Maybe.'

They ate their lunch without much conversation. Megan scrolled through her phone, and Louise took the opportunity to review the notes she had on Penny in her trusty notebook.

'What do we do now?' Louise asked, closing the notebook.

'Find Stan? I think we've exhausted the investigative avenues here in Gosford.'

'I was thinking about that. I guess we go speak to Stan, but what's he really going to tell us? Especially if he didn't tell the cops anything useful.'

'Some people don't like cops and won't tell them stuff on principle.' Megan drummed her fingers on the table, a habit that Louise found irritating, though it usually meant she was thinking something over.

'True. We're detectives. It's our job not to take what the police do at face value. We're being paid to do the running around.' Louise sighed. 'I wish I didn't feel quite so out of my depth, though. It's a lot when you're investigating a missing person, one who might be dead. Really feels high stakes, you know?'

'Yeah. If it was anyone else, I would have said they needed to go to another agency.'

'Would you? You were the one telling me how stale our jobs were, following adulterers about and taking sneaky pictures of them. Have you changed your mind?'

Megan shrugged. 'It's all a bit heavy. Like, the cheaters are always upset they get caught, and the divorce proceedings are disruptive and expensive, but no one dies.'

Louise stood and gathered her things together. Megan followed suit. They paid and left the café. She went a couple of doors down and stopped to look in the window of a second-hand shop.

'What are you doing?' Megan asked.

'Waiting to see if that sticky-beak waitress is going to follow us to tell us something or was just trying to pick up gossip.'

'What?'

'She spent an awful lot of time wiping the table next to ours while we were there. I got a snooping vibe, but I couldn't decide if she had info on Penny she wanted to deliver or was just nosey.'

'Oh.' Megan turned to look in the store window as well. Louise watched for the waitress in the reflection, but after several minutes, she hadn't run down the street to tell them anything.

'Alright, let's go find Stan.'

It was nearly three in the afternoon when they got back to the motel. They had paid for the night and could figure out where Stan was and check out in the morning. Louise had looked over his social media posts since Penny's disappearance but had been looking for signs he was lying, or references to Penny. Now she needed to turn her investigative intent towards where he was living. Stan wasn't particularly careful about hiding where he was, but he also didn't advertise it since he and Penny parted ways, and the travel vlogs had dried up.

'Do you have anything that tells us where he's staying?' Louise asked.

'He seems to have gone north. I don't think he knows how to use geotags, but we can check, and there might be something in the background of one of his recent posts that will give us an idea.'

Louise pulled out her laptop, and they started rewatching the vlogs Stan had made since Penny's disappearance.

'He's not very good on camera without her, is he?' Louise said after the first couple of videos. Stan was stilted and awkward on camera.

'Clearly Penny was the star of the show; maybe she was the director as well.'

'And these pauses, surely he could edit those out.' Megan sighed.

'Today I'm at, uh, Nobby's Beach here in Newcastle,' Stan addressed the camera. Wind whistled in the microphone as he panned across the sand. Too bad he hadn't done the voiceover in post, Louise thought.

The videos were ten minutes or so long, mostly regurgitating local tourist information or giving reviews of pub meals he'd eaten along the way. The most recent video was almost a week ago.

'Hi everyone, here I am at Tacking Point Lighthouse, built in 1879—'

'That's one of the smallest lighthouses I've ever seen,' Megan exclaimed as the lighthouse came into view behind Stan. It was squat and barely two storeys tall but had recently been painted bright white.

'That's near Port Macquarie. I wonder if he's still up there, of if he's moved on?' Louise wondered aloud. She opened Stan's Instagram and scrolled through the posts and saw he'd posted a steak he'd cooked on the beach, using the kitchen in the van. The café behind him was called the Sandbox. Louise paused the vlog to bring up the café on the maps.

'Hey Megan, check out this post; looks like he's still in Port Macquarie, assuming he's posting contemporaneously.'

Megan looked at the photo and the map and agreed. 'If he's up in Port Macquarie, that's another couple of hours up the coast. Should we drive up and take the risk he won't talk to us?'

'What else can we do? Call him? He's not more likely to talk to us on the phone than in person.'

'Yeah, but we know his number; we don't know where he's staying, or even if he's still there. We could get up there, and he's moved on, and we'd have to follow him all round Australia on Sue's money.'

Louise thought for a moment. 'Let's give him a ring, and see if he'll take a phone call, or better yet, a video call.'

'Alright.' Megan found Stan's phone number in her notes; perhaps Sue had it from when the two of them left on their grand adventure. 'Here it is. Should we call now?'

Louise shrugged. Megan placed the call, then put it on speakerphone. It was early evening, so he would probably be off work, if he had any, and not so late they were in danger of waking him. The call rang and rang; Louise was sure it would ring out or go to voicemail.

'Yeah?' a male voice answered, it didn't sound much like the man in the videos; rather, the gruff, irritated version.

'Is that Stan Warding?' Megan asked.

'Who wants to know?'

'My name is Megan Carter. I'm calling about Penny Bean.'

Silence came down the phone line except for Stan's breathing. 'And?'

'I was hoping to speak to you about her disappearance. Is now a good time?'

Stan sighed. 'Not really, but it's as good as any other time.'

At least he hasn't hung up, Louise thought to herself.

'My sister is on the call too.'

'Hi. I'm Louise,' she said.

'We've been asked to look into Penny's whereabouts by her family.'

'Right.'

'Uh.' Megan frowned and looked at Louise, perhaps flustered at his monosyllabic responses.

'Would you mind if we turned this call into a video call?' Louise asked.

'Nah. I'm like, not really dressed right now.'

'Okay, fair enough. I understand you spoke to the police about Penny?' Louise asked.

'Yeah.'

'Were you… uh, confident in their abilities?'

'Shit no.' Stan chuckled mirthlessly. 'Those guys thought I'd killed her. I kept asking them why would I? She was my girlfriend. I loved her.'

'You were the last person to see her,' Louise said.

'Yeah, yeah. I know it's their job to suspect me. Wife-beaters and all that. But they didn't even look at anyone else. Seemed to be totally fixated on me, and when I kept telling 'em that I had nothing to do with it, they had to let me get on with my journey.'

'Did you have to stay in Gosford long?'

'Coupla weeks. I kept hoping Pen would turn up, but she didn't. I even turned her phone on a couple of times, but I don't know the code, so it wasn't much help.'

'Did you tell the police you had her phone?' Megan asked.

'Yeah, they didn't seem that interested. I thought they'd want it, or her stuff, but they said I could hang onto it.'

'That's odd.'

'I reckon. I mean, what am I supposed to do with all her stuff? Every time I look at it, I remember how happy we were together, and how I'll probably never see her again, all 'coz I got the shits and she hitched a ride with a serial killer.'

'There was some speculation that she may have left of her own accord, maybe to live off the grid somewhere. Did she ever indicate she wanted to do that?'

'Off the grid? That doesn't sound like her kind of thing. She kept complaining about how the van didn't have a proper shower. I don't blame her for not being super happy about the shower but nah, she doesn't seem like an off grid kinda girl.'

'So, you didn't go to Blue Granite Farm?'

'That place? Yeah, we were there, Pen went a few times, I didn't like the guy running it much, but apparently I didn't *get it.*'

'Did you check whether she was there?'

'Course I did, but that Allan guy is a real tough cunt and wouldn't let me in. I didn't see anyone there; I figured he didn't know anything.'

'I see. Did you ever notice that Penny was using drugs?' Louise asked.

'We had our share of y'know, social lubricants, and I like a bit of weed. Nothing serious though. The cops asked me that too.'

'So, she wouldn't have had connections to sell drugs? It was just for personal use?'

'Penny didn't sell. Her friends knew she had stuff, and she'd facilitate that y'know, instead of sending them to her sources, but she never sold.'

Louise shook her head; Stan was describing dealing, but apparently his definition of dealing only applied if you sold to people you weren't friends with. 'I see.'

'Have you heard from her at all since she went missing?' Megan asked.

'Are you kidding? She's missing; like isn't that the whole reason you're calling me?' Stan's pitch rose.

Louise worried Megan was antagonising him and he would hang up.

'We just meant, perhaps she'd reached out. The fact she's not speaking to her parents doesn't mean she's not speaking to her friends, or her boyfriend.'

Stan sighed. 'I don't think she'd want to speak to me even if she was still around. The last time I saw her, I said some things I regret. Now I'll never be able to tell her I'm sorry, and that I was being a prick.'

'That must be hard.'

'It is.' Stan sniffled. Louise was surprised how much emotion he was showing. Perhaps being on the phone instead of in person allowed him to be more candid. 'Is there something I can do about her stuff though? I have her phone, bags and clothes. They make me sad. I thought about throwing them in the rubbish, but then I thought her mum might want it all back, y'know?'

'Her family would very much like to have her things back, especially if you are not planning to keep them. There must be very limited space in that van,' Megan said.

'Yeah, it can get pretty cramped. When there were two of us, Penny was really fastidious about putting things back into the cupboards and whatever, but now it's just me I've… I guess I've let things go a bit and it feels smaller than when we were both in here.' He laughed, but it was a sad sort of laugh.

'Can you mail it? We can give you the agency address in Melbourne.'

'I guess so. Text me the address… and can you send some money or whatever to cover postage? It'll probably cost a bomb.'

'Of course, we can arrange that for you. Send us your bank details in the text and we'll make a transfer.' Louise was sure Sue would be willing to pay the expense on their account. She was surprised by how much Stan was telling them, and that she believed him. He seemed clueless; the idea that Penny had masterminded the whole van life idea was gaining traction in her mind after speaking to him. Though it didn't give her any further information on what might have happened to Penny, she wasn't sure Stan had anything to do with it.

Megan looked at her, raising her eyebrows as though to say do you have any other questions? Louise shook her head. She didn't.

'I think that's about everything we need from you for now, Stan. Would it be okay if we call you again later if there are any developments or if we have further questions?'

'I guess.'

'I'm sure Penny's family really appreciates all the help you've provided, and your continued engagement with us.'

Stan sighed again. 'I miss her. Doing the vlogs and stuff, living in the van, it's all way less fun without her.'

'I'm sure it's been really difficult. We'll be in touch if we have news,' Louise said, though she wasn't confident she would actually call him back.

'Alright, hooroo for now then.'

'Yep, bye,' Louise said, and they hung up the phone.

'Do we believe him?' Megan said.

Louise shrugged. 'I am inclined to think he's truthful. He sounds like a bit of a twit, but I don't get killer vibes from him at all.'

'Would've been better if we'd been able to see his face.'

'Yeah, but we can't have everything.' Louise bit her lower lip briefly. 'Is it worth trying to get a face-to-face?'

'I don't think so. I feel like we've exhausted all our leads and we've come up with exactly what the cops did—babkas.'

'I know what you mean.'

'Do we call Sue and tell her we've hit a dead end?' Megan stared at her hands as they hung between her knees.

'Yeah. We should head home tomorrow, wait for Penny's stuff to arrive from Stan, to see if there's anything of use in her effects. Until then, I'm stumped.'

'I'd kill to sleep in my own bed again.' Megan flopped onto the motel bed, which gave her a forlorn bounce.

'Maybe not the best choice of phrasing there.' Louise flopped onto the other bed and flicked on the TV. Calling Sue could wait until morning.

*　　*　　*

Megan woke up with a headache. She felt defeated and had tossed and turned much of the night before. They needed to call Sue that morning and update her on the progress, or more accurately, the lack of progress, of the case. She squeezed her eyes shut, but sleep was gone.

The conversation with Stan had been almost entirely fruitless—though he was a good suspect on paper, she just couldn't reconcile the sad, scatterbrained man and the barely competent vlogger they spoke to with a murderer who managed to hide the body from everyone.

She looked at the clock; still before seven and too early to do anything, so she stared at the ceiling and mulled over her anxious thoughts until she heard Louise's alarm going off.

'Morning.' Louise was up and getting dressed.

Megan grunted.

'What's that mean?'

'I hate that we've come up with so little. I'm not looking forward to calling Sue and telling her that with all the money she's paying for us to be up here we haven't done any better than the police.'

Louise made a sound of agreement. 'We did tell her it wasn't our area of expertise. But when there's been several weeks since the disappearance the trail has kind of gone cold. She must have known it was a long shot.'

Megan propped herself up on her elbow. 'She did. I know I told her that when she first approached me, but I wanted to find Penny.'

'It's hard to come up with nothing, but keeping on the case in the state it's in now will likely be futile and just a further waste of money.'

'You're right. But I don't like it.'

'Neither do I. Let's get out of here; check out and get on the road as soon as we've spoken to Sue.'

'I'll get something for breakfast while you shower.' Megan threw on the clothes she'd left lying on the chair next to her bed and headed out. She didn't want to make small talk with her sister; she wanted to sulk and wasn't looking forward to the ten-hour drive back home.

The coffee shop they'd frequented a few times was doing a bustling business this morning. She got coffees and toasted sandwiches for each of them and headed back. Now she was more properly awake, she was more prepared to make the call.

'Should we call from my phone?' Megan said, after her toastie and coffee were finished. She'd put most of her stuff back into her duffle bag; it had only taken her a minute or two. She wasn't keen on folding or neatly arranging things, especially when she was feeling down.

'Yeah, you ready?'

Megan shrugged and dialled. The call rang a long time, and Megan wasn't sure Sue would pick up.

'Hello?' she sounded harried.

'Sue, it's Megan and Louise. Is now a good time?'

'Oh, yes, um, okay. I was just getting out of the shower.'

Louise looked at Megan, her eyebrows raised in a question; Megan shrugged.

'We wanted to update you.' Megan sighed. 'We've come up against a bit of difficulty in progressing the case.' Megan cringed at her own weaselling words.

'What do you mean, difficulty?'

'She means we're stumped,' Louise said. 'We've looked into every lead we can find here in Gosford, and there are no further signs of Penny.'

'You've looked into everything? Have you interviewed everyone?'

'Sue,' Louise's tone was soft, 'I don't think that would be a good use of anyone's time. Penny wasn't a local. We've done everything we reasonably can, and we have found nothing that would indicate where Penny is. I'm sorry.'

'Are you giving up?' Sue's voice rose in pitch; she sounded as though she might cry.

'It's time for us to come back to Melbourne. I think it would be best to close the case, or at least put it on hold, until such time as new evidence or leads come up.'

'If it's about money, I can increase your fee.'

'It's not about the money,' Megan said. 'I mentioned that we couldn't guarantee results. It's not our usual sort of case, and to be honest, there wasn't much to go on to start with.'

'The police did their best, and they have more resources than we do. If they weren't able to find anything substantive after a few weeks, there may not have been anything to find,' Louise said.

Sue sobbed, her breath catching in great sighing wails. 'You can't give up. She's out there somewhere.'

'That might be true, and I certainly hope she's started a new life somewhere, having her teenage rebellion late, and she'll walk back into your lives at any moment, but for now, it's time to stop.'

'O-okay. I'm sure you're right,' Sue said, sniffling.

'We're going to check out of the motel this morning; we should be back in our offices late tonight. We spoke to Stan, and he's going to post Penny's belongings to us. We'll go through those when they arrive, and it's possible that will give us fresh leads, but again, I can't promise.' Megan pinched the bridge of her nose; she knew Sue would be upset, but had expected anger, not sadness.

'If anything more comes up, or if you hear anything, get in touch and we'll look to reopen the investigation,' Louise said.

'Thank you.' Sue blew her nose, sounding a little more together. 'I have to get going. Send me your invoice, and I'll be sure it gets paid.'

The phone call ended, and Megan stared at the handset in her hand.

'Could have been worse,' Louise said.

'Yeah, could have been better though.' Having made the call, there was nothing left for them in Gosford. Megan shoved the last few of her things into her duffle and zipped it closed. No doubt if she had folded things neatly, more would have fitted better, but she couldn't find the energy to repack it.

The Carter & Carter Detective Agency checked out of the motel and were on the road before ten that morning, heading back to their office and the jobs they knew how to do. No more missing persons.

You failed to find Penny. Go back and try again.

Chapter 16

'I think we should go to the falls. We probably won't see much, but to rule out anything obvious. You said yourself the woman in the cop shop seemed stoned, so she could have seen Penny there weeks ago, if at all,' Megan said.

'You're probably right. Did you bring any walking shoes?'

'I have these.' She pointed to the sneakers she was wearing, old and scuffed but serviceable. Not hiking shoes, but they would do as long as the path was well maintained.

'Let's hope it's not too rough then.' Louise's usual shoe was a chunky, black, Mary Jane style. She'd been wearing the same for years but had packed some lace-up shoes that were somewhere between sneakers and hiking boots.

Megan drove up to Strickland Falls, about fifteen minutes north of Gosford. The drive was pleasant, the trees were beautiful, though if she were there alone, at night, and lost she thought they would easily become sinister. She'd seen enough bush horror movies to know the forest wouldn't always be friendly and innocent.

They pulled into a carpark, the Banksia Picnic Area according to the green painted sign, a large flat clearing in the middle of the eucalyptus forest. They stopped in an unmarked parking spot on the gravel surface and got out of the car. A couple of trails left from points around the carpark, and a small, covered area with a couple of picnic tables and some wood fired barbeques that had seen better days sat in a grassy area next to the carpark.

'Do we know exactly where Stan last saw her?' Louise asked.

'I don't think so. Just in this car park. Sue didn't have many specifics. Given the size of the van, that would have been here somewhere, Penny got out and Stan drove off. Forty minutes later, by the time he'd calmed down and come back to look for her, she was gone.'

Louise put her hands on her hips. 'He had her phone, and her wallet—still does it seems? So, she didn't have those with her. If she left of her own accord, she would have needed another phone and some money.'

'She might have been meeting someone.'

'Could have been.' Louise scuffed the ground with her foot absently. 'How long had they been in town for?'

'I'm not sure, they were spending a week or two in each town.'

'Long enough to meet someone from the farm and formulate a plan. It would have to be a bloody great connection to decide to leave your boyfriend and go live on a hippy farm in a week or two.'

'Maybe she knew someone there already?'

'Could be. It's possible the entire van life plan was an elaborate ruse to get her away from her parents and run off to a farm where no one could find her, but we don't have much evidence to support that theory. Occam's razor says she met with foul play, and that Stan did it. He killed her and then lied about her leaving.'

Megan wandered over to the picnic area and looked around. 'If he killed her, he could have done it anywhere and just said she was here when he last saw her.'

'I hadn't thought of that—fuck. Well, that puts a spanner in the whole thing.'

'Yeah. Let's have a wander around a couple of the trails, look for anything that might indicate she was here—'

'Like what?'

'Clothes? A bag? Blood stains? I don't know. It's probably a waste of time, since the police did it, but I want to go over the area anyway. We can't very well go back to Sue without having even tried.'

The three trail heads each led to a looping path starting at the carpark; Cabbage Tree Track, Stoney Creek Track and Strickland Falls Track.

'Where do you want to start?' Megan asked. 'Cabbage Tree and Stoney Creek can be combined into the one walk; the Falls is independent.'

'Want to split up? I can take the longer one, and you can go around the falls?'

Megan bit her lip. 'The bush is giving me the creeps. I know it'll take longer but I say we stick together. Even if we have to do the farm tomorrow.'

The sun was high overhead, though the weather was mild, as they set off down the Cabbage Tree track. The trail was harder than Megan had expected, and her shoes were getting a real workout, though the trail was mostly wide and covered in gravel or tanbark.

They took their time, each scanning the track and surrounding bush for anything that might have belonged to Penny. The circuit was nearly four kilometres and took them well over an hour to complete and by the end Megan really needed a drink and a sit down.

'Nothing on that track.'

'Agreed, thought after a month it was a long shot. Did you bring water?' Louise asked.

'I thought you did.'

Louise sighed. 'I've only got the bottle I usually have with me in the car. There's a tap over there though.'

They rested for about twenty minutes, each drinking a litre or so of water. Despite the mild temperature, Megan had worked up quite a sweat on the trail.

'I wish we'd thought to bring snacks.' They'd grabbed toasties from the café on the way past, mostly because Megan had wanted a treat after waiting around for the police.

'The falls track is shorter, and then we can have an early dinner. What do you reckon?'

Megan nodded, her legs were already tired, but they were on the job and needed to keep the investigation going. 'Lead the way.'

The track down to the falls was steeper, but better maintained, than the other track. Both Carters looked around as they walked, but just as with the Cabbage Tree track, there wasn't much to see or evidence to collect.

The falls themselves were not what she expected; smaller and more subtly beautiful that the great crashing falls she'd seen. Megan wasn't exactly an outdoors type, she had done very little bush walking, so her experience with waterfalls was restricted to the ones she saw on television, or in people's garden water features. She sat for a moment on one of the drier rocks and listened to the gentle rumble of the water. 'It is nice here,' she said.

'You sound surprised,' Louise replied.

'I am a bit. I don't usually go out into the bush and it's nice that there's something pretty to look at.'

'Not the sort of deserted deep forest one would expect a body to be dumped in.'

'Not really, no.' There had been no other people in the carpark when they arrived, but at some point while they were on the other track another car showed up. A few minutes after they arrived at the falls other hikers appeared; a man and a woman, both in their late fifties or early sixties.

Grey nomads, Megan thought, looking at their spotless hiking attire, sturdy boots and walking poles.

'Afternoon,' the man said.

'Nice day for it,' the woman added.

'Yes, lovely,' Louise said. She looked at Megan in a meaningful way that meant they should leave so they weren't there while the other two are having a rest. Megan wondered whether they would have a rest, they weren't even a little out of breath, but none the less she pushed herself up, groaning.

'I'm not used to all this outdoorsy business,' she muttered.

'It's the greatest, Nance and I do a lot of hiking, really keeps the body in tip top shape,' the man said.

'Yes, we weren't very active before we retired, both had desk jobs, very bad for the health, but since we've taken up bushwalking, we've felt so much better,' Nance said. Megan wondered if they knew they sounded like they'd lost the plot but decided they probably didn't.

'Are you local?' Megan asked.

'We live in Point Clare, near enough to local.'

Megan said nothing, hoping one of them might explain where Point Clare was.

'You could call it a suburb of Gosford,' Nance said. 'George here is being rather obtuse on purpose saying that's not local.'

'Now, now, I was just having a bit of fun,' George said.

'I was wondering, we're here looking for someone, a young woman who was last seen in the Banksia Carpark up there, you might have heard about it—Penelope Bean?'

'We wouldn't know anything about that.' George planted his walking pole in the ground and rested his elbow on it in a defensive manner.

'Of course, I just thought it might have been local knowledge, something perhaps someone didn't think was important enough to tell the police but might be helpful none-the-less.'

Nance briefly looked at George, who shrugged with his mouth. 'We heard she'd been up at the farm. Do you know the one?'

'Blue Granite Farm?' Louise asked.

'Yes.' Nance sniffed and curled her lip as though disgusted.

'Do you know much about it? Is it liked by the town?' Louise continued.

'Not exactly,' Nance said.

'Us locals, and close-to-locals, are not at all keen on it being there. There are drugs coming out of that farm, mark my words. They don't produce enough crops, or anything else useful, to feed that many people, and they have all sorts of satellite dishes and whatever up there. It's suspect if you ask me.'

'That sounds very concerning. Any idea what sort of drugs? Are they growing them? Making them? Distributing them?' Megan asked.

'I couldn't tell you. It's not pot though; you'd smell that from miles away.' Nance smiled.

'You're probably right. Thank you for your help.' Megan started towards the track that led back to the carpark.

'I hope you find her; we don't like to think there are bad apples in our midst,' George said, a serious but friendly look had replaced the defensive scowl he'd worn earlier.

Louise and Megan walked in silence for a while, not wanting to say something in earshot of the two walkers. 'That's three times someone has mentioned this Blue Granite Farm, twice in the negative.'

'I know,' Megan said, turning to look back down the trail before going on. 'When the dreadlocked woman mentioned it, I was cautious, the cop couldn't really confirm or deny anything, but he made it as clear as he could they were not keen on the area, and now these two saying it's drugs. We need to get out there.'

'I agree, but we'll need to be cautious too. If they're a drug operation, they might have weapons and we don't want to end up stabbed or worse, shot, because we went in there too hard.'

'You're right, but I don't like it.'

'Neither do I.'

By the time they were back at the car it was half past four, the day had gotten away from them, the walks were more strenuous than Megan had expected. She felt a bit sick and dizzy, she needed to eat, and probably drink a bunch of water, she'd sweated a lot on those trails.

'I can't do the farm today.' Megan slumped into the passenger seat.

'Neither can I. I know we're trying to get through everything efficiently, for Sue, but I'm dying. I need some food, and possibly a nap.'

'I still need to call Yolanda too.'

'We could do that now, but let's wait till we're back at the motel.'

As Louise drove them back from the national park to the motel, they were both quiet. Megan had plenty to think about, though her mind was mainly occupied by ways the drug dealers at the farm would murder her.

She sat on the lumpy motel mattress looking at Yolanda's phone number, Penny's friend who would apparently know more about her life than her parents or Belinda did. Megan's thumb hovered over the call button, undecided, until Louise flushed the toilet and she startled, her thumb landed on the call icon.

It's ringing now, I may as well.

The tap ran in the bathroom as she waited for an answer. Young people weren't keen on phone calls, especially from an unknown number, and she wondered if it would go through to voicemail. After about twenty-five rings, finally someone picked up.

'Hello?' a young woman said, her voice husky and irritated.

'Uh, hi, hello. My name is Megan Carter, I'm looking for Yolanda Petrakis.'

'What do you want?'

'Is that you, Yolanda?'

'Yeah. Look I don't want any of whatever you're selling.'

'I'm looking for Penny Bean,' Megan blurted out, hoping to keep Yolanda on the line long enough to explain herself. 'I'm a private investigator; my sister and I have been hired to look into Penny's disappearance and we thought you might have some insight into what had been going on with her up until April.'

'Where'd you get my number?' Yolanda was still guarded but seemed curious now as well.

'Belinda. She thought you might know—uh something that would help us to find her that her family might not.'

'That a fancy way of saying I'm a bad influence?'

'No, no. I didn't mean that at all. It's just, her mother thinks she's an angel, which is all well and good, but doesn't give us much to work with in terms of finding people who might want to hurt her.'

Yolanda sucked air through her teeth, Megan wondered if perhaps she was vaping on the other end of the call. 'Her mum was a real helicopter, wanted to be all up in her business all the time. Pen had to be super selective with the people she talked about in front of her mum. I doubt she even knows I exist, though we were best friends.'

'I'm sorry to hear that.' Megan made a note on her pad.

'Story of my life, that. I'm never what parents think is good enough for their precious upper-middle-class babies. They got no idea what happens in the real world.'

'I hear that. Did you meet Penny at uni?'

'Kinda. I'm not a student; I work in one of the cafés. I'm good at listening and I know how to spot someone who's struggling. I've thought about applying for mature age entry, but Melbourne Uni are real cunts about letting people in.'

Megan laughed uncomfortably. 'Sounds about right.'

'Anyway, so me and Pen started hanging out when she got a job at the café, lots of students work there for a little while. Penny was a hard worker, and sometimes I gave her a ride home—I live pretty close to her parent's place and drive in—anyway we got close on those drives, and we started hanging out on weekends and stuff.'

'Did you know Stan?'

'What a waste of space.'

'You weren't a fan?' Megan wrote this down too.

'He's not, like, a problem, but she wouldn't stay with him forever. He was, what's the word, temporary… a dalliance, not marriage material.' She chuckled.

'Right. Were you surprised when she said she was going on this round the country trip to be a vlogger?'

'Not really. Penny was full of big ideas. She wanted to be someone important you know, a lot of young people do, but she was willing to do the hard yards to get there.'

'Had she been planning it?'

'I guess so, we'd talk about where she would go, what towns were good for a few days, and where she should stay a bit longer. I have a lot of relatives in a lot of weird country towns, so I helped out where I could.'

'Was it Penny's idea, then?'

'Yeah, Stan never had a good idea in his life.'

'Interesting. That's not the story we got from her family.'

'Oh, you wouldn't have. Even when Penny told them it was her idea, they decided Stan was corrupting her. She was much sneakier than they gave her credit for.'

Megan made a note, this was juicy, but it wasn't helpful other than making Stan seem like a total doormat. 'Did you ever see Penny use recreational drugs?'

'Yeah, she liked to party did that girl. She was always the one with the good supply, I think some of her connects were through Stan, but others she made herself.'

'People would come to her to get what they needed then?'

'Mostly she only had what she needed, but her friends, her classmates, if they wanted something they knew she could hook them up.'

'She was dealing?'

Louise had been listening to the conversation on speaker but hadn't said anything. Her expression was both worried and sceptical.

'I wouldn't have called it that, but I supposed in a way she was. She would sell her mates party favours when they needed them. She didn't do it for profit, just for fun.'

'Thanks for the information, we certainly weren't aware of that… element of her lifestyle before,' Megan said. She wrote on the pad asking if Louise had any questions, but her sister shook her head. 'I think that's probably everything we need to know for the moment.'

'Okay.'

'Before I let you go, there was one thing. Have you heard from Penny at all since she left Stan?'

'What do you mean? I thought she was like, dead or something?' Yolanda sounded suddenly worried.

'It's something we're asking everybody. No one has had any contact from her so far, but there is a possibility Penny has gone missing on purpose, as it were. If that's the case, and she's safe, but doesn't want to go back to her old life for whatever reason, we would respect that— no need to tell her family where she is—but it would be reassuring to know she hadn't come to any harm.'

'I get you. She's definitely clever enough to disappear on purpose, but I haven't heard from her for months.'

'Thanks for your help again, Yolanda. If you think of anything we should know, you can call this number.'

'No worries. It's good you're looking into this. The cops never give it enough resources, especially if they think they're a runaway.'

Megan ended the call and looked at her sister. 'The more I hear about Penny, the less I feel like she makes sense. She's an academic high achiever who's dealing drugs to her mates, she's an angel who would never get involved in anything dodgy, but she runs off in a van with a no-hoper like Stan.'

Louise frowned and didn't answer for a long moment. 'I think we're starting to get a more accurate picture of Penny now we're onto her friends. If we were in Melbourne I'd want to go see them in person, you get so much more information from people face to face, but we're up here in the ass end of nowhere and we can't.'

'We can go to the farm.'

Louise looked around and met Megan's eye, sighing. 'Yeah. We can do that.'

'Tomorrow though, I'm starving and I don't think even the friendliest of farm owning, drug dealing hippies wants us to turn up at dinner time.' Megan had intended the comment to be amusing, but instead of laughing, her sister pressed her lips together and stood up. *Clearly, I've said something wrong.*

'I think we've bitten off more than we can chew.' Louise had started pacing up and down in front of motel window. The sheer white curtain blocked the view into the room from outside, but the cream cement blocks of the other motel buildings were still visible.

'What does that mean?'

'I regret getting into something that's much more in the police's wheelhouse.'

'You said they were useless.'

'That was before I tried putting together a sequence of events and trying to find a young woman who may not want to be found.'

Megan stood and looked out the window onto the bleak, bright brickwork of the buildings. There was something about country motels that seemed desolate, even if they were new and full. 'If I really believed she was hiding, or had started a new life somewhere, then I would be happy to leave it, but the statistics of intimate partner violence are horrific. The fact is she's much more likely to have been killed by Stan and dumped somewhere than to have "Gone Girled" herself.'

Louise made an indecipherable grumbling sound. 'You might be right. Let's get something to eat.'

Gosford had several places open for dinner, including a couple of pubs close by and an RSL club near the motel that served counter meals. Louise and Megan were both too knackered to bother searching through online reviews or driving around town looking for the best deal, so they ate at the club.

The interior was the same as every other RSL Megan had been to; carpets with a dark green and red pattern, lots of timber on the walls, and a trophy cabinet filled with various plaques and awards lists. The dining room held around twenty tables, the square wooden type, with heavy wooden chairs. Only a few other patrons were in the dining room, plus a couple of old fellas who looked like regulars on the stools at the bar.

They ordered at the bar, chicken parmigiana for Megan, and roast of the day for Louise.

'Anything else for you?' the man behind the bar asked when they had ordered. Leon, according to his name tag, looked to be in his early sixties, very tall with a pot belly that looked like half a basketball stuck to his abdomen. His uniform polo shirt was clean but showed signs of wear and age around the collar and cuffs.

'That's it for us,' Louise said.

'Unless you have any information on Blue Granite Farm you want to share, we're supposed to be going out there tomorrow.' Megan wasn't convinced he would tell them anything, but it was worth a shot.

Leon wrinkled his nose. 'What're you going out there for?'

'Business,' Megan said.

'Dunno what kind of business two respectable people like you would have out there.'

'We're looking for someone,' Louise said.

Leon's eyebrows shot up his forehead. 'Now that I would believe. There are a lot of people who get seduced by whatever they have going on over there. Folks reckon it's a cult, or possibly a drug den. Some folks think both. Not a nice place, but the local law doesn't give a toss.'

'Really?' Megan asked. 'You think they're dragging their heels intentionally?'

'Maybe, maybe not. They reckon they're hamstrung by all the bureaucracy, having to have probable cause, warrants or whatever, to go searching through the place.'

'They do have to follow the law; otherwise, what good are they to anyone?'

'Back in my day, we would've run the lot of them out of town. But you can't do that anymore either.'

'No.' Megan was starting to think this old guy wasn't going to let them go and regretted opening this line of conversation.

'Anyway, enough about that lot of bohemians. I'll get those meals on for you and have them out in a jiffy… well, perhaps two jiffies.' Leon smiled broadly, revealing yellowed teeth.

They walked back to their table, Megan's mind full of Leon's vehement dislike of the farm.

'Another fan, then.' Louise sat heavily in her chair.

'Yeah, I thought we might end up stuck listening to a rant or something, thankfully he let it go pretty quickly.'

'This farm is a real problem around town… though small towns can be very change resistant, so maybe it's just a matter of people not liking difference.'

'I don't know whether to hope for that or not. If they are a cult, we're more likely to find Penny out there, but if they're just a bunch of people trying to start an organic food revolution, then we're back to Stan probably having killed her.'

'Great.' Louise sat back in her chair and was quiet. Megan turned the case over and over in her mind until their food came, then she tried to move her thoughts on.

*   *   *

Their meals were not great, more like passable. Louise's roast beef was a bit dry, and the gravy was made from powder, but the potatoes were delicious; crispy outside and fluffy inside. She'd been pondering what could have happened to Penny if she hadn't been killed. It had been her assumption from the start of the case that Stan had done her harm, and despite some of their new information, the likelihood of it being another outcome was small.

He had her phone, her wallet, her clothes, and no one had heard from her. Not only her family, but her friends, the sort of people who might be expected to know if she'd gone off the grid. On the other hand, it was possible she'd had some sort of breakdown, or revelation, depending on your point of view, and left to start a new life with no connection to her old friends or family.

'Is there any history of mental illness in the family?' Louise said to Megan as they were getting ready for bed.

'Mental illness?' Megan frowned. 'I don't know. Sue didn't mention anything about it, why?'

'I was just thinking there are certain serious mental illnesses that can have their first onset in adolescence, up to the early twenties. If Penny has had a psychotic break or something, that would explain why she's disappeared.'

'I hadn't thought of that. I guess it's possible.'

'I had a friend whose older brother had a breakdown in his second year of university. Turned out he was schizophrenic and started having hallucinations, people were trying to steal his thoughts to feed into some sort of machine. One day he was fine, the next day he left and never came back.'

'How did they find out about the hallucinations?'

'He'd been telling friends about it, that ASIO was after him and whatever. They thought he was joking, but when he left, they told his parents. My friend looked into her family tree, and there were suicides on both sides that were likely the result of something like schizophrenia.' Louise shook her head; she couldn't imagine having thoughts that made the world so scary you had to run away from your family and your life.

'I'll ask Sue.' Megan typed out a text message. 'What do you think of this?'

> **Hi Sue, we're up here in Gosford looking into Penny's last sightings. We wondered if she'd ever had any mental health concerns. Or if there was any mental illness in the family? It might help us eliminate some possible avenues of investigation.**

'Looks good. Let me know what she says,' Louise said.

They had decided to go to Blue Granite Farm first thing the next morning. It was about twenty minutes out of town towards Central Mangrove. The route took them right past the Strickland State Forest, which felt like it meant something.

Megan was driving, the smell of eucalyptus was strong as they drove through the forest, then as they came out the other side, it was back to farmlands and paddocks, where the only smell was a vague hint of manure, so Louise rolled her window up.

The farm was signposted with large, blue, fabric standing flags, which had become tattered at the edges after flapping in the wind for years. A hand-painted sign welcoming them to Blue Granite Farm was attached to the fence, also a little worse for wear.

'Are you getting a sinister vibe? Or is it just me?' Louise said.

'Nah, it's full horror movie stuff,' Megan agreed.

Louise couldn't have exactly said why she found the driveway creepy, perhaps it was the combination of aging welcome signs and razor wire that sent mixed messages. The farm, a hundred metres or so down the driveway, was a collection of low wooden and mudbrick buildings. They were sprawling and haphazardly arranged; Louise suspected building regulations were only loosely consulted, if at all, in their construction.

'You see anyone?' Megan asked as she brought the car to a crunching stop on the gravel in front of the largest building. It could have been a big house, or possibly a hall or gathering place.

'Not unless you count chickens.' A few loose chickens were roaming around the farm, along with a skinny black dog watching them.

'I get the feeling they don't like visitors.' Megan stepped out of the car, Louise followed, and they made their way towards the building. As they approached, Louise spotted a series of large, low greenhouses down the slope of the hill, along with a vast metal packing shed.

'Maybe they're down in the shed?'

Megan shrugged, and Louise started down the hill towards it; if people were working on the farm, that's where they would be. Though if the farm was a front for something more sinister, her assumptions could prove dangerous, especially if the shed was full of equipment for processing meth.

'Help you?' a deep, male voice called from behind them. Louise turned and faced a long-haired, bearded man in his late forties. He was remarkably handsome, even in his unkempt state, and she could imagine he would be a magnet for young people.

'We were hoping to speak to someone in charge, I guess the uh… manager?' Louise said.

'You can talk to me.'

'Great. Uh…' Louise stumbled. This man was not happy to be greeting unannounced strangers; all his body language seemed to be directed at making them go away.

'We were talking to someone recently, in Gosford the other day, who thought they might have seen someone we're looking for, Penny Bean?' Megan said.

The man crossed his arms over his chest and lifted his chin. 'And who have you been talking to then?'

'Cindy said Penny might have been working here.'

'Why are you asking about this Penny Bean person?'

Louise glanced at Megan briefly before answering. 'Her family is concerned, they haven't heard from her for some time, and we've been asked to look into it.'

'Her family? I see. Well, that's none of my concern, and I think you should get off my land.'

'You're not interested that people are pointing fingers at you?' Megan said, taking a half step forward.

'Pointing fingers?' He scoffed. 'That's all they ever do around here. We're trying to create a community where people who don't fit into society's rigid, stifling expectations can be free, where we respect nature, and develop our spiritual connections. If we were Catholic contemplatives, no one would bat an eyelid, but because we're not affiliated with any of the Christian ideologies, people think we're plotting to take over the world. I can assure you, the only thing we're trying to take over is the patch down the back of that paddock that's been overrun with blackberries. Those things will really tear you up if you're trying to dig them out.' He had uncrossed his arms to gesture widely while he made his speech. 'We've had the cops up here more times than I care to mention, and every time they have walked away empty-handed.'

'You haven't seen Penny, then? What if I showed you her photo?' Louise asked, something about the rant struck her as manipulative, as though yelling about country towns with small minds would distract them from the reason they came, and he could avoid answering the question.

'If you like, but I don't think she's been here. We don't get many visitors.'

I can't imagine why not, Louise thought, as she pulled out her phone and swiped to the photo of Penny. The photo showed Penny's tall, slim frame in black slacks and a white shirt, dressed for work at a catering company, one of her many university jobs, her long brown hair tied back neatly in a ponytail. 'You haven't seen her?'

A flicker of emotion ran across this man's face; a slight downturn of the mouth, a flare of the nostrils, he'd seen her before. 'I told you, we don't get many visitors.'

'Right, thank you mister… uh?' Louise said.

'King, Allan King. If that's all, you can fuck off and let me get back to my planting.'

'If you think of anything, Mister King, that might help us find Penny, or if she shows up looking for work, you can give us a ring.' Louise held out a business card with their names and phone numbers.

'Righto.' King shoved the card into the back pocket of his weathered coveralls and folded his arms again. It seemed he was planning on standing there and watching them leave. Louise nodded to Megan, and they headed back into the car.

Chapter 17

Once back on the highway, Megan drove a few hundred metres back towards Gosford before pulling over onto the verge.

'He knew her.' Megan gripped the wheel tightly and looked straight ahead.

'Definitely.' Louise looked back towards the waving blue flags. 'No wonder the town doesn't like him; he's an absolute charmer.'

'Yeah. No love lost there. He's clearly got something going for him if he's attracting young people to live with him and join his "spiritual community". He's got cult leader written all over him.' She let go of the steering wheel to make sarcastic air quotes.

'Mmm. What do you want to do now? If he knows her, maybe she's in there, alive and well. And if she's not there, maybe he, or one of the other residents, knows where she is.'

'He's never going to tell us anything.'

'You're probably right.'

'Would you mind if we just sat here and watched the comings and goings for a while? If someone comes out, we could follow them, maybe see if Cindy's going to the shops or something and if she wants to talk some more.'

'Sure, it can't hurt. I'll have a look for Stan on his social media while we wait.'

They sat on the side of the road for almost two hours; at least the late autumn sun didn't make the car into a sauna too quickly. Megan watched the farm driveway in the mirror; it would have been too obvious to turn around and face it directly. As they waited, Louise rewatched several of Stan's more recent vlogs—though they were shorter and less frequent than when Penny was with him.

'I think he's in Port Macquarie; he's tagged himself in the pub there on Instagram. And he's doing some sort of construction work; there's a shot of the building site behind him in one of the videos.'

'Nice.' Megan didn't look away from the rearview mirror. 'I think someone's heading out from the farm.'

Louise turned to look behind them and saw a beaten-up white van turn out of the driveway and onto the highway behind them. Megan started the car and pulled onto the road behind the van.

'Write down the plates,' she said.

'Yes, boss.' Louise made a note in her notebook, though it was unlikely they'd need the number plate for anything; they couldn't search like the police could.

The white van drove into Gosford and turned into a large, dark green and red building supplies store. Megan cruised past the van and parked in the next row over, watching again in the rearview mirror.

'Supply run?' Megan said.

'Maybe they need more razor wire.'

The young woman with the dreadlocks, Cindy, jumped out of the van. It was quite a drop for her petite frame from the high van seat. She looked directly at the Carters in their car before walking towards the store.

'She saw us,' Louise said.

'Isn't that your friend from the police station? Think she wants us to follow her in?'

'That's my guess.'

The store was an enormous shed-warehouse style; it felt industrial and impersonal, but the greeter at the door said good morning, as did several other staff members in their dark green and red uniforms.

Louise scanned left and right, having lost sight of Cindy after they entered the building. 'I think she's down with the plants.' She pointed to the right.

They both walked past the huge aisles of stuff: paint cans, toilet seats, pipes, screws, and garden furniture until they came to the humid, covered outdoor area which housed the plant nursery.

'Cindy, right?' Louise said, approaching the young woman.

Cindy darted her eyes around before replying. 'Yeah.'

'What are you doing here?'

'I umm… saw you talking to Allan, and I remembered you from the police station.'

'Okay.' Louise waited. Cindy would need to tell them whatever she had to say in her own time.

'I waited till you left, and then I told him I was coming out for some machine oil; I was going to come find you, and then I saw your car on the side of the road and I hoped you would follow me.'

'You were right.'

Cindy looked around once more, her hands twisting over themselves. 'Do you have a photo of the girl you're looking for?'

'Sure.' Louise pulled out her phone and showed Cindy the photo of Penny in her white shirt and black slacks. 'Do you know her?'

'Yeah, I mean, she looks a bit different now, and when you asked if her name was Penny, I didn't click, because we call her Mandy. She's a farmhand, working for Allan.'

'You mean she's there now? On the farm?' Megan said, her voice loud, almost a shout.

Cindy took a step back. 'Um, yeah, she lives there.'

'How long has Mandy been on the farm?' Louise asked, putting out her hand to indicate Megan needed to tone it down.

'A couple of weeks, I guess? I'm not good with time, or names, or really with faces. I'm sorry it took me so long to realise.'

'It's alright, you've told us now. If she's safe and well on the farm, that's excellent. Do you think you could get her to come talk to us? So, we can tell her family we found her?'

Cindy looked at her hands, having pretzelled fingers in anxiety, then back at Louise. 'I don't know. She said she's having some time away from the world. And Allan really doesn't like visitors, or people leaving the farm without him.'

'You did well to come talk to us in that case. How did you know to do that?'

'Well, when I left my family and came to live on the farm, no one came looking for me. I knew they didn't want me, and so I have a new family now, but if someone's looking for her, and, like, don't know that she's okay, I'd want them to know.'

'That's understandable. Thank you for telling us.' Louise looked at her sister. 'How do we go forward from here?'

Megan shrugged. 'Not sure. We can't tell Sue we found her unless we have something direct, a meeting preferably, or Penny makes a phone call to Sue or Kate…'

'We're not allowed to have phones on the farm. Allan says they cause cancer,' Cindy said.

'Sounds about right. No landline either, I guess?' Megan said.

'There's one in the main house, but it's for emergencies. You have to be on the special list to make phone calls. When you join, Allan asks you if you have any ties to the outside world, and if you do, you have to give them up.'

'So, he wouldn't like her talking to us, or her family?' Megan said.

'No. He's pretty strict.'

'You can say that again,' Louise said. 'If we gave you one of our phones, and you asked Penny, or Mandy, to call us, maybe take a photo of herself, and then we can come take the phone back without getting anyone in trouble. Do you think you could do that?'

Cindy's face blanched, and she looked around again. 'I… I guess I could try.'

'If she wants to stay on the farm, we won't try to stop her, but her mother is very upset thinking her baby has died. It would really mean a lot for her to know she's alive.' Louise put her hand on Cindy's shoulder. The poor girl was trembling, but she was being very brave.

'Take my phone, it's got nearly a full charge,' Megan said. 'Once we've spoken to Mandy, and she's sent us a photo, we can come by and collect it from the letterbox, what do you think?'

'Okay, I can do that.'

'Well done. If you ever need help, or want to leave the farm, and need somewhere to stay in Melbourne, you can call us.' Louise held out a business card. 'This has our mobile numbers on it. You can call anytime if you need to, okay?'

Cindy nodded, taking the card and Megan's phone and slipping them into the pockets of her overalls. She took a deep breath and straightened her posture, as though having decided she was going to defy her leader, she had more courage. 'I'd better get back. Allan doesn't like us to be away for too long, plus I have chores I need to get to.'

'Thank you for your help, Cindy. We really appreciate it.' Louise let her hand linger on Cindy's shoulder before letting it drop. The young woman walked away, back through the store to buy machine oil.

'I still think it's a cult,' Megan said, her voice low.

'I can't fault you for that; it seems pretty culty. But it's not illegal to join a cult; it's not illegal to disappear, either. If we can get proof she's alive and choosing not to talk to her family, then we've done our job.' Louise touched a nearby monstera plant; its smooth, glossy, deep green leaves were soothing to her fingers.

'We'd better get back to the motel then.'

'I guess so. Do you need anything while we're here?'

'Nah, I'm okay for machine oil.' Megan smiled.

*　　　*　　　*

All the way back to the motel, and for several hours afterwards, all Megan could think about was the fact that Penny had chosen to leave. What had prompted her to do that? How had she done it? Did Stan know? Or was he as clueless as he seemed, and had she left him specifically so he would be suspected of her death? What was it that Allan King had that made young women flock to him and abandon their previous lives?

'How long do you think it will take for Penny to call?'

'I dunno. Why?'

'I'm starting to regret giving Cindy my phone, because now I don't have a phone. And she could be doing all sorts of stuff on it, like posting on my social media or something.'

'Oh.' Louise bit her lower lip. 'I hadn't thought of that. We should have gotten a cheap new one for the purpose.'

'Hindsight is twenty-twenty, I guess.' Megan drummed her fingers on the laminate tabletop.

Louise's phone rang a little after nine o'clock. Megan's name showed on the screen.

'Hello, this is Louise Carter,' she said as she put the phone on speaker.

'Umm… hi. Cindy said you wanted to talk to me?' The voice on the phone was hushed and sounded like a very young woman, not at all like the voice Penny had in the vlogs.

285

'Yes, who's this I'm speaking to?'

'My name is Mandy now, but you'd know me as Penny Bean.'

'Thank you for calling us, Mandy. It's good to hear your voice. My sister is here too; you have her phone.'

'Hi Mandy,' Megan said.

'Your mother and aunt are really worried about you,' Louise said.

Mandy sighed. 'I thought they might be. I don't want them to worry—when I came to live here on the farm, I intended it to be only a couple of days, but then it turned into a week, then a couple of weeks, and I didn't know how to tell Mum I wasn't coming back.'

'I understand. It can be hard with parents.' Louise kept her voice low and even.

'What happened before you came to the farm?' Megan asked, unable to keep her silence.

'Oh... We'd been here in Gosford, I mean me and Stan, for like two weeks, and I'd run into a few of the other farmies in town, and we'd, uh, partied a little, you know. Stan isn't really keen on that stuff; he smokes pot, but like, nothing else. So, he didn't want to hang out with everyone, and we kept fighting. He wanted to go north, thought we needed to be making more money, and keep moving around Australia, except it was my plan to travel. If I wanted to stay in Gosford, why did it matter to him?'

'I hear you,' Megan said, though she definitely didn't understand why it had caused such a fight.

'So that day in the picnic area, I was supposed to be meeting Allan and one of the other blokes, and Stan decided they were trying to sleep with me—they were, but I knew that and I wasn't going to do anything with them. Anyway, he said some unkind things, I stormed off, he left in the van, and Allan turned up about five minutes later.'

'What happened then?'

'I got in the van with Allan, told him what had happened, and I was crying. I said I didn't have any of my stuff, my wallet, phone, or ID. He said I didn't need it. I could just come stay on the farm for a few days and chill out, and if I wanted to chase up Stan, he'd help me out, lend me a phone or whatever. I dunno.'

'Right,' Megan said.

'Did you know your mother had reported you missing?' Louise asked.

'Well…' Mandy sounded vague; perhaps she was high on something. 'I haven't really been into town since then; we have everything we need here on the farm, and I'm in a relationship with Allan and this other guy Dylan, most people here are in multiple relationships, it's very freeing.'

'You didn't know the police were trying to find you?'

'They've been to the farm a couple of times, but they're always trying to bust us for drugs, so I avoided them. I guess they could have been looking for me.'

'Allan never said they were there for you? We were there earlier today looking for you too, and he chased us off.'

'He didn't say; he's got a lot on his mind. I don't blame him for thinking it wasn't important.'

'But Cindy told you about us, and gave you the phone,' Louise said.

'Yeah, Cindy is—well, she's been here a lot longer than I have, but she hasn't really fitted in like I have. I sometimes think Allan wants her to leave so we can be more harmonious. She's a bit of a sad sack, to be honest.'

Megan mouthed the word, 'wow.'

'Would you meet with us? So, we can tell your family we've seen you and you're okay?'

'No. I don't think that's wise. I haven't been off the farm for a while, and Allan won't let you in. It's not going to work.'

'Okay… Do you think you could take a selfie with Megan's phone and send it to me? To send to your mother?'

'Yes, but I have a condition.'

'Go on?'

'You can't tell her where I am. She'll want to come up here and find me, and I can't bear it. I just need some space—like that's why I went off in the van in the first place, and then I needed space from Stan too. Will you promise you won't tell her?'

Louise looked at Megan, her eyes questioning, and shrugged. Megan shrugged back.

'That seems reasonable,' Louise said. 'We'll come collect Megan's phone tomorrow morning, if you want to leave it in the letterbox, by the front fence.'

'Yeah, that would be good. Allan would be furious if he knew I was talking to you, but I also know my family, and they really don't like taking no for an answer. If you didn't talk to me, I was sure you'd keep pestering us and I'd never get the peace I came here for.'

'I'm sorry we had to intrude on your decision to isolate yourself, but you must understand why your family were worried?' Megan said.

'I do. I just wish they'd leave me the fuck alone.' Mandy's tone was surprisingly bitter.

'When they know you're not dead in a ditch somewhere, I'm sure they'll be a lot happier with your absence. And possibly the cops will stop hassling Stan.'

Mandy gasped softly. 'I hadn't thought of that. I didn't mean for Stan to get in trouble. Will you tell him I'm sorry?'

'If we have contact with him, we'll let him know,' Louise said. Megan was losing patience with Mandy's slow, soft-speaking voice; it was hard to hear, and she wasn't really saying anything useful. They knew where she was, and she wouldn't meet them. She made a circling gesture with her hand, prompting Louise to wrap up the call. Louise rolled her eyes but then nodded.

'Do you have anything you want to say to your family?' Louise asked.

'No. Just tell them I'm fine, and I don't want to be found. When I'm ready, I know how to reach them.'

'Alright. Thank you for speaking to us, Mandy. Cindy has our phone numbers on the business card we gave her if you ever change your mind or need help with anything.'

'Yeah, yeah. Thanks for that.' Mandy wasn't listening.

'I'm glad you're okay,' Megan said.

'Of course, why wouldn't I be?' Mandy chuckled softly. 'Bye.' She hung up the phone.

Megan stared at the now silent phone in her sister's hand for a long moment; neither of them spoke.

'That… did not go the way I expected,' Louise said.

'You can say that again.'

'Was she high, do you think?'

'I wondered that.' Megan stood up and walked to the window. The view over the dark water had a sprinkling of lights around the edge, but nothing like Melbourne, which was constantly a dull orange colour at night. 'She can't possibly have thought no one was worried about her. She just disappeared.'

'Yeah, that was weird. Maybe Allan didn't say there were people looking for her, like that would make sense for him, but she should have known her parents would be worried. Even if they'd had a fight, surely Stan would be worried. He had all her stuff.'

'Do you think she's… I dunno, had a psychotic break or something?'

'Maybe? I don't know. We're not shrinks, and to be honest, I'm glad to be able to put this one to bed. We've found her. She's alive. She's not being held against her will. Job done, time to go home.'

Megan chewed her bottom lip. 'I don't like it.'

'I don't either, but Penny or Mandy is a grown-up. She can decide to run away from her life if she wants to. I think it's a load of shit and she should have let someone know she was okay, even if it was to tell the cops to lay off, but—'

'Do we need to tell the police we've found her?'

'Probably. I guess we wait till we get the phone back from the farm tomorrow and drop in on the way home.'

'Home.' Megan sighed. 'I'll be glad to get back to the usual cheaters and insurance injuries when we get home. Let's not do a missing person again, at least for a long while.'

'Agreed.' Louise came to stand at the window with her sister, looking out over the water.

*　　　*　　　*

The next morning, they were up early and out of the motel before eight o'clock. Louise drove up to the farm, and they retrieved Megan's phone from the letterbox. Of course, by then the battery had died, and she had to plug it into the car to check they had the selfie.

Penny had managed to remember to take the photo; she had lost weight, her eyes were slightly glazed, and the photo was a bit grainy in the low light, but despite being a bit thin and scruffy, it was clearly her and she appeared to be well.

'Do we send this to Sue now? Or wait till we get back?' Megan said, showing Louise the photo.

'I would rather tell Sue in person that we found her, but we'll have to wait till tomorrow. We won't make it all the way back to Melbourne tonight, especially if the police want to interview us.'

'True. Let's see what the police say first.'

Louise nodded, and they were silent for the twenty minutes or so it took to drive back to the police station. It looked exactly the same as it had the day before; its grey concrete walls and awful brown décor were still

291

depressing. Finding Penny didn't bring Louise the joy of success that she thought it would. She was glad it was solved, but somehow it was just as sad Penny had disappeared on purpose and didn't care that her family were worried about her welfare.

The same gangly youth was behind the glass in the police station, though he didn't seem to recognise them when they introduced themselves.

'Is Sergeant Burt Collins here?' Louise asked.

'I'll have to check. Have a seat, Ms Carter, and we'll let you know.'

They only had to wait about ten minutes for Collins to amble out the door and beckon them down the grey corridor in the station.

'You have something else to tell me, I take it?' His face was expressionless as he sat in the hard plastic chair nearest the door in the same stained interview room they'd been in previously.

'We thought you should know, we found Penny,' Louise said.

Collins' eyebrows raised for a moment before he schooled his face back into its neutral expression. 'Is that so?'

'Yes. We went to Blue Granite Farm and spoke to the guy who runs it, Allan King. He's a real piece of work, I'm not surprised the locals are trying to find ways to get him run out of town.'

'I see,' Collins said.

'He didn't give us anything, but when we left, the woman I'd seen in the reception area here earlier, Cindy, followed us out, and we eventually got from her that

Penny has been living on the farm ever since she left the Strickland Falls car park.'

Again, Collins' eyebrows moved slightly upwards, and he made a note on his little pad. 'We had our suspicions, but never saw her there, and weren't able to get anyone to verify they'd seen her. Is that all?'

'No. We lent Cindy Megan's phone, and asked Penny, who is calling herself Mandy now, to call us and take a photo of herself. We've spoken to her, and we have this picture.' Louise showed Collins the photo. 'I'm confident that's the same woman.'

'I'll need a copy of that photo,' Collins said.

'Of course.'

'Did she say what happened?'

Megan shrugged. 'Apparently, she and Stan had a fight, and she was meeting someone from the farm anyway, and when Stan had gone and the farm contact turned up, she decided to live on the farm.'

'Without taking any of her things or telling anyone.' Louise said.

Collins sighed. 'I'm glad she's not dead. On the other hand, it would really have been better if she'd told someone she was on the farm and saved us a few weeks of running around trying to find her. I'm sure it would have saved her family a lot of grief too.'

'Yeah. I'm not looking forward to telling her family we've found her and she doesn't want to come home. Oh, and she said she didn't want the family to know where she was, so you won't tell them, will you?'

'No, we can't give that information out without her consent. I'll have to go up to the farm and try to confirm she's there before I can close off the report; I'm sure I've got Buckley's of that, but thank you for letting me know.'

'Of course.' Louise leaned forward in her chair, ready to stand up, but Collins remained in his chair. She waited for him to signal the interview was over; instead, he sighed loudly and took his time closing up his notepad before standing.

Collins walked them out, and Megan and Louise headed straight back to the car.

'It's a ten-hour drive; we might be able to make it home tonight,' Megan said. It was a little after ten in the morning.

'Let's see how we go, but that would be ideal. I'd love to be back in my bed.'

They drove hard all day, stopping only briefly every couple of hours to eat and pee. Louise was on the final leg, and they arrived back at the agency a bit before eleven that night.

'I've never been so stiff. I'm going to sleep for a week,' Louise said as she levered herself out of the car.

'Agreed. Let's only take local cases from now on.'

'Yep. Local cases that are cheating or injuries. Just the basics.'

They dragged their bags inside, and Louise was ready to fall asleep as soon as her head hit the pillow. The cats didn't show themselves, perhaps hiding, or resentful at being left behind, but Louise knew Maz would be like Velcro once she'd got over the initial betrayal.

The next morning, she woke at nine, allowing herself to sleep in and recover from the drive. Maz was curled up on the end of the bed but wasn't interested in pats. They needed to contact Sue today and give her the news, though Louise was dreading it.

She got up and made herself a pot of coffee, leaving enough for Megan before putting her head into her sister's bedroom. 'You need to get up.'

Quince, Megan's cat, was sleeping on the pillow next to her head, partially on top of Megan. She cracked her eye open, registered Louise's presence, and closed it again.

'I'm serious. We need to see Sue; I want this case closed. It's giving me anxiety and indigestion.'

'Five more minutes.'

'No, now. Come on.' Louise had lived with her sister long enough to know that five more minutes would mean she fell asleep again. It was hard to explain her impatience, but Louise needed to get this chapter of their lives closed.

'Alright, fine. I'm up.' Megan flung the doona off herself and groaned. Quince looked very put out.

'There's coffee in the kitchen.'

Despite Megan's slow start, they were on the road again by ten. Even though the trip was only about twenty minutes, Louise's body hated getting back into the car after so long in it yesterday. They parked out the front of Sue's Edwardian home, and Louise took a deep breath.

'Let's do it.' Megan's voice was dull and lacked enthusiasm.

Louise sighed and stepped out of the car.

'Louise! Megan!' Sue exclaimed when she opened the door. 'I didn't realise you were back.'

'I'm sorry we didn't call ahead; we have some news and wanted to deliver it in person.'

'Oh no. Did you find her body?' Sue's face drained of colour; her eyes widened and she seemed panicked.

'It's not that. Can we come in?' Louise took Sue's elbow and ushered her back through the house into the enormous, renovated kitchen.

'I'll put the kettle on,' Megan said. Sue had regained a little of her colour by the time she sat down at the rustic kitchen table.

'Let's start with the headline: we found Penny.'

'That's wonderful. Where is she? Did you bring her back with you?'

'The thing is, there are some caveats that I think you'll find hard.'

'What do you mean?' Sue swivelled her head from one Carter sister to the other; the panic she had earlier started to return to her eyes.

'We found her, she's safe and well, but she doesn't want to come home.'

'Well, that's not too bad. I'll just call her.'

'And she doesn't want to be in contact with the family.'

Sue froze, her mouth half open as though about to say something. She closed it again, and the kettle switched itself off in the background.

'I'll make the tea,' Megan said. As she clanged around the kitchen, Sue watched on in silence.

'She doesn't want to speak to us?' Sue said, her hands now wrapped around the mug of tea, though she didn't seem to have registered its arrival.

'We spoke to her, and the decision to step away from her previous life was deliberate. She wants to be left alone.'

'But where is she?'

'We can't tell you that.'

'What? Why not?' Sue frowned at Louise.

'She asked us not to.'

'We have to respect her wishes. I know you wanted us to find her and bring her home; we did the first part, but we'll have to admit failure on the second part,' Megan said.

Louise brought her tea to her lips and blew across the top. It was still far too hot to drink. 'I'm sorry we don't have better news.'

'And you're sure she's safe?' Sue said after a long pause.

Louise looked briefly at her sister. 'As much as we can say anyone is safe, yes. She has food, shelter, money, all the necessary things.'

Though no phone, or contact with the outside world, Louise wanted to add, but didn't.

'I'm sorry; it's all rather hard to understand. Why would she do this? Does she really hate us this much?'

'I don't know. I think it's about her feeling free, to explore herself, create a life outside her family and the structure of university.' Megan shrugged.

'To be honest, we didn't get a very good answer from her about why she did what she did and why she didn't tell anyone she was okay, so I can't tell you anything more,' Louise said.

'You're telling me the case is closed. I guess this means you'll be sending an invoice?' Sue said.

'We've done everything we can. Again, I'm sorry we don't have a better outcome for you.'

'She could have been dead in a ditch. I've been worrying myself into a stick for weeks. That's what I feared all along, so I'm glad that wasn't what you'd come to tell me. I need to get in touch with Kate. If you can send me your account, I'll settle it up as soon as possible. I'll show you out.' Sue stood up, her tea still mostly full, and started herding them towards the door. It was abrupt, but Louise supposed it made sense when you'd had bad news.

Back in the car, Megan turned to Louise. 'Case closed then?'

'Yep.' Louise sighed, turned over the engine, and they headed back to the office.

Congratulations, you found Penny.

Chapter 18

You decide to admit defeat and go back to Melbourne.

'I need to think about it for a while. I'm going for a run.' Louise didn't want to give up on the case, but Megan had a point. She changed into her running gear and headed out. Gosford was a pretty sleepy town, and the late autumn weather had a slight chill.

Louise started heading in the direction of the police station, but instead of turning inland, she followed the shore of the Brisbane Water past the sailing club to Pioneer Park before turning around and heading back. The rhythm of running had always helped her think things through; while her conscious mind was busy putting one foot in front of the other, her subconscious sifted through information, turning and twisting it, trying to make it fit. She would often come back from a run with a new perspective or idea, and it annoyed Megan the way she would "flip-flop" after one of her runs.

She wasn't worried about that; being able to change your mind in the face of new facts had always seemed like a virtue, not a fault. Despite the cool weather, she was sweating under the long-sleeved T-shirt by the time she got back to the motel.

Megan wasn't inside; perhaps she'd gone for a walk, or more likely, given the time, had ventured out to get lunch. Louise showered and changed, leaving her sweaty running clothes hung over a chair in the room.

That'll annoy Megan, probably. But there was no other place to put her gear, and leaving it damp would turn it mouldy. Once she was clean and dressed, her stomach started to grumble; she hadn't eaten anything since breakfast. She walked back out toward the little café where they'd met the two young hippies.

As she approached, she saw Megan sitting at a table by the window and tapped on the glass. Megan jumped and gave her the finger.

'I thought I'd find you here.' Louise took a spot at Megan's table; she'd already finished what looked like a big breakfast.

'How was your run?' Megan said, sneering the word "run".

'It was great.'

'Have you thought about what I said?'

'Yeah—'

'Can I get you something?' a waiter asked, having appeared at their table without Louise noticing.

'I'll have a ham, cheese, and tomato toastie, please. And an Earl Grey tea with milk.'

'Sure. Anything else for you?' The waiter turned to Megan.

'No, thanks.' Megan watched the waiter walk back to the counter before continuing. 'So?'

'I think you're right. Stan isn't going to give us anything new. We could call him, but we aren't law enforcement, and he's probably sick of answering questions about Penny. The comments sections under his videos were full of them too.'

'Yeah, his content has gone down the tubes since Penny left.'

'I suggest we call Sue and tell her we think we've exhausted all reasonable avenues, and didn't get any further than the police.'

'Sue won't like that.'

'No, I don't suppose she will. Maybe she'll even get another agency to look into it, but for my professional peace of mind, I can't keep charging her when I know we're at a dead end.'

The waiter brought Louise's meal and left them to it. The sisters were quiet, Louise was dreading the conversation with Sue, and assumed Megan was the same.

*　　*　　*

'I'll call Sue. She came to me, it should be me who tells her,' Megan said, breaking the silence when they were back in the motel room. She had spotted Louise's stinky running clothes on the chair, but since they were heading home soon, she didn't say anything.

'Put it on speaker. I can back you up.'

Megan nodded and dialled. The phone rang for a long time, and she was sure it would go through to voicemail.

'Hello?' Sue's breathless voice answered.

'It's Megan Carter,'

'Yes… I can see that. Hello, Megan.'

'Have I caught you at a bad time?'

'No, it's fine, I just had to run inside from the garden.'

'I can call back later—'

'No, you've got me now. What is it?'

301

Megan swallowed; Louise did a thumbs-up beside her. 'I've got Louise here too.'

'Hi, Sue,' Louise said.

'Tell me what's going on. This feels weird.'

'The thing is…' Megan swallowed again, her mouth suddenly dry, 'we're thinking of wrapping up the investigation.'

'What? Why?' Sue's voice squealed down the line.

'We've run down all the leads here, plus a few other lines of enquiry, and I have to be honest, we haven't come up with anything more than what the police did.'

'I thought you said they were useless?'

'I did say that, but now we're here, and we see what they were working with, we can't do any better. I'm sorry.'

There was silence on the other end. Megan looked at Louise, who shrugged.

'We'll head back to Melbourne today. I'm sorry we weren't able to give you better news.'

'What if I said I didn't want you to stop investigating? Money is no object; I can keep paying you.'

'I understand that, and you're welcome to engage the services of another agency, but I feel—we both feel—we've done all we can, and to keep taking your money would be unprofessional.'

'I see.' Footsteps echoed through the phone as though Sue was pacing on her hardwood floors.

'It's been a difficult decision to make, but we're at the limit of our expertise.'

'If you do engage another agency, we'll happily provide them with any reports and materials, assuming you give us consent to do so,' Louise said.

'I don't mind telling you I'm very disappointed. I had hoped there would be an outcome, one way or another. This not knowing is killing me, and Kate's worse.'

'I understand. It must be torture,' Megan said.

'I know you're only doing what you think is best. I'll have to consider what to do next. Send through your invoices or whatever the normal process is, and I'll let you know if I engage anyone else.' Sue hung up the phone without waiting for them to say goodbye.

'I think that went as well as can be expected,' Louise said.

'Agreed.'

*   *   *

The sisters drove back to Melbourne in a haze of quiet defeat. They made it as far as Goulburn that first day and stopped in another motel and were back to their office in Melbourne late the next day.

Maz and Quince ignored them that evening, as though angry to have been left behind, but when Megan woke up the next morning, Quince was lying on her bedcover in the crook of her knees.

Louise and Megan worked together to get the invoice sorted out and sent off to Sue. It had come to an extraordinary amount, even for only those few days. Seeing the figure reassured Megan that they had made the right call to end the investigation.

Over the next few weeks, they went back to their usual trade of following people around with cameras, and the world seemed right again. The excitement of a high-stakes case had been replaced by the knowledge that Penny was still missing and her family was in limbo, unable to grieve her death or stop worrying about what had happened.

About six weeks after Megan returned to Melbourne, she received a call from a private number.

'Hello, Megan Carter here.'

'Ms Carter, it's Sergeant Burt Collins here, from Gosford Police.'

'Yes, Sergeant Collins, what can I do for you?'

'I just wanted you to know that we've identified the remains you and your sister found. A twelve-year-old girl from Newcastle called Heather McConnell. She went missing on her way home from school three weeks before you found her.'

'Thank you for letting us know.' Megan frowned. She hadn't expected to hear from the police about the remains.

'It seems her soccer coach had developed something of a fixation on her, and when he tried to molest her, she struggled so hard he killed her unintentionally. It took him a couple of days to figure out what to do with her, then he left her in the forest.'

'I see.'

'We know all that because he's confessed. I just thought you'd want to know. Will you tell your sister the news?'

'Of course, thank you for the call, Sergeant.' The call ended, and the empty feeling in Megan's stomach abated a little.

You failed to find Penny, but you did find justice for Heather. Go back and try again.

Chapter 19

You get started on the drive to Gosford immediately.

Megan flipped her notebook closed; she'd decided.

It's been over a month already. I need to get going as quickly as possible. She put the car into gear and drove back towards the office in Northcote. The roads were busy with the school pickup rush; four o'clock was a bad time to try to get anywhere.

Louise wasn't in the office when Megan walked in; the two cats were in opposite corners of the room, and she wondered if they'd had a disagreement. Quince was much bigger than Maz and sometimes bullied her. Megan knelt to stroke Quince's fur as she went past. 'What a good boy you are. Has nasty Maz been getting in your way again?'

Quince meowed plaintively and pushed his head into Megan's hand.

'I'll put some food out for you for tonight, but Louise will feed you while I'm away.' As she said it, it occurred to Megan that she would need to tell her sister that she was heading out of town. Since their disagreement earlier, Megan didn't want to text or call, so she found a pad of paper and a pen and scribbled a message.

> **Sue's given me a lead on Penny's last known location. I'm going up to Gosford, NSW, to check it out**

tonight. I don't know how long I'll be, but will call if there are any developments.

Megan frowned at her blocky handwriting. *Good thing I don't have to write much these days.* Upstairs in the apartment they shared, Megan pulled out her duffel bag. She tried to be economical with her packing; having a big suitcase only led to taking more crap with her. Clothes, a change of shoes, underwear, toiletries, and chargers—all went in without much thought to order. There was still a little bit of room after all that, so she added another jumper—just in case—though it would probably be warmer as she went north.

'Bye, Quince, my boy. Bye, Maz, you tart.' She teased the other cat, since they didn't get on, though she hadn't figured out why. Maz liked everyone else, including some of Louise's questionable boyfriends.

The whole visit had taken her about twenty minutes, and then she was back in the car. She put Albury into the maps function on her phone and slipped it into the dashboard mount.

Four hours. Okay, I can do that. Might even have time to get a bite to eat and a relatively good sleep.

She set up her phone to play indie pop through the car sound system before pulling out into the rush hour traffic. At least driving was something she enjoyed.

Once she was on the Hume Highway, and out of the suburbs, the traffic lightened up and she cruised along.

The sun was setting, and the paddocks were bathed in the warm orange-yellow light of the golden hour. She'd never been one for poetry, unlike Louise, but it was gorgeous watching the landscape go past, singing along to her favourite tunes.

When it was fully dark, the road ahead seemed to disappear into the blackness. This far out of the city, there were no streetlights, and even with high beams on, the black night swallowed up the light completely. She shivered a little and turned the heater up a notch.

Her music had stopped for some reason; maybe reception had dropped out, so she switched to the radio, only to get static.

Must be out of range for that too.

As she was trying to tune in to a local radio station, out of nowhere, she saw a huge shape bounding towards her.

'Fucking hell!' she yelled, yanking the wheel to the right to try to avoid the enormous grey kangaroo that had bounced onto the road in front of her. Everything started to happen in slow motion; the roo was too close, she'd swerved too hard, and when she tried to correct, the back of the car fishtailed across the asphalt.

The car slid across the road and collided with the kangaroo, which had stopped dead still. The crunching, heavy thud of flesh against metal was sickening. The car jolted and tumbled over the roadside barrier. There was a brief moment of calm before another louder crash as the car hit one of the tall straggly gums beside the road.

Megan couldn't really feel the parts of her that were broken, but she was dimly aware she wasn't doing well.

She struggled to keep her eyes open and tried to reach for her phone to call for help, but it had fallen into the footwell of the passenger side, out of reach. When she tried to move towards it, nothing happened; her arm didn't respond, and then suddenly all the pain she hadn't felt came rushing over her.

It took hours for Megan to die, stuck there in her car, pinned against a gum tree in the middle of nowhere along the Hume Highway.

You failed. Go back and try again.

Acknowledgements

This book was the result of an off-hand comment by one of the Carter sisters (the real ones) that I should write a book about them as private detectives. Well, Louise and Megan, here it is! I hope you have enjoyed the fictional version of you contained here. If we're all very lucky, I'll write a sequel with the Carter & Carter Detective Agency. I met Louise on a night out in St Kilda in 2006 and met Megan a while later. I've also met both Maz and Quince, though I'm allergic to cats, and they both seem disinterested in my existence.

The process of writing a branching narrative, in the style of the *Choose Your Own Adventure* novels is especially difficult, what with trying to keep the different streams of action straight and making sure the continuity is right. It is, however, very popular among readers of a particular generation. I guess the childhood experience of having your fingers stuck in all the pages where we've made choices while trying not to die is formative.

My thanks to Louise and Megan Carter, both of whom provided feedback on the manuscript (again, the cats Quince and Maz did not respond to my emails). In particular, thank you to Louise for writing an excellent foreword and to Megan for the cover design.

I would also like to acknowledge my writing colleagues, members of the Melbourne Romance Writers Guild, and Romance Writers of Australia, my mum, Jenny, who proofreads all my work, and all my friends and family who have helped in my journey. I would have struggled to keep at this weird business of writing without their love, support, proofreading, beta reading, and handholding.

About the author

Fleur Blüm, a Melbourne-based writer, performer, and musician, crafts fiction with a romantic twist, infused with feminist themes. Balancing light and dark, she adds humour to narratives exploring tough topics.

Fleur has ten published books and three poetry collections.

You can find out about Fleur, including book links and upcoming releases, at her website: www.fleurblum.com